Families in the compound waited for a sign from heaven

The cult members had been brainwashed to expect a government assault, and the sect had stockpiled weapons. When push came to shove, the men would fight—and maybe the women.

And their children would be caught in the cross fire.

That was enough for Bolan to oppose a full frontal assault, and Brognola had finally relented. The Executioner knew, however, that Justice wouldn't simply watch if The Path turned suicidal, taking out its disciples the way of Jonestown or Heaven's Gate.

"Five miles," Grimaldi announced. "I think—"

"Never mind," Bolan said. "It's down to me." He had to get inside to stop the action.

And he'd have to live with it, no matter how the hand was played out.

*Other titles available in
this series:*

DON PENDLETON's
MACK BOLAN.

Termination
POINT

BOOK III

A GOLD EAGLE BOOK FROM
WORLDWIDE.

TORONTO • NEW YORK • LONDON
AMSTERDAM • PARIS • SYDNEY • HAMBURG
STOCKHOLM • ATHENS • TOKYO • MILAN
MADRID • WARSAW • BUDAPEST • AUCKLAND

First edition June 1999

ISBN 0-373-61466-7

Special thanks and acknowledgment to
Mike Newton for his contribution to this work.

TERMINATION POINT

The fruit of the tree of knowledge always drives
man from some paradise or other; and even the
paradise of fools is not an unpleasant abode
when it is habitable.

—William Ralph Inge
The Idea of Progress

Belief in a Divine mission is one of the many
forms of certainty that have afflicted the
human race.

—Bertrand Russell
*Ideas That Have Harmed
Mankind*

Experience has only made me certain of one
thing: Brute force may never be desirable,
but sometimes it is still the only means of dealing
with fanatics.

—Mack Bolan

To the survivors of Jonestown, Heaven's Gate,
the Order of the Solar Temple and all other cults.
May they find peace in this world,
as well as the next.

CHAPTER ONE

"That's Roswell," Jack Grimaldi said, raising his voice to be heard over the engine noise of the Cessna Centurion. "You want to stop and see the little green men?"

Beside him, double-checking gear before the jump, Mack Bolan said, "Been there, done that. The target lies northwest of town, another fifteen, sixteen miles."

"Roger."

Grimaldi made a minimal adjustment to their course, while Bolan stole a glance at Roswell, down below. Their altitude was close to half a mile, enough to make the moving vehicles on the ground resemble ants seen through the wrong end of a telescope, while individual pedestrians couldn't be seen at all by the naked eye. They hit an air pocket, the Cessna dipping, jolting. Bolan brought his eyes and mind back to his gear, the final check before he stepped out into empty space and plummeted toward God knew what.

"I don't suppose you've changed your mind about this deal," Grimaldi said, half shouting. Even so, there was a hopeful quality about his voice, as if he had been speaking in a normal tone.

"You're right," Bolan said to the man who was his second oldest friend alive. "I haven't."

"Because I was thinking," Grimaldi went on, as if the Executioner hadn't responded to his first remark, "we could go back and grab a chopper, maybe an Apache or Sikorsky. We could load it up with everything they've got at Bliss and do this whole thing from the air, you know?"

Fort Bliss, the U.S. military reservation located some sixty miles southwest of Roswell, New Mexico, had been their jumping-off point for the present mission. Bolan knew that loading up a helicopter gunship with a fair selection of the works would have made a damned impressive package.

But it simply wouldn't work.

"No good," he said, still checking gear. "The lab is too far underground. You'd never touch it."

"So, we send in Marines, a military decon team, whatever. Hell, those guys *built* the place, remember? Let *them* take it down."

Bolan made no reply to that. He knew that Grimaldi was testy, nerves on edge, not for his own sake, but for Bolan's. They had gone through so much hell together in the past, sometimes it felt like one more forward step, the slightest move, would stretch what passed for luck beyond the breaking point, and one or both of them would plunge headfirst into the dark abyss of no return.

Grimaldi kept his mouth shut after that, until a long, low building suddenly appeared in front of them, its bland paint job as good as camouflage down there, against the arid, sun-bleached background of the desert.

"This the place?" Grimaldi asked.

"Affirmative."

Bolan was up and moving, even as he spoke. It took him seconds flat to don the parachute, which he had packed himself that morning, with nothing left to chance or someone else's negligence. He snugged the straps and triple-checked both rip cords, making certain there was nothing in the way to foul them when it came time to deploy the chute. He had two chances; the main chute and a reserve if anything went wrong. Two strikes, and if they both failed somehow, in defiance of all odds, his entry to the compound below would be a rather different show than he had planned.

He moved back toward the Cessna's door, half crouching from the weight of the gear he carried and the lack of headroom in the Cessna's cabin. Snug against his side, slung muzzle-down, was a Colt Commando carbine with a 40 mm M-203 grenade launcher mounted underneath its barrel. Its 100-round drum magazine, weighing close to twenty pounds, was firmly in place. He also carried extra magazines—the standard 30-round variety—along with several kinds of 40 mm rounds to feed the launcher: high explosive for the doors, buckshot for personnel and some incendiaries for the lab. Add fragmentation grenades, a Ka-bar combat knife, two pistols—the Beretta 93-R slung beneath his arm and a .44 Magnum Desert Eagle on his hip—and Bolan had bumped his normal weight by close to eighty pounds. He felt the burden

in his legs and shoulders, but he wouldn't let it slow
him.

Too much depended on this jump and its result.

Too much was riding on the line for him to drop
the ball.

THE TENSION HEADACHES were becoming worse, and
while Auriga knew their cause—he was a doctor, after
all—there seemed to be no way for him to ease the
pain that burrowed in and throbbed behind his eyes.
Auriga knew the headaches were distracting him, perhaps affecting his performance on the job, but there
was little he could do about it, since his biggest headache at the moment *was* his job.

The world knew him as Dr. Joseph Campbell, on
the rare occasions when its mindless denizens considered him at all. He was, in fact, a double doctor, sport-
ing both an M.D. and a Ph.D. behind his name. At
MIT and Stanford Medical School he had been something of a wunderkind. His special training, since the
government had recognized his worth and snapped
him up, had been in CBW—chemical and biological
warfare, including both agents and antidotes.

Auriga was, in short, a specialist in death.

He didn't serve the government these days. He had
resigned. At the bottom line, it all came down to opting out of chaos and devoting all his mental energy
to something greater than himself, greater than any
institution organized by mortal men. Auriga knew the
truth about his race, its origins, its fate. He knew exactly what was coming down the road, how it was

meant to play, and he was working overtime to help the end come sooner. To do his part.

Unfortunately, something had gone wrong.

They might be isolated at the compound, but there was still TV and radio, Dan Rather, Peter Jennings, Katie Couric, CNN. Auriga still kept up with national and world events, because he wasn't just a member of the audience these days. He didn't just receive the news and drink it in; with those who helped him in the lab, Auriga *made* the news.

And lately, all of it was bad.

Los Angeles had been a failure, worse by far than he had ever privately imagined it could be. Auriga reckoned it wouldn't be out of line to call the mission a disaster, not because so many lives were lost, but rather on account of the pathetic body count, because there were so few.

The team had been expendable, of course. Its loss was nothing that Auriga hadn't counted on. The sacrifice had been in vain, however, since only a handful of its so-called innocent civilian targets had been killed—and those by gunfire, if the media reports were true. Apparently the sarin gas Auriga had supplied was never used at all. Someone, somehow, had met the team and managed to destroy it with the canisters of creeping death still sealed.

The failure wasn't his fault, granted, but Auriga felt it like a deadweight draped across his shoulders. There would be finger-pointing soon, there always was when things went wrong, and if the finger wound up pointing his way...then what?

The logical response was that no blame should attach to him or his product, since according to the media, the team had been wiped out before it started to release the gas. The sarin worked; he knew that for a fact. Was it Auriga's fault if something or somebody else—some traitor in the ranks, perhaps—had found a way to sabotage the mission?

Even looking at the problem logically, however, he could still see holes in his defense. No one outside the lab, outside the team itself, had known about the plan. No one, that was, except The Two, and clearly they wouldn't betray the mission when it had been their idea, their dream, from the beginning. That could only mean that someone on the Roswell end of things had bungled, maybe even blown the game deliberately, and as the scientific supervisor of the project, now that Nimrod was among the dead, Auriga bore the full weight of responsibility for any problems that originated at the lab, whether those problems were mechanical or human.

He could try to lay the blame on Nimrod, maybe even on the Arabs now that all of them were dead, but it was still too much to hope for any sympathy. Dead men were perfectly immune to criticism, much less punishment. The cause had suffered several setbacks in the past few weeks, and while Auriga didn't think a human failure could divert the path of destiny, he understood that someone, somehow, had to be called to account for the string of recent failures. It was only right and fair.

Which didn't mean the punishment would be apportioned fairly. That was simply life, and there was nothing he could do about it. Not until the Ancients came again, restoring perfect peace and justice to Earth.

Meanwhile, it might be helpful if he could devise some scheme for getting even, try to break the losing streak that had afflicted agents of The Path so grievously. He didn't have authority to launch a mission on his own, of course; that would be treason, punishable by the severest of penalties.

Correction, Dr. Campbell thought. It would be treason only if he failed. Conversely, if he should succeed, produce results that roughly balanced out the losses in Los Angeles...well, it was always easier to ask forgiveness than it was to get permission. A display of true initiative might be rewarded handsomely, at that.

They still had a supply of sarin left, and there were extra canisters in stock. It wasn't all that far to Albuquerque, Tucson, maybe even Denver. All he needed was a group of volunteers—three ought to be enough, he calculated—who would risk their lives to save the cause.

Three volunteers, and he had eight subordinates on staff. How difficult could that be, choosing three of them to die?

If necessary, he could always flip a coin.

"I'LL MAKE ANOTHER PASS," Grimaldi said. "We're steady at five thousand feet. You pick your time."

Bolan responded from the doorway, with a thumbs-up signal and a flash of teeth that could have been a smile. The black helmet and goggles made him look like something from an old war movie, like he should have been emerging from the turret of a Panzer tank, instead of leaping into thin air a mile above the arid wasteland of New Mexico.

Grimaldi didn't like it, but he didn't have to. He had been around the block with Bolan frequently enough to know he couldn't talk the big guy out of anything, once the man's mind was set. The Executioner knew his capabilities and limitations, understood his enemy, the ground he would be fighting on, and still, the Stony Man pilot couldn't shake the feeling that one time—perhaps this time—Bolan's strategic calculations would fall short of keeping him alive.

He circled back, holding the Cessna steady as a rock. The blockhouse below them didn't look like much from his perspective, smaller than a postage stamp. Grimaldi couldn't tell if guards were sweeping the grounds, but Bolan didn't seem concerned.

Hell, Bolan *never* seemed concerned.

That wasn't strictly true, of course. What Bolan never really seemed to be was frightened. Grimaldi had seen his old friend risk horrendous death more times than he could count, offhand, and never once had Bolan hesitated out of fear for what might happen to himself. He weighed the odds, of course, then went ahead regardless, even when another man of roughly equal skill might well have changed his mind, backed off to seek a more propitious moment. Bolan had a way of getting in the Reaper's face, pushing his luck with everything he had, and every time they worked together, Jack Grimaldi worried that it might turn out to be the last time, that he would be forced to watch his best friend die.

This time, of course, he wouldn't see a damned thing, not circling like a hawk, five thousand feet above the action.

"Ten seconds," Grimaldi called out, not glancing backward. It was more important that he hold the Cessna steady, than for him to be swiveling, waving goodbye.

It would be better, cleaner, if he didn't watch the jump.

"Five seconds!" Grimaldi raised one hand, the fingers splayed, and kept his eyes fixed dead ahead on nothing.

Bolan didn't want to land directly *on* the blockhouse, but he had to know when they were passing over it, and even wearing the goggles, it would be difficult to see the target from his present vantage point. Once he vaulted from the plane and opened the parachute, there would be time enough to pick a landing site, maneuver as he fell through space.

And time enough for someone below to mark a target, more than enough time for alarms to sound, gunners to cock their weapons—maybe sighting on the chute at first, to try to kill him that way. Well before he reached the ground, though, Bolan would be close enough for any decent marksman to complete a quick and easy kill.

Regardless of the odds, Grimaldi wouldn't bet against his friend in that eventuality. Too many men had faced the Executioner, all assuming they were strong, mean and quick enough. Too many broken, lifeless bodies marked his trail. Whenever someone underestimated Bolan, Grimaldi thought, it was the beginning of the end.

The blockhouse was behind them now, three seconds, four, five. Finally, the pilot half turned in his seat and glanced toward the open doorway. It was empty. Jack Grimaldi was alone.

He flew straight toward Roswell for another quarter of a mile before he turned the Cessna, circling well east of the site. He hadn't seen a radar dish down there and wasn't worried by the prospect of surveillance. There were no SAMs at the target, no air force to come and rescue them. In a few more moments, the crew down there would have its hands full, all the trouble they could handle.

It was Grimaldi's lot to watch and wait, whichever way the game went down. When it was over, he would either land and pick up his old friend, or fly back to Fort Bliss alone and place a scrambled call to Washington. If it went *that* way, though, he vowed that it would make no difference what the orders were from Wonderland. Grimaldi knew what he would do.

If it came to that, he would be coming back to give the men who killed his friend a little taste of hell on earth.

TUCANA HAD BEEN PLEASED when Ares had appointed him to head security at the New Mexico facility. It was a great responsibility, a huge step forward, and while no one on the staff received a salary, the job meant higher rank, the kind of real authority he had craved since childhood.

That had been nine months ago, however, and Tucana, in his private moments, had long since admitted to himself what he would never tell another living soul on earth: the job was boring. Nothing ever happened at the lab, aside from the occasional visit by assorted VIPs. There had been two of those while he was on the job, and since the visitors had barely spent two hours on the site each time, Tucana and his soldiers were reduced to something like a beefed-up welcoming committee.

It was pitiful.

Sometimes he almost wished that something would go wrong at the lab, and provide him with a break from the monotonous routine. Oh, nothing serious, mind you. Trespassers would be nice, preferably the sort of worthless transients Tucana could rough up a bit before he sent them on their way. On rare occasions Tucana wished that he might have a chance to execute some prowlers, spies from the Establishment, creeping around the place and trying to undo the great work of The Two.

It was a strange wish, granted; possibly, it should have been a warning flag, an indicator of some psychological disturbance, but Tucana didn't see it that way. He had trained to be a soldier for the cause, vowed to do everything within his power to promote the swift, successful reappearance of the Ancients. That meant stoking the pilot light for Armageddon, Judgment Day on Mother Earth, and there was no damned way that job would be completed without spilling blood.

So, basically, Tucana had decided he was simply

zealous to achieve great things, not only for himself, but for The Two, the Ancients, all the remnants of humankind. And what was wrong with that?

It seemed that he would never get his chance out here, though. Even knowing that the lab was critical to everything The Two had planned for these chaotic final days, Tucana still felt sidelined, like a substitute player confined to the bench while his friends hit the field.

Considering what had become of all those first-string players in their last few outings, though, Tucana had to stop and wonder if his present detail wasn't vastly safer, even if it bored his ass off and he wound up hunting scorpions at dusk—the big ones, that would grapple to the death if they were placed inside a mason jar with no room to maneuver. Betting wasn't a sin, according to The Two. The Ancients, after all, had gambled on their choice of Earth, and look how that was paying off, at last!

The lab crew had access to satellite TV transmissions, so they knew about the incident outside St. Louis, the federal raid in Boulder, the highway massacre in Arizona, now the failure in Los Angeles. It was tricky stringing some of those together, but Tucana had long since grown adept at reading between the lines. What it boiled down to, in the proverbial nutshell version, was that Tucana's side had been getting its ass kicked in four different states, and all The Path had to show for it was a depleted army.

Better safe than sorry, Tucana thought, but then he was instantly ashamed. The fear of death, and his acknowledgment of same, was tantamount to failure in

Tucana's mind. The fact that he was torn between self-preservation and self-sacrifice made him ashamed. A true committed soldier of the cause would have no second thoughts. He would embrace death like a long-lost friend, if it would help edge his comrades one step nearer to their goal.

To hell with that, Tucana thought, and he couldn't suppress a tremor racing through his body. His grandmother had once told him that when you shivered that way for no reason, it meant somebody was walking on your grave. Tucana hadn't understood that as a child, but he was all too conscious of its meaning now.

The trick, he knew, was hanging in until the time of tribulation was behind him, and the faithful who survived were blessed with immortality. Of course, Tucana still believed that those of the righteous who fell beforehand would be gifted with new astral bodies as part of their reward, but he had grown attached to his own flesh and blood. He didn't plan to—

The shrill alarm caught him reclining in his chair, feet propped on one corner of his Army-surplus desk, his ankles crossed. The first note of the warning nearly pitched him over backward, chair and all, before Tucana caught himself, arms flailing, lurching from his seat.

He found a pistol in his hand before he was aware of drawing it. His mind was racing, wild surmises crashing into one another, then careering off toward new collisions, making him feel dizzy as he stood there, surrounded by the loud, discordant shriek of panic.

Tucana hoped it was a false alarm, but he would have to find out, either way. The worst scenario that he could think of was a sarin spill, although the lab had airtight doors that ought to save those who were topside. What else could it be?

Still carrying his pistol, cocked and locked, Tucana left his office and was turning toward the elevator when a powerful explosion rocked the bunker and he stumbled, going down on hands and knees.

BOLAN HAD LEFT the Cessna at an altitude of some five thousand feet and plummeted toward the ground, arms pressed against his body, while the weight of his gear seemed to accelerate the fall. That was a fallacy, he realized; two solid objects dropped simultaneously from the observation deck of the Empire State Building would land at the same instant, whatever their respective weights.

He yanked the rip cord at an altitude of fifteen hundred feet. Bolan felt the parachute deploy, was ready when the harness jerked him backward, so that he was dropping feetfirst toward the target zone. Tugging the risers left and right to guide himself, correcting his approach, he came in fifty feet behind the blockhouse, the frosted windows on that side closed up tight against the midday heat. He touched down on his feet, knees bent, and followed through the landing with a practiced shoulder roll that helped absorb the impact and brought him upright once again. His fingers found the quick-release latch and snapped it open. He stepped out of the harness, felt it swept away behind him as a desert breeze filled the chute, propelling it across the open wasteland like some giant jellyfish, long tendrils streaming out behind.

Already moving toward the blockhouse, covering the sightless windows with his automatic rifle, Bolan was alert to any signs that would reveal he had been spotted coming in. There was no trace of anyone outside the bunker, which was one more reason for his timing on the drop, since he had known, from personal experience, that members of the Roswell team preferred to spend their days inside the air-conditioned building, if they had a choice. With any luck at all, that just might be the edge he needed to successfully complete his mission and survive.

The blockhouse had two exits, required by federal safety guidelines at the time it was constructed as a government facility. The front door faced southeastward toward an access road that linked with the nearest highway, well beyond the reach of the naked eye; another opened on the bunker's northeast side and served the kitchen, granting access to a garbage bin planted there. Both doors were made of steel, and both were always locked.

When no alarm was sounded, no shots fired, no soldiers sent to greet him, Bolan made his choice, deciding it would be no harder going in the front door than around the side. A few more loping strides and he was there.

He barely had to aim the 40 mm grenade launcher, loaded with a high-explosive round designed for penetration. He was thirty feet away when he let fly, and hit a crouch immediately, just in case. The HE round went in on target, detonating with a smoky thunder-clap, and he was on his feet a heartbeat later, charging toward the open doorway, triggering a burst of automatic fire to clear his way before he ducked inside.

CHAPTER TWO

Tucana was relieved, at first, when someone in the lab below responded instantly to his query via intercom. It sounded like Auriga, but he wasn't sure. Canned voices never sounded quite the same, and this one made no effort to conceal an undertone of fear.

"There's nothing wrong down here!" the voice squawked at him, from the square wall-mounted transceiver. "It must be something on your end."

The words had barely registered before Tucana heard a brisk metallic rattle that could only be the sound of automatic weapons' fire. He smelled smoke, then, the kind his mind associated with munitions and explosives.

One of his soldiers—Cepheus—ran into Tucana's field of vision, nearly passing him, oblivious, until Tucana grabbed an arm and hauled him back. The young man gaped at him, disoriented for a moment, then he recognized his boss and stiffened to a vague approximation of attention, though he left off the salute.

"What's going on?" Tucana challenged his subordinate.

"Attack!" the soldier blurted. "Front door!" He seemed incapable of forming sentences until Tucana grabbed him by the shoulders and shook him violently.

"Goddammit, Cepheus! Tell me what's happening!"

"Front door," the young man said again, then caught himself. "Somebody blew it, sir. There's shooting. I don't know…"

The explanation trailed off there, Cepheus looking dazed and troubled, as if he had somewhere else to be but couldn't quite remember where it was, or why he was supposed to be there.

"Well, go find out, dammit!" Tucana barked. "You're wasting time!"

"Yes, sir!"

The order seemed to help him focus, and the young man took off running toward the entrance, as if anxious to discover who or what was waiting for him there.

Tucana should have followed, but he had another errand first. If they were truly being raided—and the steady sound of gunfire left no doubt on that score— he didn't intend to meet the enemy with nothing but a pistol in his hand. Tucana ran back toward the weapons locker, found it standing open and removed an MP-5 SD-3 submachine gun from the rack inside.

The wicked-looking weapon was double illegal under state and federal statutes. It was a full-auto weapon with a factory standard suppressor, used on nocturnal security patrols, when it was feared the sound of gunfire might carry for miles across the open desert. Mere possession of the weapon was a felony, but what the hell. The only way police or federal agents would discover it was if they pulled a raid, in which case charges based on the illegal manufacture of nerve gas would make a simple firearms rap pale by comparison.

The MP-5 was loaded when he took it from the rack. Tucana jacked a round into the chamber, grabbed three extra magazines out of a drawer below the gun rack and stuffed them awkwardly into his pockets.

Tucana had prepared himself for this moment—or tried to—from day one at the lab, still never quite believing it would happen. Now that he was in the middle of it, moving toward the sounds and smells of mortal combat with a submachine gun in his hands, he wished that he had some idea of who was attacking. It seemed irrational, insane, to kill or be killed in a fight with total strangers, and that notion almost made him laugh, imagining a world in which the men who wanted you dead took time to introduce themselves, make small talk, prior to pulling out their guns.

The firing slackened, suddenly, before he reached the corner that concealed the killing ground from view. Tucana hesitated, overcome with the desire to drop his gun and run away, do anything he could to save himself. It would be futile, though, he realized. This skirmish might go either way, but the outcome of the final clash at Armageddon had been preordained. Whether he lost his life today or not, the one sure way to lose his soul, his place in paradise, would be to cut and run, forsake his duty in the face of danger.

Stiffened with a new resolve, he swallowed hard and started forward once again, advancing toward the killing ground.

THE SAME HE ROUND that had cleared the doorway also took out two of the blockhouse defenders, dead before they even realized that they were coming under fire. It was a combination of the blast and shrapnel from the shattered metal door that killed them, left their bodies lying twisted in the corridor, oblivious as Bolan swept the entryway with automatic fire and made his way inside.

Two down, but others were responding to the racket of his entry to the bunker, startled voices shouting questions and commands, somewhere around the elbow of a smoky corridor that branched to right and left, some twenty feet in front of him. Instead of rushing it, risking a cross fire that would cut him down in seconds flat, he chose a spot midway between the entrance and the intersection of two hallways, kneeling as he thumbed a 40 mm buckshot round into the M-203 launcher's open breech.

It took more discipline to wait, sometimes, than to attack, especially when waiting meant ignoring the sound of enemies in unknown numbers racing toward you, any one of whom could drop you with a single lucky shot. He could have lobbed a frag grenade into the corridor ahead of him to slow them down and thin the ranks, but that meant pitching blind before he knew their number or their capability.

The time Bolan had spent inside the desert lab before he blew his cover in Los Angeles told him that six or seven guards made up the usual contingent, with another four or five cultists assigned to work the lab itself. The latter batch were noncombatants, in the strictest sense, but Bolan had no doubt they were prepared to fight to defend their crazy cause.

If he could reach them, they would have that chance today.

His adversaries came around the corner in a rush, three men exploding from the corridor on Bolan's left, and two more on his right. He fired the M-203, not bothering to aim as he depressed the trigger, spewing fifty lead pellets, each one the size of a .33-caliber bullet.

Two gunners went down in the face of that blast. Others were stung by the shot but retained their balance, unloading on Bolan with a variety of small arms. His advantage of surprise, combined with drifting smoke that partially concealed him from his enemies, wouldn't last long once they had found the range. Rather than wait for them, he started milking short bursts from his Colt Commando, resisting the temptation to simply hold down the trigger and empty the 100-round drum in a searing nine-second burst. It took more discipline to regulate the rate of fire, while bullets sizzled past his head and spent brass rattled on the concrete floor.

There was scant time for picking out targets as individuals, but Bolan did his best. The two men standing who were armed with automatic weapons posed the greatest danger, and so he shot them first, blessing dumb luck that they were side by side. The 5.56 mm tumblers Bolan drilled into their bodies had sufficient force to penetrate some Kevlar body armor at close range, and Bolan's enemies weren't wearing any. Both of them were slammed backward by the impact, still unloading on the walls and ceiling with their burp guns as they fell.

That left one soldier on his feet, already wounded by the spray of buckshot pellets, but he still had strength and grit enough to blaze away at Bolan with a semiauto pistol. The Executioner stitched him with a rising burst that opened him from groin to sternum, spinning and slamming him against the nearest wall. He left a glossy crimson smear across the beige paint of the hallway as he slithered to the floor.

Bolan was on his feet and cautiously advancing when a sixth man barged around the corner, breaking stride and gaping at the carnage that met him. His "star name" in the cult was something that reminded Bolan of a jungle bird—Tucana, that was it—and he had been in charge of the on-site security when Bolan left to join the raiding party in Los Angeles.

Tucana recognized him now, shock and betrayal written plainly on his face, but by the time his thoughts could translate into action, it was too late for the younger man to save himself. He tried, regardless, swinging up the SMG he carried, muzzle-heavy with its sound suppressor, but Bolan dropped him with a 3-round burst before Tucana had an opportunity to fire. He died without a sound and toppled backward, sprawling on the blood-slick floor.

Cautious, alert for any soldiers late in getting to the

party, Bolan made his way around the corner, stepping over corpses as he homed in on the elevator. It required a certain code to operate, and Bolan hoped the code hadn't been changed within the past two days. He tapped the keypad with his index finger, waiting for the chime that would announce success.

It came a moment later, and the door slid open to reveal an empty car. He stepped inside and touched the only button to be found there. He was slipping an incendiary round into the M-203 launcher when the elevator started moving, dropping smoothly toward the lab below.

AURIGA SLAPPED a button on the intercom and killed the sound of static hissing from the surface world above. It was a fluke that he had heard the first explosion, someone having left the channel open, since the lab was too far underground for occupants to hear—or feel—such things. After his brief exchange with Tucana, Auriga had deliberately keyed the line open, allowing himself and his companions in the lab to listen while the battle raged. It had gone silent now, and oddly, after all the shooting, shouts and curses, silence was the most unnerving sound of all.

He felt the others staring at him, waiting for him to assert himself, flex his authority and come up with a plan. Inside the lab, his word was law, and even on the surface, he deferred to orders from Tucana only if concerns about security were evident. Auriga had the rank, the brains, the dedication to command respect.

And none of it was worth a damn right now.

"What's happening up there?" one of the others asked, a mousy little tech whose star name—Lyra—didn't seem to fit, somehow.

Auriga scowled at her for asking, mainly since he didn't know what in the hell was going on. Cessation of the killing sounds could only mean resistance had been overcome by one side or the other. And, the doctor told himself, if it had been Tucana on the winning side, surely they would have been informed by now, an all-clear signal broadcast to the lab.

"We may—" Auriga choked on the words, was forced to clear his throat and try again. "We may assume the base has been attacked," he said. "In fact, as you're aware, we've been preparing for this day."

"Attacked by who?" another of his techs—Lacerta—asked.

Auriga overcame the impulse to correct the man's grammar and responded to the question. "By the government," he said. "Who else? The state condemns us for our faith and lives in fear that we will pave the way for a triumphant second coming of the Ancients."

There were mumbles from the group of six that stood before him, all of them committed to the message, some still obviously hoping that the fires of Judgment Day would somehow pass them by. Auriga looked beyond their circle toward the elevator and the two security men who stood before its silent door with automatic weapons in their hands. It struck Auriga that their presence didn't make him feel particularly safe, nor did the fact that he and his companions were buried underneath thick layers of steel, concrete and earth. If anything, he felt entombed.

"What happens now?" Lyra asked, staring at him with the wide eyes of a lost and frightened child.

"We wait," Auriga said. "You ought to know the drill by now." His tone was harsh, deliberately so, attempting to snap the others out of their incipient panic and force them to focus, remember what they had been taught. "If necessary," he continued, finishing the order, "we resist."

"With what?" his biochemist, Antlia, demanded. Glancing toward the soldiers near the elevator, he went on, "They've got the only guns."

"We don't need guns," Auriga said, directing a meaningful glance toward the shiny canisters of sarin that were lined up in a rack, two dozen of them, primed and ready. They were working on another batch, but it was incomplete.

No matter, Auriga thought. Even one container, properly deployed, would wipe out any trace of human life inside the blockhouse—and if it escaped, depending on the wind, for something like a mile downrange. Two dozen canisters would turn a patch of desert ten miles square into the freaking dead zone.

If they got a chance to use the gas, that was.

"The elevator's coming down!" one of the sentries blurted.

His lab techs started moving toward the elevator, drawn as if against their will. Auriga barked at them, "Stay where you are! Avoid the line of fire."

That held them for a moment, scared eyes shifting back and forth between Auriga and the silent elevator door. There were no numbers, since the car made only two stops—at the lab and the surface—but an amber light went on above the door whenever someone used the elevator, and that light was burning brightly now. Auriga felt a sudden, childish urge to smash it, grab the nearest heavy object and destroy the light, as if it were the enemy, instead of whomever or whatever was coming down in the elevator car to greet them.

He understood that it might turn out not to be a human being. All the better SWAT teams used some kind of robot these days for reconnaissance, dismantling bombs, whatever. If the government had come to shut down his operation—and who else could it be?—it had to mean they knew about the nerve gas. At the very least, they would be wearing decon suits, rebreathers, something to protect them from the sarin. That could pose a problem, but Auriga told himself that it was likely only members of the final penetration team would be decked out that way. Their comrades on the surface would have come prepared for battle, with their small arms, body armor, helmets and the like.

He had to get the canister upstairs, then. Let the two young sentries deal with any opposition on the elevator, clearing the path for an all-out counterattack. Inspired by the notion, he started snapping orders at his circle of subordinates.

"Each one of you, go fetch a canister of sarin," he commanded. "Bring them over here. Hop to it, now! We have no time to waste."

The words had barely slipped from between clenched teeth, his people moving reluctantly toward the rack of doomsday cylinders, when the elevator door slid open with a muffled whoosh. Before the two young guards could open fire, weapon chattered from inside the car and bullets cut them down where they stood.

Auriga recoiled from the sight of their bodies, their blood, stumbling backward as some kind of lightning bolt erupted from the car, streaking across the lab and bursting into brilliant flame.

BOLAN EXPECTED TROUBLE when the elevator door slid open, standing to one side with the Colt Commando braced against his hip. He cut loose with a burst before he had clear target acquisition, sweeping 5.56 mm tumblers left and right without regard to a specific mark, clearing the way, and saw the two guards crumple as his bullets chopped them down.

There was a risk to shooting in the lab, and Bolan knew the gas mask he had slipped over his head a moment after entering the elevator wouldn't help him if got so much as one drop of the deadly sarin nerve gas on his skin or clothing. Still, it was a risk he had to take, determined that the threat posed by the Roswell lab would end right here, right now.

Bolan didn't wait to find out if there were any other gunmen in the lab. He caught a glimpse of movement to his right, a desperate scuttling, but ignored it as he triggered the incendiary round already loaded in his grenade launcher. The M-203 had no recoil to speak of, its report a muffled pop in comparison to normal gunfire. The result was most dramatic, though, a crimson fireball suddenly erupting on the far side of the lab, enveloping a workbench loaded with equipment, spilling tentacles of flame across the polished floor.

He heard the lab techs screaming as the fire broke out, though none of them were close enough to really feel the heat. Not yet. One of them rushed the elevator in a panic, arms outstretched as if for an embrace, and Bolan shot him in the chest, the short burst pitching his human target backward, dropping him into a crumpled heap.

No mercy.

He couldn't allow these zealots, who had been content to slaughter countless thousands in L.A. and elsewhere for their twisted faith, to have another chance at pulling off their scheme. In their extremity, he guessed that they would promise anything, lie through their teeth to save themselves, but they had stepped too far beyond the pale, and there could be no turning back, no pardon or reprieve.

He fired another burst across the room to keep the others at a distance, while he slipped another HE round into the launcher. As it chambered, Bolan reached out with his free hand for the button that would close the elevator door and send him back upstairs. It would require precision timing, but if he pulled it off…

The door began to close, eclipsing Bolan's view of the wall-mounted rack that held the sarin canisters. He waited through another heartbeat, stroked the M-203's trigger when he had a fraction of a second left and heard the muffled blast after the door had closed, the elevator car ascending with its solitary passenger. The scattered bodies on the ground floor offered no resistance as he passed them and made his way outside, already reaching for the walkie-talkie on his belt.

The desert sky above seemed marvelously clear. What evil could befall humankind on such a day as this?

Unfortunately Bolan knew the answer to that question—more than one, in fact—so many ghastly answers that the cloudless day at once seemed overcast and grim.

"We're finished here," he said into the radio, and heard the Cessna's drone somewhere behind him, circling back.

But only here, he thought, adopting an unconscious frown.

The worst, he knew beyond a shadow of a doubt, was still to come.

CHAPTER THREE

Celeste Bouchet had waited for a phone call, so wrapped up in worry that she dared not leave her motel room for fear of missing the report from Michael Blake. She always thought of him that way, although she had long since convinced herself that it wasn't his name. The label scarcely mattered, now that she had come to know the man.

After the man had saved her life, not once, but twice.

But she was waiting for a phone call, and she nearly jumped out of her skin when someone knocked three times on her door. It was too early for the housekeeper, she thought, and she had ordered nothing from room service, since the motel didn't have room service. Guessing, she decided that it was a man's knock, but she was expecting no one. Only two men in the world knew where she was, not counting the peculiar little dweeb who had been working at the registration desk the previous night.

Lurching to her feet, she took her pistol from the nightstand and proceeded toward the door. The Glock was almost too much gun, but it was fairly light as pistols went, simplicity itself to operate, and with a live round in the chamber it would give her eighteen shots before she had to ditch the empty magazine.

Bouchet was trembling as she looked through the peephole, leaning forward from a yard away, as if afraid the little fish-eye lens would strike at her somehow. She held the pistol in her right hand, squarish muzzle inches from the door, her left hand braced against the painted wood to keep herself from falling forward on her face.

Speaking of faces, she was startled and immensely relieved by the one she saw outside, half turned away from her to watch the parking lot and street. Bouchet would know that profile anywhere—in light or shadow, in a crowd, or in the dark were she required to trace its lines by touch alone.

She fumbled with the security locks, hampered at first by the gun in her hand, then stuffed it inside her belt and threw the door wide open, stepping back to let him pass. So doing, she was treated to another quick glimpse of the outside world, mostly a stream of traffic passing by outside, chrome glinting underneath the desert sun.

The Bide-a-Way Motel was half a block from Highway 17, the interstate located in the southern part of Phoenix with its backside pressing up against the dry Salt River's bed. The rooms were carbon copy, fairly clean and furnished in a style Bouchet perceived as early drifter.

Still, Blake didn't seem to mind. She closed the door behind him, double-locked it, turned and faced the man to whom she owed her life. His face was haggard with a fresh but shallow cut scabbed over on one cheek, an inch or so beneath his eye. Otherwise he was presentable and more or less relaxed.

Bouchet thought he looked great, and was afraid it might show on her face, which only made her blush.

"How did it go?" she asked to keep her thoughts from rambling.

"It went," Blake said. "The lab is history, but there was no sign of The Two."

"You weren't expecting them to be there," she reminded him.

"I know," he grudgingly conceded, "but I kept my fingers crossed regardless."

"So what's next, then?"

"That's what troubles me," he said. "Without a target, I'm severely limited in how I can proceed. Some other time, I might go out and rattle cages, shake some trees and see what tumbles out. Except this time our playmates have already hidden all the cages, and they've cut down all the trees."

"Hiding has always been their specialty," Bouchet replied. "Sometimes they do it in plain sight."

"I guess I haven't looked in the right places, then," he said.

"You're tired. Who wouldn't be?" she said. "You need some rest, and I don't mean those twenty-minute catnaps you call catching up on sleep."

Bolan forced a weary smile and said, "I'm not exactly swamped with leisure time."

"Make time," she told him, trying to make it sound like doctor's orders. "You deserve it."

"I'll deserve it when I'm done," he answered simply. "When the score's all settled."

She had known it would come down to that. Her own thoughts, even now, didn't stray far or long from the image of Andy Morrell, their comrade who had fallen in Los Angeles, giving his life to frustrate a bizarre nerve gas attack on L.A.'s subway system. Blake and Andy had been working different trains, Blake unaware that Andy was a player in the doomsday game until the smoke cleared and the body count was calculated. Short of reading Andy's mind and locking him up in protective custody, there had been nothing anyone could do to stop the former G-man's final play.

But it had cost his life, and the survivors simply had to live with that. Which meant that they would live with pain, a sense of loss and guilty feelings that didn't qualify as rational.

"It's not your fault," she told him gently, wondering if it would help at all. "You couldn't know what he was planning. Hell, *I* didn't know, and I was with him damned near every minute that he wasn't in the bathroom. You're absolved."

"It's not about what you call absolution," Bolan replied. "I can't just leave a job half done, not knowing what The Two have planned between now and their holy Armageddon."

"From what we've seen so far," she said, "I think that's pretty obvious. They're shooting for an incident or string of incidents that will unravel old alliances and push the major players of the world into a final, all-out war. Each step they've taken so far has been escalating, moving up the ladder.''

He glanced at her, looking thoughtful, and she didn't like the smile that played across his handsome face.

HERMES—BORN AS Galen Locke a thousand years ago, or so it seemed that afternoon—sighed wearily and closed his eyes. He had been smoking marijuana for the past half hour, but he guessed that either he had scored a bad batch or his nerves were simply too strung out to let him finally relax. Instead of soothing him, the air-conditioning inside the safehouse had raised goose bumps on his flesh, reminding him unnecessarily that he wasn't immune to fear.

"Don't worry," Circe told him from across the room. She occupied a wicker throne of sorts, positioned so that sunlight spilling through a tall, green-tinted window, framed her like an emerald spotlight. Hermes wondered whether she had planned it, worked out the position of her chair down to the hundredth of an inch, but he refrained from asking. Long experience had taught him that his soul mate left nothing to chance, nor would she talk about her plans, preferring that observers view the stage-managed events as natural occurrences, with just a hint of destiny thrown in to keep them guessing.

"Worry?" he replied. "Why should I worry, dear? We've only had three massive failures in a row, with heavy loss of life. All of our known retreats have either suffered raids or are surveilled around the clock. We're hunted like dumb animals across the land, and now we've lost the Roswell lab. Why should I worry, love? I'm on the verge of ecstasy. It's all that I can do right now to keep from breaking into song."

"Sarcasm doesn't suit you, Hermes," she replied, unruffled by his outburst.

"No, that's true enough," he said. "But I'm hard-pressed to say what does suit me, these days. It's clearly not success."

"I will not listen to defeatism," she told him sternly. "You are destined to succeed in this and bring the Ancients home. We weren't promised that the effort would be simple or devoid of conflict. We were promised victory, and that makes all the difference in the universe."

She was dead right, of course, as usual. And yet...

Hermes wouldn't admit it even to himself, but there were moments, recently, when part of him—the sluggish part once known as Galen Locke when he was in and of the world—nagged him with questions, muttering with some dark purpose in the corner of his mind where useless things were tucked away. Increasingly, of late, those questions made their way from his subconscious into daylight, and he had to deal with them, if only privately.

Questions like:

Hey, what if you're wrong? What if this whole gig with the Ancients is just a pipe dream, nothing more than damaged brain cells shorting out on overload? What if there is no mother ship, and you've been jerking off like a demented idiot the past few years, scheming to bring about a catastrophic war for no good reason whatsoever?

There was medication that could mute the voice inside his skull, if only for a time. Hermes didn't enjoy its side effects—the lethargy, disoriented thought patterns, sporadic impotence with Circe. He had given up the pills for good, eight months earlier, and damn the voice. It was part of him, the part that he had so far failed to subjugate, and he would take it as a challenge to command himself as he commanded others in the cause.

What better way for him to set a bold example for the faithful than by grappling with and finally defeating inner demons of his own?

Except it wasn't working out so well, thus far.

Hermes had come to question even his own skill at prophecy of late, caught himself wondering if he had ever really been in personal communion with the Ancients—and, more to the point, if there were any Ancients with whom to commune. That kind of doubt was nothing short of blasphemy and placed his soul, his cosmic role in the eternal scheme of things, at risk.

Each time the doubts had gone that far, he pulled himself back from the brink, albeit with increasing difficulty. Hermes felt that he was weakening, the string of losses like sucking wounds inflicted by some loathsome parasite, sapping his strength, his will, draining his vitality. If it kept on that way…

And suddenly, he knew what he had to do.

The abrupt change in his attitude had to have been

visible in the expression on his face. Circe blinked at him, only once, and then began to smile. "You have it, don't you?" she asked softly. "The solution to your puzzle."

"I believe I do, my dear."

"Don't keep me in suspense," she chided him.

"I have to find out if it's possible before we start to celebrate," Hermes replied. "There might be obstacles that I haven't foreseen."

"But you see everything," she said without a hint of sarcasm.

"I used to think so," Hermes said, "but now, I'm not so sure. The flesh is weak, you know."

"Not for much longer, love." Her eyes were shiny bright with love for him, excitement over his new mood, the plan that he had dredged from who knew where inside him. And she didn't even know, yet, what the plan would be. Her perfect trust thrilled Hermes, as it always had.

"Before I share," he said, "I need to get in touch with Icarus and see if he can help me make this happen."

"Icarus." She almost whispered as she spoke the name. "He is a man of great determination and ability."

"I'm counting on it," Hermes said. "He's just the sort we need right now, to turn things back around."

She came to sit beside him, one hand settling lightly on his thigh. It stirred him, as she always had and ever would. "A hint, before you call," she said. Her smile was teasing, promising rewards for value rendered. "Would your plan, by any chance, involve…"

She leaned close and whispered in his ear, her breath like feathers, tickling him. When she leaned back again to measure his response, her smile was confident.

"Sometimes I think you really *are* a witch," he said. "You must be careful, dear one, when you read my mind."

"Would I find something to surprise me there?" she asked, still teasing him.

Hermes could barely meet her eyes as he replied, "You never know."

THE DAY ICARUS WAS initiated to The Path, his first choice for the future was to file retirement papers and be done with all the military trappings of his life, which had been good enough to satisfy him for the past two decades. It was only after some discussion with The Two that he decided to remain in uniform, paying lip service to the country of his birth, while working overtime on the behalf of principles that ruled his new and secret life.

His time was coming, Icarus had faith in that, but there were days and weeks he could only sit and wonder when? Late-life conversions to a new faith frequently produced more zealous true believers than a lifetime learning wisdom, from the cradle up. Latecomers always felt a sense of wasted time, life spent in vain before they saw the light and learned the truth. Such men and women came complete with energy to burn, a need to make up for lost time, and it was doubly aggravating, then, for Icarus to simply sit and wait, anticipating orders that were never issued.

Another, weaker man might well have turned to alcohol, perhaps illicit sex, to occupy his mind. For Icarus, the safety valve was exercise. He had been logging more time in the gym these past twelve months, than he had spent there in the other nineteen years of his career, combined. He was a new man, in more ways than one, and women had begun to look at him again, the way they did when he was in his teens and early twenties, wanting him.

Not that it mattered. Icarus had no more interest in their sweaty little bedroom games, just now, than he would spare for watching *Big Time Wrestling* on TV. Both pastimes were a waste of precious time, which he could better spend in private preparation for the coming day of fire and judgment. When the word came down at last, Icarus told himself, he would be ready. And he wouldn't hesitate.

He had two hundred pounds up on the bar, and he was starting on his second set of fifteen reps, his chiseled torso bathed in sweat and glistening, when Icarus was suddenly distracted by the cordless telephone he carried everywhere. It had rung only once before since he had purchased it, and that had been a negligent wrong number. His disappointment had been such that it exploded into fury, and he had launched into a raving tirade, bellowing obscenities into a perfect stranger's ear until the caller had had enough and finally hung up on him.

This time, he let the telephone ring twice before he dropped the heavy barbell, listening to the vibration of its impact echo through the empty gym. He had the whole place to himself, because he liked to work out at odd hours, with no one else on hand to stare at him and wonder why the "old man" pushed himself so hard, so mercilessly toward a goal they couldn't even comprehend.

He picked up on the third ring and didn't speak in case it was another idiot, perhaps an enemy. His name was spoken on the other end, softly, respectfully, and his anxiety evaporated in a rush.

"Here, sir!" he said.

"We need your help," his master's voice declared.

"Whatever I can do," he said, and meant it, without any reservation in his heart or mind.

Hermes explained his need, the urgency behind it. There was just a beat of disappointment, Icarus discovering that this wasn't to be *the* day, but it was coming, soon now, if the preparations were this far advanced. It pleased him greatly that he was the only one on earth who could supply The Two with what they needed.

Hermes finished his brief recital with a question. "Can you do it?"

"Not a problem, sir," the answer man replied.

"I'm glad to hear it."

"By this time tomorrow, it will be done," Icarus said. "Unless, that is, you need it sooner?"

"No, my son. Tomorrow will be fine."

"It's done."

"Always a pleasure, Icarus. You've never let us down."

"And never will," he told the humming dial tone,

not insulted in the least that Hermes would hang up on him, thus gaining the last word.

Icarus had a job to do. In truth, he had a job to delegate, since he wouldn't perform the task himself, but it was all the same. He had selected, screened and trained the brother who would serve him now, assured that there would be no negligence or insubordination from the younger man. His word was law among the troops that served him, but this one was special, a believer like himself, and thus adept at following a certain special order that would be their little secret, hidden from the unit and the world at large.

It wouldn't be concealed for long, of course, but by the time his agent had performed the task assigned, it would be simple to create diversions. Why, in any case, would anyone in his or her right mind suspect The Path could be involved in something so apparently unlike the other recent efforts that had failed? If carried out precisely in accordance with the plan, it would appear to be an accident, and the inevitable rehash by committee would take days to organize, long wasted weeks to sift through incomplete or planted evidence.

With any luck, the trap would have been sprung before the ineffective bastards were within a month of even a preliminary verdict. And by that time, it would be too late for all of them.

Icarus left the barbell where it lay and moved with easy grace into the shower room, stripping off his sweaty T-shirt with such unconscious force that it was ripped along one seam. He kicked off shoes, peeled off his shorts, jock strap and socks, leaving a trail as he approached the nearest shower stall.

Inside, he turned the water on full-blast and icy cold. It was the way he had to make himself, inside, to carry out the mission that awaited him. And there was never for a moment any slightest doubt that he would carry out his mission. Failure meant that his whole life had been a waste, a futile lie. His soul would spend eternity in torment, and he couldn't stem the rising tide by any act of his, even if he had been inclined to try.

Which he wasn't.

Icarus knew exactly where his future lay, and he would stop at nothing to advance that golden day, to make it real. Soon, now, he told himself.

THE SECOND CALL to Hal Brognola told Bolan nothing more than he already knew—specifically, that there were no new leads on Galen "Hermes" Locke or Helen "Circe" Braun—and he cradled the receiver with a sense of apprehension, taking a moment to unhook the scrambler from the telephone and stow it in his bag.

Not knowing was the problem; losing touch was dangerous. His enemies, this time, weren't the sort who would retire once they were beaten in the field. They weren't mercenaries who would fold their tent and try to find another game, nor were they rational enough to take their mounting losses as an indication of defeat. The problem with a true believer, most particularly in bizarre religions, was that faith sustained him, and no earthly evidence of failure was enough to shake that faith in final victory. No matter what defeats the home team suffered, it could always be rationalized as ''part of the plan,'' a test designed to separate the worthy from the weak. A true believer knew that he could never really lose the game, since God or some equivalent of same was on his side.

Most cults, he realized, depended upon a charismatic leader to provide a sense of unity and order. The theology was secondary, sometimes incoherent, often flexible to the point that basic tenets were revised from one day to the next, even discarded on a whim, according to the wishes of the man or woman in control. Cult leaders held such power in the eyes of their disciples, because they were touched by the divine or the demonic, as the case may be. In some cases, they claimed to *be* divine, all evidence to the contrary, and believers still ate it up, trusting their feelings over common sense. Indeed, if common sense were utilized, how many sects could last five minutes in the unforgiving light of day?

There was one thing that Bolan was prepared to say with certainty after his infiltration of The Path, a.k.a. Millennial Truth: as long as Hermes and/or Circe were around to call the shots, their drones would follow orders to the bitter end. It went beyond brainwashing, into areas of trust, belief, a private sense of mission that fell somewhere between commitment and a kind of shared insanity.

The folks at Jonestown had displayed that kind of dedication to their self-appointed god, when they died in Guyana after imbibing a cyanide-laced drink. Years later, lethal faith had reared its ugly head again at

Waco, and in Europe, where adherents to the Order of the Solar Temple killed themselves en masse to get a jump on Judgment Day.

The Path was different, though, in that respect. If members of the cult had simply been content to kill themselves, it would have been a simple sanitation problem: tag and bag the bodies for disposal after they were found. There would have been no public danger, and the problem would resolve itself eventually, when the cult ran out of members willing to participate in suicide. Unfortunately for the bulk of men and women who weren't insane, The Two had come up with a rather different plan. Instead of dying for their holy cause, disciples of The Path were honor-bound to kill for it, if called upon to do so by their leadership. How better to prepare Earth for the second coming of the Ancients than to help accelerate the prophecy of Armageddon and ignite the final conflict that would purge the planet of its unbelievers and consign them to the lake of fire?

So far, their efforts had been unsuccessful—thanks to Bolan—and their targets hardly qualified as global or apocalyptic, but the stakes had visibly increased with each new effort. In Missouri, they had taken half a dozen hostages, demanding airtime from the media to spread the doomsday message. Later, with the plan to detonate a truck bomb in Las Vegas, there had been no effort to communicate beforehand, and their use of transient allies from a paranoid militia group had clearly been designed to shift the blame, promote conflict in the disaster's wake. Most recently, with the attempt to unleash sarin nerve gas in Los Angeles, the cult had switched to front men from a Palestinian commando unit, angling toward an incident of international proportions.

They were learning fast, and Bolan had to ask himself—

"What next?"

He blinked and turned to face Bouchet. "Excuse me?"

"I was wondering what we do next," she said.

The Executioner responded with a frown. "I wish I knew."

"It's not your fault, you know," she said, surprising Bolan as she shifted gears.

"What isn't?"

"Andy, in L.A.," Bouchet replied.

There had been three of them when they began the mission. Bolan was the pointman and presumably the sole combatant, going under cover as a new recruit for Millennial Truth. Celeste Bouchet, as a defector who had seen the light and done her utmost to convince the government of some impending danger from The Path, had helped him understand the way the cultists thought and acted, how they could participate in acts of terroristic violence as a means for reaching paradise. Andrew Morrell had been a former special agent of the FBI, the one insider who had listened to Bouchet and helped to plead her case where it would do some good, with Hal Brognola. He wasn't supposed to meddle on the killing side of things, but he had jumped in with both feet to save Los Angeles from an impending suicide attack by cultists and their part-time Arab allies, armed with nerve gas. Morrell had been instrumental in averting the catastrophe, but it had cost his life.

"I know it's not my fault," Bolan said, but a part of him was unconvinced. Morrell had made his own decisions, but at the same time, he wouldn't have been in a position where the sacrifice was called for, if he hadn't been involved in Bolan's war.

"If anyone's to blame," Bouchet went on, "it's me. I got him into this, remember."

"There's no blame," Bolan replied. "It just gets old, sometimes."

"What does?"

"Outliving all my friends." He stood from his chair. "I'd better go. We both could use some sleep."

They had booked separate rooms at the motel. His room was two doors down, next to the ice machine.

"Speak for yourself," she said, unbuttoning her blouse. "I'm wide awake."

"This might not be the best idea," he said.

"I'll be the judge of that," Bouchet replied. "Get over here."

CHAPTER FOUR

The morning he awoke to change the course of human history, Captain Earl Stant, USAF, felt as fine as frog's hair. He couldn't help smiling at his own reflection in the bathroom mirror while he shaved his handsome, youthful face. He would be twenty-seven on his next birthday, come April, and he had no plans to age at all beyond that point.

What good was immortality, for Christ's sake, if a guy was so damned old and wasted that he couldn't even get it up?

He was excited, keyed up by the orders that had come down yesterday through channels that the Air Force didn't even know existed. It was time for him to do his part, step up and give the cause that boost it needed to initiate the final countdown. He was honored to be part of it, a crucial part, and he had faith enough in his own capability to know he wouldn't fail.

The Two were counting on him. Stant wasn't about to let them down.

One last grin for the mirror, as he slapped on aftershave. His military buzz cut spared him any need for combs or brushes, an ironic touch, considering that he would have been similarly shorn, even without the uniform he wore. Short hair was mandatory for disciples of The Path, unless they had some covert mission in the dead world that demanded a disguise. In Stant's case, there had been no need to improvise. The Air Force uniform he wore was all the cover he required.

His star name, "Janus," said it all. The two-faced Roman god was perfect for his role within the Air Force. On the surface, Captain Stant was true-blue all the way, a pilot known for nerves of steel, self-discipline, plus an engaging sense of humor. Underneath, he was a different man entirely, though some measure of the boyish personality remained intact. The warrior known as Janus took his orders from the ultimate authority, light-years beyond the petty Air Force brass, and waited for the coming day when self-appointed "leaders" of the human race would be consumed by righteous fire.

That morning, he was going to advance the doomsday clock and bring that day much closer. Kissing close, in fact.

It was supposed to be another practice mission for the B-2 Advanced Technology Bomber, designated "Spirit" by the Air Force, popularly designated "Stealth." The plane was one of only three in active service at the present time, full-scale production stalled between the never-ending budget crunch and dissolution of the Soviet Union, deemed to represent the "loss of a structured nuclear threat" to the U.S. of A. With all the standard World War III scenarios in mothballs, Air Force strategists had refined the B-2's mission to emphasize long-range conventional strikes, but even that took practice to keep the handful of trained pilots and weapons officers on their toes.

Lieutenant Philip Gleason was already waiting for him by the time Janus arrived, himself a good half hour ahead of schedule. Gleason was an eager beaver to the core, possessed of an enthusiasm that exceeded standard macho posturing among his fellow pilots, verging on the status of a toxic irritant.

No sweat, Janus thought, as he joined his weapons officer and they prepared to board their craft. He had the cure for that.

It was supposed to be the usual radar evasion exercise. The B-2 ATB achieved invisibility to radar and infrared sensors by reducing the aircraft's radar cross section—RCS—and decreasing engine exhaust gas temperatures through innovations in design. Overall, the B-2 resembled earlier Northrop "flying wings," a configuration with the smallest possible head-on and side view RCS. A further RCS reduction was achieved by use of surface skins constructed from a composite ferrite-based carbon-fiber honeycomb— the "radar absorbent structure"—over a titanium skeleton. Sixty-nine feet long, with a maximum height of seventeen feet and a 172-foot wingspan, the Stealth-Spirit had more than five thousand square feet of wing area. The whole package was powered by four General Electric F118-GE-100 nonafterburning turbofan engines, two in each wing, with a top speed of Mach 0.85 and a range in excess of 6,000 miles.

But Janus didn't plan on flying nearly that far.

They took off from Nellis Air Force Base at 0728 hours, two minutes ahead of schedule, Janus plotting an eastern course to begin with. Their exercise was basically a game of hide-and-seek, with the B-2 attempting to avoid the many radar screens at Dugway Proving Grounds, in Utah, but Janus had plans of his own.

Unfortunately for his weapons officer, those plans didn't include one Philip Gleason. He was strictly excess baggage, and as such, he couldn't be allowed to interfere with something so much greater, more important, than himself.

Which meant that he would have to die.

Across the open desert, day or night, Janus would often take the B-2 Spirit as low as sixty feet above the deck. There were no trees to speak of, and the only thing he really had to watch for were the power lines that typically ran parallel to highways, the exception being files of giant pylons better than a hundred feet in height that marched across the desert, coming down from Boulder Dam to Bullhead City, Arizona, and from there turned westward, toward L.A. Janus had flown below those power lines a time or two, just for the hell of it, but Gleason didn't take well to that kind of stunt.

He didn't take well to their change of course that morning, either.

"There's something wrong here," he announced at 0742 hours, staring at the indicators on the bright heads-up display.

"What's that?" Janus asked, feigning curiosity, although he knew the answer going in.

"Unless this readout's wrong, our course is off by thirty-six degrees," Gleason replied.

"No shit?"

Gleason half turned to face him, just had time to register the mocking smile, before a Parabellum slug from the Beretta Janus held drilled through his cheek and snapped his head back sharply. At that range, even loading hollowpoints, the bullet would have exited his skull, except for Gleason's crash helmet, which stopped the mutilated slug and spared the two-man cockpit from a major crimson splash. The weapons officer twitched once against his safety harness, feebly, then his head slumped forward, chin on chest, the face wound dribbling blood into his lap.

"Don't sweat it," Janus told the corpse. "It's nothing personal."

"WE SHOULD BE DOING this at night," Poseidon said. He frowned and scanned the flat horizon from behind his jet-black shades. "Somebody's gonna see us, I just bet."

"And who would that be?" As the leader of the pickup team, Antares felt a need to keep the lid on any gripes and nagging from his soldiers.

"How the hell should I know?" Poseidon groused. "Somebody. You never know who's out here in the desert. Hell, the Manson family was out here for a while."

"That was Death Valley," Antares said. "As in California, you know? Two hundred miles due west of here, all right? Besides, they're all in jail."

"Prospectors, then. Boy Scouts. Girl Scouts." Poseidon couldn't seem to let it go. "You ever see that movie with the cannibals? *Mountains with Ears,* I think it was."

"The Hills Have Eyes," Pictor corrected him. "That's fiction, Posey, and the cannibals were in Nevada."

"All the same."

Antares turned to face Poseidon, measuring his words. "If you're so fucking scared," he said, "you should have passed and let somebody else come in your place."

"Who said I'm scared?" Poseidon bristled at the accusation. "I'm just thinking of security, is all."

"Uh-huh."

Security had been on everybody's mind when they were laying out the mission. They had done some hasty planning, granted, but Antares was convinced that they had also done their best. The target zone was in the northern corner of Mohave County, Arizona, sandwiched between the Virgin Mountains and the Black Rock range. The nearest town was Littlefield, ten miles away, across the Virgins, and Grand Canyon National Park was forty miles due south, beyond the Grand Wash Cliffs. If there was anyone at all out there to see them, whether grizzled hermit or some off-road biker, he remained invisible.

And if he showed himself, Antares thought, the four of them were well equipped to take him down. The four of them, including Pictor and Columba, leaning up against the second Blazer, were armed to the teeth—three semiautomatic rifles, one 12-gauge shotgun and five pistols among them.

If anything went wrong, they were prepared to kill—or die; yes, there was always that—to see the mission through.

Hermes had made it crystal-clear that nothing could go wrong this time. Antares knew it was an honor and a privilege for him to lead the mission, though in truth, it felt more like a burden at the moment. He was working on a nervous headache and had swallowed half a dozen painkillers already, without any hint of relief. It would get better, he was certain, once they had the cargo loaded and were on their way. But for the moment, he would just have to ignore it and get on with his business.

"He's late," Poseidon said. And then again, when no one answered him, "I said, he's late."

"Your watch is fast," Antares told him, glancing at his own watch to make sure. "It's two more minutes, yet."

"You sure?" Poseidon asked him, sounding peevish.

"Yes, I'm sure."

But was he? And if the delivery was late, what could it mean? A hundred different possibilities—all bad, some dreadful—seemed intent on crowding every other thought out of his mind just then, until he closed his eyes and made a conscious effort to dismiss them all. It seemed to work, after a fashion, though the vanished images still left him with a sense of vague anxiety about the cargo, its delivery, its transportation to the drop-off site.

Reluctantly, he lit a cigarette to help himself relax,

immediately grateful as the nicotine kicked in, providing him an artificial sense of calm.

"I thought you gave up smoking," Poseidon commented.

"No."

"Hey, sure you did. Last week—"

Antares turned and blew a cloud of smoke directly in Poseidon's face. "Does it appear that I've quit smoking? Really?"

"Hey, relax, okay? Excuse me for living."

"You're excused," Antares said, and smiled in secret satisfaction as he turned back toward the north.

Waiting.

They still had time, he thought, and if the cargo was delayed, then they would wait. There was no law against that, after all. Four fellows standing in the desert, staring at the sky. If someone came along to question them or tell them to move on, it would he his tough luck, and no mistake.

Antares wouldn't contemplate the possibility of failure. Everyone was counting on him to succeed— The Two, the Ancients, everyone. He reckoned it was no exaggeration when he told himself the very future of the planet might depend upon his own performance here today.

If he succeeded, there would be no stopping the return.

And if he failed…

He lit a second cigarette from the ember of his first, then ground the old butt underfoot. If anyone asked, he would have to say the cargo was late now, but no one—not even Poseidon—dared to interrupt his silent reverie.

Pleased with himself, Antares kept his eyes fixed on the vast horizon to the north and settled in to wait.

THE RADIO WAS DRIVING Janus nuts, so he switched it off. At first it had been Dugway, asking him if there was any problem, checking in to see why he was late for the beginning of their little game. When that brought no response, Dugway got on the air to Nellis, and then Nellis started nagging him, as well. They weren't tracking him on radar; Janus knew that much, or else they wouldn't have been asking him for his location every fifteen seconds until he switched the damned receiver off.

There. That was better. He was in control.

Now all he had to do was concentrate on what came next.

Landing the B-2 was impossible out here, of course, unless he found himself an open stretch of desert highway, and that simply wouldn't do at all. There was a possibility that he could touch down in the desert and survive it, if he sacrificed the landing gear, but even then the odds were marginal, at best. And even should he be successful, touching down that way would block the weapons bays, preventing those who waited for him up ahead from salvaging the cargo.

There was only one course open to him, worked out in advance. He would be forced to jettison the load himself, then blow the canopy and leave the Spirit to come down as best it could, unmanned. Having disabled the transponder early on, Janus was confident his radical departure from the scheduled course, together with the mountainous terrain ahead, would buy him several days, while search-and-rescue teams were scouring the countryside.

His payload on this "practice" run, as usual, consisted of two AGM-86B air-launched cruise missiles. Each measured twenty feet, nine inches overall, from tip to tail, and two feet in diameter, with a twelve-foot wingspan. Propulsion, if launched, was provided by a six hundred pound Williams Research F-107-WR-100 static thrust turbofan engine, with a top speed of Mach 0.7 and a maximum effective range of 1,550 miles. Each AGM was fitted with a two hundred kiloton W-80-1 oralloy-supergrade plutonium warhead—that was to say, the "dirty" equivalent of some twenty thousand tons of TNT. They were pop guns, as far as nukes went—no radiation to speak of, beyond a mile or so from ground zero; minimal damage from shock waves outside a six-mile radius—but either one of them could still wreak bloody havoc on a properly selected target.

None of that mattered at the moment, however, since Janus wasn't about to fire the missiles. Rather, he intended to drop them, a procedure worked out in advance for safety's sake, in case the B-2 had to crash-land, as he meant to do that morning. Neither missile would be armed, which meant they couldn't detonate on impact, even if they slammed into a granite cliff or dropped into the middle of a raging forest fire. A rupture in the heavy insulated casing could be dangerous, but AGMs were built to take some vicious shocks, and each would automatically deploy a built-in parachute when it was dropped without a firing signal from the plane.

All that remained, then, was to find his mark and come as close to it as possible before he triggered the ejector seat and left the B-2 on its own. Gleason had no objection to the plan, slumped in his shoulder harness like a crash-test dummy, with an ugly crimson puddle in his lap.

Janus was hoping that the plane would blow on impact. At the very least, he could expect it to break up, with wreckage strewed across a quarter mile or more of open ground. He made a mental note to un-latch Gleason's safety rig last thing before he pulled the pin and blasted out of there. That would insure maximum damage to the corpse—perhaps decapitation, if he caught a break—and could delay a finding on the cause of death.

Not that it really mattered, either way. Janus was bound to face some kind of charges when his body and the AGMs all turned up missing from the B-2 wreckage, but it wouldn't matter, then. He only needed time enough to join the pickup team, and they would take him out of there, to his reward. The team and AGMs would be long gone before the searchers gave up hunting in Nevada and Utah, expanding their range. A day was all they needed. One good day, with proper transportation, and the missiles could be any-where.

They could reach anyone.

The B-2's instruments told Janus when he had crossed over into Arizona, just as surely as a highway sign would have advised an earthbound motorist. He stayed well north of Littlefield, then turned due south, the Virgin Mountains coming at him swiftly on his right, the Black Rocks slightly farther off and on his left. He didn't have to see the pickup party below; he knew where they should be, and if they weren't on target, that would be their own damned problem.

It was no sweat, dropping the AGMs. Janus had practiced it a hundred times with dear departed Gleason, using dummies on the other runs, but it was all the same. He needed altitude, two hundred feet or so, to make it work. No sweat, Janus thought, since the mountains flanking him on either side would shield him from the countless electronic eyes already sweeping the horizon, searching far and wide for the invisible.

Smart bastards, building planes the Russians couldn't see, and then the Russians fell apart, swept up whatever scattered marbles they could find and left the game. Now there were planes the good guys couldn't see, if someone like himself should take it for a spin and accidentally forget to bring it back.

The one regret that Janus had about the plan was that he couldn't keep the plane itself. What havoc he could wreak in the last days, what blows he could inflict upon the enemy with such a fighting chariot at his command. Still, Janus had his orders from The Two, and he wasn't about to disobey. Not when he stood to lose his soul and any prospect of eternity.

He hit his mark and threw a switch to open the weapons bays. All systems go, according to the indicator lights. The AGMs were gone like that, in no time at all, and Janus held the B-2 steady on its course, another mile or so, before he reached out for the button that would trigger his ejector seat. He threw a last glance at Gleason, slumped forward now, without the taut straps of a shoulder rig to hold his body upright.

"No hard feelings, right?" he quipped, then blew the canopy.

There was a rush of air and sound that nearly deafened him. He kept his eyes closed, even with the goggles on, in case he took a faceful of debris by accident, but in another instant he was free and clear. An almost graceful somersault, nearly a hundred feet above the hurtling aircraft he had just abandoned, then the parachute snapped open, jerking him back into contact with reality.

He had to fight the risers briefly to keep from being smashed head-on into a cliff, and even when he gained the open ground, his altitude was such that he came down with painful force. He would be black and blue by sundown, from his shoulders to his buttocks, but the bruising was a minor price to pay for victory, much less eternal life.

As soon as he could stagger to his feet, Janus released the harness on his chute and left it where it lay. According to the rule book, he should hang around and bury it, but nothing in the book had planned on this specific situation. He had twenty minutes, tops, to find the pickup team, or they would drive away and leave him to the desert, on his own.

Determined not to miss that rendezvous, Janus took

out his compass, double-checked what he already knew and started hiking to the north.

"I'M TELLIN' YOU, it was a fucking UFO!"

"Yeah, right!" Deke Moseley had been taken in by crazy stories in his time, but he wasn't about to buy that shit.

"Hey, man, you saw it, right?" Jerry Jones was angry that his friend would question his veracity. "You gonna claim you didn't see that shit?"

"I saw something," Moseley admitted, punctuating the admission with another belch. Corona beer always hit him that way, but he loved it all the same. He finished off the bottle, and pitched it out the driver's window of his Cherokee.

"So, what the hell you think it was?" Jones demanded.

"Some kind of plane. What else?"

"You need to watch the *X-Files*, man," Jones replied. "That show'll open up your fucking mind."

He had been leading Moseley by two to one on the Coronas, and had sparked up a joint moments prior to the arrival of a sweeping shadow, swallowing the Jeep before it swept away and took on solid, bat-wing form, then disappeared to the south. He wasn't absolutely wasted yet, but he was getting there, and no mistake.

Moseley humored him. "So, what the hell am I supposed to do about it?"

"Go check it out, man. Maybe it went down, you know? It happens all the time. Remember Roswell, man? The Air Force doesn't want you to believe they got a saucer, but the world knows, man. I know."

"Roswell was over fifty years ago," Moseley said, asking himself if maybe he should have another beer.

"So what, man? Jeez, I'm tellin' ya, they come down all the time. You ever read the papers?"

"Not that supermarket trash you mean," Moseley replied, deciding that another beer would definitely hit the spot.

"Well? Are we goin' after it, or what?"

And suddenly, Moseley thought why not? It wasn't like they had all kinds of things planned to do that morning. They were out of school and out of work, with nothing much but time to kill. The Jeep was nearly full of gas, though, and regardless of the fact that Moseley was sure it couldn't be a UFO, much less a freaking crash, what was the harm in looking?

"All right, then," he said at last, "let's make it interesting. I'll bet your sorry ass a six-pack of Corona that it's no damned UFO."

"You're on, bud. Fire it up!"

He put the Cherokee in gear and took off down the canyon, four-wheeling over rough ground at speeds that made Jones bounce in his seat. The second time he almost slid right off, dropped the joint and had to scramble for it, bending down. Moseley saw his opportunity and gunned the Jeep, then tapped the brakes, bouncing his best friend's head off the dashboard.

"Fuck me!" Jones wailed.

"Not a chance, bud. You'd have to grow tits, first, and maybe some hair."

"You're particular now?" Jones leered at him. "Hey, I remember when—"

"Whoa!"

Coming over a low rise, the Cherokee almost slammed into a couple of guys who were standing there, out in the middle of nowhere, eyeballing some nondescript object laid out on the ground. Moseley cut the wheel sharply to miss them and slammed his foot on the truck's no-lock brakes, raising a cloud of dust and dumping Jones on the floorboards by the time they came to rest, some thirty feet off to the left.

"Goddammit, Deke, I don't know why the hell—"

"Who are those guys?" Moseley interupted, twisting the rearview mirror to catch another glimpse of them, assuming that the dust would ever settle.

"What guys?" Jones was scrambling back up to his unsteady seat. "I didn't see—"

"Those fucking guys," Moseley cut him off, jerking a thumb back toward the four men who were lined up now behind the Cherokee. "The ones with guns."

"Say what?" Jones turned to scope them out. "They must be out here shootin' cans or rabbits, don't ya think?"

"They look pissed off."

"Hey, you'd be pissed off too if some asshole nearly runs you down in the middle of nowhere." Suddenly, it seemed that Jones had a bright idea. Moseley almost saw the lightbulb floating in a comic-book balloon above his friend's head. "I'll bet they saw the saucer, too!"

"Hang on—"

But the warning came too late. Jones was out and

moving toward the gunmen in a flash, wearing that loopy smile that seemed to keep him out of trouble, more often than not.

But not this time.

All four of them cut loose in unison with rifles, rapid-firing from the hip. They seemed to focus all their fire on Jones first, his body twitching through a crazy little dance before he toppled over on his back.

His best friend's death bought Moseley the time he needed to crank the truck's steering wheel around and gun the engine. He could feel the fat tires digging in for traction, nearly lost it when he felt the truck thump across some kind of moderate obstruction that he figured had to be Jones, but he concentrated on the need to get away from there and tell the cops they had a gang of crazy people on the loose.

He might have made it, too, if those old boys were any slower on the trigger, but they swung their weapons right around and started pumping slugs into the Cherokee as he made the turn, presenting them with something very like a perfect target. There was barely time for him to scream before the bullets found him, smashing through the tinted windows, others drilling through the door like it was nothing, seeking flesh.

Deke Moseley never felt it when his Cherokee struck the rocky wall ahead of him, the air bag opening in time to spare him from a broken nose, but much too late to save his life.

CHAPTER FIVE

The news reached Icarus as it reached ninety-five percent of all Americans that afternoon: he switched on the television and channel-surfed until he found his way to CNN, letting the talking heads brief him on what had happened in the past few hours. Elsewhere in the nation, military men ensconced in offices much like his own would have received the word directly from the field, but Icarus wasn't involved. It was beyond his jurisdiction and his need to know.

That was the beauty of his plan.

And it had been *his* plan from the beginning; there was no denying that. He could allow himself a moment of reflection, basking in the pardonable pride of his achievement. Even though he hadn't flown the plane himself, had come no closer to the scene of action than a thousand miles or so, he was responsible.

Which made him guilty of at least a dozen major felonies, most of them federal crimes or violations of the U.S. Military Code of Conduct, starting with the theft of government property and progressing toward—what? Seditious conspiracy? They couldn't call it treason, technically, unless a war had been declared against The Path, in which case Icarus would certainly be guilty of offering aid and comfort to the enemy. Without that declaration, though, there *was* no enemy in legal terms; that rule of law had been established during the Korean "conflict," and again in Vietnam's "containment action."

Still, he was a traitor in his heart. And it felt wonderful.

His "brother" officers would never understand how Icarus had changed, but he didn't require their understanding. Why should he debate the point with fools who let themselves be duped by years of propaganda and deceit? He had been skeptical himself, of course, despite the sighting he had made three years earlier, during a routine flight from Washington to Texas, but the incident had set him thinking, set him searching. In his spare time, he had scavenged through the Project Blue Book files—his rank had paid off there, in gaining access to the data—and determined for himself that the Air Force had lied repeatedly about its findings in the field of UFOs. He had found that out of several thousand sightings, something more than one in ten was labeled "unexplained" in Air Force files, when they had finished heaping on their labels: swamp gas; migratory waterfowl; weather balloons; the planet Venus. Ten percent the Air Force would admit to, and that told him there was something out there.

The remainder of his journey had been solitary searching: reading every book that he could lay his hands on, from the scholarly to the bizarre; watching a hundred different TV documentaries that rehashed old reports and told him nothing in the end; shedding his uniform as he sat in on assorted lectures, seminars, what have you.

All of it in vain until he found The Path.

Most of the men and women Icarus had worked with over twenty-three long years in uniform would think he was insane. That knowledge didn't faze him in the slightest. He had been where they were, seen the world through their eyes, and he knew that each of them would have to find the truth in his or her own time.

Except that they were running out of time. His plan had seen to that.

In order for the Ancients to return, their prophecy to be fulfilled, it was essential that disciples on the planet Earth hold up their end of the arrangement and prepare the way for Armageddon. Recent efforts to proceed in that direction had been frustrated, by one means or another, and while Icarus hadn't been privy to those schemes, he guessed that part of the problem had been shoddy planning, perhaps a tendency to think small.

The spark for Armageddon's cleansing fire couldn't, in his opinion, be ignited on a local scale. Icarus grasped the strategy of building tension through a string of incidents spread over time, but it could only take the cause so far. The final battle of humankind was clearly meant to be a clash of principalities and powers, not some penny-ante game of cops and robbers. That meant cranking up the volume until it shattered glass—and international relations.

They would have to go all-out, if they were going to succeed.

And with the plan devised by Icarus, they did exactly that.

There was no turning back from this point, short of full surrender and a prison sentence that would run to several hundred years. His faith told Icarus the Ancients would devise some way to make their prophecy come true, in any case, and where would that leave those who failed along the way? Some losses were much worse than any sacrifice of liberty or mortal life.

If there was anything that irritated Icarus about his own bold plan, it was the fact that he couldn't participate directly. It required a younger man with special skills and a particular assignment in the Air Force: someone like brave Janus, who as luck would have it was a loyal disciple of The Path himself.

But luck, in this case, had received covert assistance from a mortal hand. It had been relatively simple, given his rank and connections, for Icarus to arrange certain transfers, steer a fellow believer in uniform toward a particular course of training and the ultimate assignment as a B-2 pilot. Like Janus, he wished they could have taken the bomber intact. What a weapon it would have made in the final conflict!

Still, there would be men and arms enough involved, when Armageddon's fire began to spread. No corner of the globe would be secure on that day; only those who kept the faith and kept it well were guaranteed to make it through alive.

Icarus planned to be among that number, booked

for paradise, and if it meant he had to set the world on fire with his own hands, so be it. It would be an honor.

He was smiling when the intercom clicked at him, and the smooth voice of his adjutant came through. "Sir, Major General Vandiver calling on line one."

"Thank you," Icarus said, still smiling as he lifted the receiver to his ear. "Good afternoon, sir. How may I help you?"

IN HIS FOUR YEARS with the NEST program, it was the second time Joe Duncan had been scrambled for an actual emergency, which seemed like twice too often, when he thought about it and considered the alleged security surrounding nuclear devices in the States and overseas. All things considered, if you ruled out the chaotic hodgepodge of warring mini-nations that had once been the Soviet bloc, there was no good reason why a nuclear emergency search team should ever be needed.

And yet here he was in the big Huey chopper, surrounded by soldiers and weapons, his own armament consisting of a side arm he had fired once in his life—at paper targets—and the Geiger counter resting on his lap.

The first time he was scrambled, as the NEST commanders aptly described this disruption of his daily life's routine, it had been 1996, in circumstances not unlike the present case. A military plane had gone down in Wyoming with some nukes onboard. It took the better part of two weeks just to find the plane, and when the weapons were recovered safe-and-sound, the brass had heaved a huge sigh of relief. Joe Duncan, for his part, had been demobilized and sent back to his day job as a consulting engineer with the Atomic Energy Commission.

Now here he was again, despite his fervent hopes that he would never get another scramble call. This time, the search had been pared down to something less than forty hours, even though the Air Force had begun by looking in the wrong location. Air Force brass had logically concluded that the B-2 should have gone down somewhere on its scheduled route, between the Nellis takeoff point and Dugway Proving Grounds, and in fact, the main search effort was still concentrated there, in Nevada and Utah. The NEST excursion into Arizona was an unexpected shift, occasioned by a grim report from local lawmen.

From the slim details available, Duncan gathered that some off-road bikers had discovered two dead men, their bodies and their four-wheel-drive vehicle shot to hell with something that resembled military hardware. Sheriff's deputies responding to the call had found a parachute nearby, which was in turn identified by military contacts as a chute used on the AGMs and certain other nukes, in case they were discarded without being armed and fired. Where there was one, the brass had reasoned, there might be another, and the supposition was correct.

Two parachutes; no nukes.

And that was bad.

The wreckage of the B-2 plane itself had been discovered some time later, as the quadrant search continued. Duncan's team had been assigned to check the

crash site first, in case—against all odds—the AGMs
were somehow still aboard, although their parachutes
had been recovered twenty miles away. He understood that no one really thought the nukes were in the
plane, but they were also manifestly not at the location where their parachutes and various suspicious tire
tracks had been found. It was incumbent on the NEST
squad to make doubly sure of where the AGMs were
not, and to discover—if they could—why any B-2
weapons officer would jettison that kind of deadly
payload over rural Arizona.

Once those questions had been answered, then it
would be time to work on who had grabbed the
AGMs and why.

Because the nukes were gone; that much was clear
to Duncan, and it made his scrotum shrivel as his
mind ran through a few of the more plausible scenarios.

So far, they knew the following: two AGMs with
unarmed warheads had apparently been jettisoned before a B-2 bomber crashed in Arizona's desert wasteland, cause unknown. Those AGMs had been retrieved by persons unknown, using at least one
four-wheel-drive vehicle. Around the same time, persons unknown had also murdered two innocent young
men, firing enough rounds in the process to suppress
a small riot. In the circumstances, and considering the
isolation of the desert canyon where both incidents
occurred, Joe Duncan was prepared to view them as
related, without waiting for analysis of tire tracks at
the murder scene and pickup sites. Presuming that the

incidents were unconnected simply strained coincidence beyond the bounds of rationality.

"Our LZ's coming up," the Huey pilot shouted back at them, and all around Joe Duncan, his companions seemed to take a firmer grip on automatic weapons. It was inconceivable to Duncan that they would find any targets waiting for them, but he understood the gung-ho military mind-set that required a bit of flash and melodrama even in the most mundane circumstances.

The chopper touched down in a storm of dust and sand whipped up by rotor wash, Duncan shielding his eyes with one hand as he dropped to the ground, ducking beneath the flashing blades. Some fifty yards to the southwest, he saw the shattered B-2 bomber—most of it, at any rate—protruding from the sand like some downed spaceship in a movie on the Sci-Fi Channel. It had broken up on impact, but a large piece of the fuselage was still intact, though twisted and deformed: a tombstone to the pilot and his weapons officer. Duncan assumed both men were dead, since they hadn't been found along the glide path of the plane.

And yet, if there was time for them to jettison their nukes, why would they go down with the aircraft?

Duncan thought it was ironic that despite the troops and guns surrounding him, he was the pointman for this portion of the mission. With his Geiger counter, he would be the first man to approach the B-2 wreckage, ascertaining whether there were nukes onboard, and if so, whether any of their insulated shields were compromised.

He could have—maybe should have—worn a radiation suit, but Duncan hated putting on the spaceman outfit that inevitably made him break out in a sweat. He would have donned the outfit even so, of course, if he had thought there was a hope in hell of finding either AGM aboard the plane. In point of fact, though, he couldn't imagine any way at all in which the parachutes from both nukes could be found so widely separated from the wreckage, if the nukes had gone down with the bomber.

"Watch your ass," one of his fellow NESTers said, as Duncan switched on his Geiger counter and started moving toward the wreck. Another said, "Take care," while the remaining four kept quiet, checking out the landscape, seeming anxious for a chance to use their guns.

He circled wide around the B-2 wreckage, holding the Geiger's wand before him, eyes fixed on the gauge that would alert him to a radiation leak. The needle jittered slightly, as it always did, but Duncan paid no mind to background radiation that was present almost everywhere, to some minute degree. He knew exactly how the Geiger counter should react if he encountered damaged nukes, and there was nothing even close to that reaction as he moved closer toward the wreck.

At last he stood beside it, touching-close, and waved the others in. They rushed to join him, circling the shattered aircraft as if planning to impound it for some parking violation. One young member of the team—Grunewald—climbed up to check out the cockpit, returning moments later with a grim frown on his face.

"What's up?" the team commander, Captain Ormond, asked him.

"One body, sir," Grunewald replied. "Looks like the weapons officer. I'm betting that he didn't have his harness on when they nosed in."

"The pilot?" Ormond pressed.

"He pulled the pin, sir. Up and outta there with the ejector seat."

"You're positive?"

"Yes, sir," Grunewald replied. "The canopy's been blown."

"I don't much like the smell of this," Ormond announced to no one in particular. "No sir, I don't like this at all."

THE TELEVISION NEWS was limited, with military censorship and all, but Hermes still took heart from what he heard. This plan, unlike so many others recently, appeared to be successful—or more properly, at least it had not failed so far. They were a long way from the finish line, he realized, but picking up the two cruise missiles was the first and crucial step toward ultimate success.

It didn't bother Hermes in the least that two young men were dead, gunned down by his disciples at the pickup site. They had been idle meddlers, worse than useless, and he questioned whether anyone would miss them. Anyway, the prophecy he was pursuing called for millions to be sacrificed before the second coming of the Ancients. These two weren't members

of The Path, and would have died regardless in the
coming days of wrath. If anything, they had been
spared potential pain and suffering.

Hermes had done the two of them a favor. It was
almost like a gift of love and mercy. He hoped they
were properly grateful.

On the TV screen in front of him, a bleach blonde
with the bluest eyes Hermes had ever seen was running down the bare-bones details of a search in
progress. Wreckage of the B-2 had been found, she
said, but there was no official word yet on the weapons it had carried on its final flight. One body had
been salvaged from the ruins of the airplane, but a
second man was missing. On the screen behind the
blonde, a photograph of Air Force Captain Earl Stant
suddenly appeared, his all-American face decorated
with the hint of a smile.

A brief and cryptic phone call, hours earlier, had
told Hermes that all was well, so far. The caller spoke
no more than forty words, no names or places mentioned, nothing that would help eavesdropping lawmen build a case, but by the time he cradled the receiver, Hermes knew the first phase of their project
was successful. His disciples had retrieved the AGMs,
along with Janus, and the weapons were aboard a
moving van, eastbound on U.S. Highway 10. Southwest of Pecos, Texas, they would pick up Highway
20, which in turn would transform into Highway 59
when they crossed into Alabama and began the journey north. Between Chattanooga and Knoxville Ten-
nessee, it was Highway 75, then Highway 81 leaving

Knoxville for the long run to Maryland and dooms-day.

Hermes knew it was undignified to gloat, but he couldn't resist the grin of satisfaction that was tugging at the corners of his mouth. There had been so much grief of late, so many setbacks, that an encouraging turn of events brought him instant relief. He felt as if a crushing weight had lifted from his shoulders—or, at least, as if it had begun to lift, the pressure easing up enough for him to catch his breath.

It was too early yet to celebrate. A thousand dif-ferent things could still go wrong, he realized, and any one of them could spell disaster for the cause, but he was hopeful all the same. Why not, when prophecy assured him that the Ancients could not be denied by any pitiful attempts of mortal man to frus-trate their cosmic design? If his belief meant anything at all, if there was any truth behind his mystic reve-lations, then the end of human time had been foretold from the beginning. Hermes was the instrument of bringing the experiment to its predestined conclusion.

In other words, he couldn't fail. And yet...

Misgivings were a weakness, Hermes told himself. Such doubts betrayed a lack of faith to which he, of all men on Earth, should be immune. It was a vicious circle, the existence of such doubts forcing Hermes to question his incipient divinity, anxiety com-pounded by uncertainty, until he felt an almost fever-ish uneasiness. If anything was wrong, if he had made some critical mistake—

"You should be pleased." The sound of Circe's

voice cut through his jumbled thoughts, returning Hermes to the here and now.

"I am," he said, with something less than full conviction.

"But you're worried, too," she said, reading his mind.

"Not worried," he replied. "Concerned, perhaps."

"That's only natural," his soul mate told him. "After all, there have been problems recently."

"You have a gift for understatement," Hermes said, unable to resist another smile.

"As long as we believe," she stated, "no problem should be insurmountable. I take the Ancients at their word."

"Suppose…" He stopped himself before his doubts came pouring out.

"Go on," she urged him. "Tell me, love."

"I simply wonder if the issue may be still in doubt," he said, cringing inside, worried that voicing any doubts aloud might somehow give them strength, an independent life. "We know that prophecy is subject to interpretation, sometimes offered as a warning, rather than a guarantee of things to come."

"Not this time," Circe said, with perfect confidence. "Not in the Final Days. How could the Ancients be mistaken? They're responsible for what we know as human life on Earth. They know the end from the beginning."

"Even so."

"We have been tested," she went on. "Our faith and our determination have been challenged, and we have not given up. We *will* survive the fires of Armageddon, and we *will* see paradise."

"And if we fail?" His voice was weak.

"I don't acknowledge failure as a possibility," Circe replied. "I won't acknowledge it. Neither will you."

Hermes drew strength from her assurance, as she took his hand and squeezed it. Even after all these years, she still amazed him with the depth of her conviction, her unmitigated nerve.

"You're right," he said at last. "Doubt is an insult to our destiny."

"So be it," Circe said.

"So be it," Hermes echoed, drawing her into the warmth of his embrace.

HAL BROGNOLA DIDN'T HAVE the luxury of watching CNN that afternoon. He had been swamped with calls, beginning with a brief from Stony Man Farm, in Virginia, followed closely by a heads-up from the White House. The events out west were shaping up as more than an unfortunate occurrence, and the Oval Office wanted the big Fed on top of it, in case things went to hell, beyond retrieval by the military or the FBI.

At first glance, it was difficult to see how anything could be that bad, when you considered all the personnel on hand, so many of them trained to cope with just this kind of an emergency. The problem wasn't numbers, though, or even expertise.

The problem was legality.

In the United States, lawmen and soldiers had a

hefty book of rules to follow, from the top down. You started with the U.S. Constitution, adding untold numbers of restrictive federal, state and local laws that spelled out just exactly what a politician, cop or soldier was allowed to do in any given situation, nailing down the how and where and when. Of course, such laws were broken every day—in boardrooms, in the halls of government, on city streets across the land— but they were broken, generally, with discretion. Those who broke the rules and let themselves get caught were typically out of luck.

That, in a nutshell, was the reason Hal Brognola had been put in charge of Stony Man—initially the Phoenix program—by another President, in other times. The White House personnel had changed since then, but crime and terrorism never went away: they just got worse. Brognola's program had been secretly continued under several administrations now, and when there was a problem that required not only bending rules but smashing them to bits, Brognola got the call.

It had been such a call, some weeks earlier, that sent Mack Bolan to infiltrate The Path. The body count on that job was still being tabulated, and it wasn't finished yet. Now this: a missing Air Force pilot and two AGMs with twenty-kiloton warheads.

Brognola couldn't help but ask himself if the events might be related. He wasn't a man who saw one great conspiracy behind the many evils of society, and yet he knew there *were* conspiracies—some trivial, some cataclysmic—all around him. A conspiracy, by legal definition, was no more than an agreement between two or more offenders to commit a crime, however great or small, coupled with some attempt to pull it off. You could conspire to jaywalk, to commit a petty theft...or to destroy the world.

Jaywalking didn't bother Brognola, but he had spent the past few weeks tracking his agent in the field, as first one plot for wholesale slaughter was derailed, immediately followed by another. Members of The Path had planned to detonate a massive truck bomb in Las Vegas, to destroy a huge resort hotel, and when that scheme went south, they instantly rebounded with a plot to unleash sarin nerve gas on the L.A. subway. Was it mere coincidence that two cruise missiles vanished in the wilds of Arizona so soon after Bolan took out the cult's lab in New Mexico?

Perhaps. But Hal Brognola wasn't betting on it.

Granted, there were hundreds of extremist groups in the United States that would have loved to get their hands on dynamite or hand grenades, much less an AGM. There were militias, Klans and neo-Nazi factions, ethnic liberation armies simmering in ghettos coast to coast, street gangs and syndicates, along with several other doomsday cults whose teachings made The Path seem halfway rational. Beyond that, there were foreign terrorists and drug cartels, and at least a dozen governments that harbored killing grudges against Washington—the list seemed endless when he ran it down.

Coincidence?

The big Fed didn't think so.

Most of the domestic candidates on his prospective hit list were the kind of half-assed malcontents who printed semiliterate broadsides on basement mimeo machines and trained with small arms on the weekends. Others spent the best part of their time wasted on drugs and alcohol, between adventures in petty crime that ultimately led them into violent conflict with police. The street gangs mostly killed each other, plus whatever innocents were fool enough to think the public streets were safe by night or day and walked into the cross fire. Various political and racist groups aspired to launch private holy wars, but most of them were small-time operations run by stunted minds. Some of them might attempt this kind of score, but they would leave a trail behind them like Godzilla on a stroll through downtown Tokyo.

And someone always talked.

Unless the nukes were found within the next few hours, up on cinder blocks in some pathetic redneck's yard, Brognola didn't see a happy ending to the quest. The missing AGMs might well have been ripped off by madmen, but Brognola knew the job hadn't been done by idiots. And that made all the difference in the world.

An idiot with nukes might set them off by accident, most likely in his basement, tinkering with things he didn't understand. A madman, on the other hand, might very possibly devote his life to coolly and deliberately unleashing hell on Earth. Both types were dangerous, but there was no legitimate comparison between the two.

The Path wasn't made up of idiots. From top to bottom, members of the cult were dedicated to the proposition that a mother ship was drawing closer day by day, bringing salvation to the nearly ruined planet Earth from another galaxy. The Ancients whom it carried were the same race that had populated Earth in prehistoric times, as an experiment of sorts, and they were coming back to put things right where they had gone awry. The Bible, the Koran and other holy books allegedly contained the message of their coming, and the need for certain loyal disciples to prepare the way. That meant an all-out final conflict on a global scale, which members of the cult were ready to provoke by any means available, to clear the decks for a return to paradise.

Brognola didn't buy it, but that was beside the point. When dealing with religious zealots, he was constantly reminded of that line about the bogeyman: "It makes no difference whether you believe in him, because the bogeyman believes in you." And he would get you, someday, if you didn't watch your ass.

Watching was Hal Brognola's job—or part of it, at any rate. Besides keeping both eyes open, he was also under standing orders to eliminate the bogeyman, whenever and wherever it appeared. Of course, the bogeyman wore different faces and espoused a wide variety of causes. He was left- and right-wing all at once; black, white, Hispanic, Asian; male and female; straight and gay.

The one thing that his clones all shared in common was a taste for blood.

Brognola knew the enemy by smell, if not by sight. He kept his fingers crossed that this time, Bolan wouldn't be too late.

His thoughts were grim as he reached to grab the telephone.

CHAPTER SIX

It took Brognola all of fifteen seconds to describe the problem, handing it to Bolan, but he had no prospects for resolving it. That wasn't news, of course. If the big Fed had known the answer, he wouldn't have made the call.

"I'll see what I can do," Bolan said, and returned the telephone receiver to its cradle. "Damn!"

Behind him, stirring sleepily beneath the rumpled sheets, Celeste Bouchet asked, "Is it bad?"

"It could be," he replied, and sketched the rough outline of Brognola's report: a military plane crash, one crew member dead, another missing, two bystanders shot and left for the coyotes, evidence that two nukes had been jettisoned before the plane went down and retrieved by someone waiting below.

"Dear God."

"We don't know that The Path's involved," he said, but it rang hollow, even as he spoke the words.

"Who else?" Bouchet demanded. She was sitting in bed, sheet loosely clutched against her chest. Despite the recent intimacy they had shared, she still retained a bit of modesty in Bolan's presence. "It's exactly what they'd try to do," she said. "Or would have, anyway, while Ares was alive."

"Ares," born Dillon Murphy, had been the leader of Thor's Hammer—the doomsday cult's paramilitary arm—until he crossed Bolan once too often and wound up dead.

"Who was in-line to run the show with Murphy gone?" he asked.

"You were," Bouchet reminded him. "I guess they've given up on you by now, though."

Bolan had replaced the fallen Ares for a time, and was assigned to lead the team that carried lethal canisters of sarin nerve gas to Los Angeles for the rendezvous with a small group of terrorist front men. He had foiled the plan with seconds to spare, and while Brognola pressured LAPD to withhold a final body count on perpetrators, there was still a decent chance that leaders of the cult might know Bolan—or Nimrod, as they knew him by his star name—hadn't been among the dead.

"Who else?" he prodded her.

"Beats me," she said. "I've been out of the loop for two years now, remember. Lots can happen in that time. All kinds of people come and go. I never had close dealings with Thor's Hammer to begin with."

"Anything at all?" he said. "I need a handle on this thing before it goes to hell."

"Well, Ares used to travel, sometimes, with a guy called Cerberus," she said. "They got that from—"

"The three-headed dog who guards the gates of hell," he said. "I still remember some of my mythology."

"Okay. Unfortunately," she went on, "I never knew his real name, where he came from, anything like that. It didn't pay to ask a lot of questions, if you get my drift."

He got it, loud and clear. "Description?" Bolan asked.

"Last time I saw him," she replied, "he would have been midtwenties, maybe six foot one or two, athletic-looking. I'm no good at guessing weight, but he looked solid for his size, no flab. He had brown hair, the standard buzz cut, but I never saw his eyes."

"How's that?"

"He always wore these sunglasses," she said. "The mirrored kind, you know? Indoors, outdoors... I never saw him when he wasn't wearing them. Some kind of macho thing, I guess."

It was a fair description, but it didn't match with any of the cultists he had taken out, so far, nor anyone whom he had met during his infiltration of the sect. Of course, the fact that Bolan hadn't seen him didn't mean the guy was gone, by any means. He might have been assigned to operations in some other area, which kept him out of Bolan's way. It didn't matter now, unless he had assumed control of paramilitary operations for the cult and had the means of leading Bolan to the missing AGMs.

"You've tracked this outfit by computer since you left, correct?" he asked.

"As much as possible. The public stuff was easy," she admitted, "but I've also hacked into their private files from time to time."

"And you have contacts," he went on.

"*Had* contacts," she corrected him. "I'm poison to them now. It's like I spit on everything they stand for and believe in."

"But you still know where to find them," Bolan said. "Outside of the retreats, I mean?"

"A few. What are you getting at?"

"I need a pigeon," Bolan told her frankly. "Someone I can squeeze for information—meaning that it shouldn't be somebody from the bottom of the rank and file."

"This kind of thing," she said, "I just don't know. They'd play it close. Most of them wouldn't have a clue."

"That narrows down the list."

"I'm thinking, dammit!" Bolan couldn't tell if she was mad at him or at herself. "Where did this happen, with the plane?"

"Mohave County," Bolan said. "I make it three, four hours north of here."

"That close?"

"That close," he said.

"Well, if it *was* The Path, they'll want to take the missiles somewhere safe, where they can hide until they're ready for whatever crazy deal they have in mind. I don't know where they'd go, but they'll need transportation, right?" She forged ahead, not waiting for an answer. "For a job like this, they'd want somebody they can trust. Somebody close enough to come through in a hurry, too. My guess would be Mercury."

"Real name?" he asked her.

She shrugged, the sheet slipping to show off delicious, deep cleavage. "All I know is where he lives— or lived, two years ago."

"And that would be…?"

"Las Vegas. Shall I pack?"

ON THE OCCASIONS when he thought about his old and half-forgotten life, Mercury told himself that every difficulty he had ever suffered was directly traceable to parents who had hated him from birth. Why else, he asked himself, would John and Janice Cobb have tagged their first and only man-child with the given name of Cornwell, knowing—as they had to have known—that everyone who met him for the next two decades would delight in calling him Corn Cobb? It was demonic, a sadistic plot…but it was all behind him now.

Thanks to The Path.

The Path had saved him, in more ways than one. Before he had his close encounter, five years previously, Cobb was cruising in the fast lane on a one-way road to sudden death or prison, wasted half the time on drugs and alcohol, dabbling in crimes that ranged from B and E and auto theft to smuggling contraband from Mexico. In fact, if he was honest with himself, he knew that *dabbling* didn't cover it. He had already been arrested twice by metro police in Las Vegas, and suspected that the Feds were watching him, just waiting for the slipup that would send him to Atlanta, maybe Leavenworth, when he was rescued by a miracle.

His close encounter had occurred on Halloween of 1994. A number of his erstwhile friends, in retrospect, attributed the incident to a distorted view of trick-or-treaters, warped by acid and a fifth of Absolut, but he was adamant that it had been for real. How could it *not* be, when the incident had turned his whole life around?

His sighting had occurred in that part of Las Vegas called "the Naked City," set back from the Strip a block or two, which tourists never saw if they were lucky. The inhabitants were mostly black, unanimously poor and plagued with crime that kept the squad cars prowling day and night in search of bad guys to arrest and youngsters to harass. Cobb had gone in to score some smoke, but never made the buy. Instead, he walked into a vision right out of *The Twilight Zone,* complete with eerie lights and short, big-headed man-things that had stared at him with eyes the size of avocados, fairly willing him to use his so far worthless life for something other than destruction of the flesh by chemicals.

Corn Cobb had been impressed, but even so, it took him several days to find what he was looking for. Hermes and Circe were delivering a lecture on November ninth, and he had gone to check it out, intrigued but not convinced that it would do the trick. To Cobb's surprise and great relief, the message put it all together for him, slicing to the center of his being like a scalpel. Cobb had known that he was home, discarding tattered remnants of his old life and emerging from his welcome to the sect as Mercury.

He had assumed, in the beginning, that his righteous newfound friends would want him to forsake his past transgressions, maybe even try to make amends. Mercury was surprised, therefore, when he was summoned to a private meeting with the leaders of Thor's Hammer and informed that he could serve the Ancients best by practicing those skills he had acquired during those dreary, best-forgotten days. The difference would be that now, when Mercury appropriated vehicles or other merchandise, he would be acting as a soldier in their holy cause, each move he made another step toward Armageddon and the second coming of the Ancients.

How could he refuse?

The Blazers had been easy in a town like Vegas, switching license tags no challenge for a man of Mercury's achievements, when you had so many tourists pouring in around the clock. Odds were, the stupid earthlings wouldn't even miss their plates unless some smoky stopped them on the road, and by the time that happened, Mercury's associates would have accomplished their design, ditched the Blazers somewhere, wiped for prints and gone on their way in clean vehicles.

Simple.

They hadn't entrusted Mercury with any details of the plan, but one of them—a youngster named Columba—had let slip that they were headed for "someplace back east" when they were done. Columba also told him that their mission, whatever it was, would move the world a long step closer to the Final Days.

"We're gonna pull the trigger," he had said. And now, watching the news out of Arizona on television, Mercury could guess what the young man was hinting at.

The thought had troubled him at first, thinking about what he had done, the countless lives that would be sacrificed, but that was war. For Mercury and other faithful of The Path, the road to paradise led through the days of tribulation and across a sea of cleansing fire. If he could help to strike that spark, permit himself and other faithful souls to reach that sacred goal, then Mercury was proud. He had no reason to be fearful.

Not unless he counted cops and Feds.

He wasn't all that worried, though. A lifetime of skirting the law—when he wasn't breaking it six ways from Sunday—had accustomed Mercury to covering his tracks. The fact that he had been arrested only twice, with both cases dismissed for lack of solid evidence, was testimony to his skill at dodging the police.

This night he meant to celebrate by taking in a show. Not one of those revues that played for suckers on the Strip, with topless dancers wearing stage makeup thick enough to stop a bullet, rouge around their nipples, with a two-drink minimum for liquor that was watered down and overpriced. No way, José. Instead of wasting time and money on a tourist scam, he would be dropping by the Pussycat, an all-night theater near Glitter Gulch—or Fremont Street, if you were looking for it on a map—that featured three hard-core triple-X flicks for the modest entry fee of $7.95.

The Path discouraged sexism, of course, but what was wrong with watching young, enthusiastic people get it on—in Technicolor, yet—if they were all consenting adults? Mercury had never seen the harm, and he avoided having it explained to him by the expedient of keeping private business to himself. What Hermes didn't know would never hurt him, and he had a feeling that the Ancients would be sympathetic to a lonely soul in search of some relief.

The Pussycat was four blocks from his small apartment, and there was no point giving up his parking space, when he could walk it just as easily. He covered less than half a block before a soft, vaguely familiar voice called out his name.

"Yo, Mercury!"

His star name, yet. There was no question of ignoring it and playing dumb. Who else, except another member of The Path, would recognize him on the street?

He turned, trying to keep it casual. A woman stood before him, and her face sparked fragmentary memories. "I know you," Mercury declared, but he was having trouble with her name. Before he could retrieve it, something else clicked in and sounded an alarm inside his head. "Hey, wait a second! You—"

He never got to finish it. From out of nowhere, someone was behind him, pressing close. The round, hard object poking at his spine, an inch or so above the waistband of his jeans, could only be the muzzle of a gun.

"We're going for a little ride," a man's voice said.

THE DAY HIS ORDERS CAME, Apollo put the damper on an urge to jump for joy. He had been sniffing after the assignment for the past two months, beginning with the first announcement of the visit, knowing that it would present the perfect opportunity. Indeed, *he* had proposed the operation that was under way right now, and while Apollo knew that he wouldn't receive the credit, he wasn't concerned.

The only thing that mattered was success, the triumph of their sacred cause.

Protecting foreign heads of state fell to the Secret Service, ordinarily, and while that crowd had primary responsibility, the job was rated too big, too important, for a single agency to handle the whole show. Enter the FBI, assigned to a variety of jobs, including background checks and interviews with crazies who might try to take advantage of the visitation, warning them that they were underneath a microscope and any hostile action on their part would land them in a cell—assuming they survived to reach the lockup. Twenty G-men had been detailed to assist the Secret Service with its work around the conference site, and it was that job that Apollo had pursued with all the subtle zeal at his command. Ass-kissing was required, but he had pulled it off. He would be watching from a ringside seat when the first blow was struck, preceding Judgment Day.

And if the plan should somehow go awry, he was prepared to strike the blow himself, regardless of the cost.

Apollo was convinced that his terrestrial facade wouldn't survive The Day. It was a measure of his dedication that he didn't care. The shell he wore was nothing but a vehicle. If it could serve a higher purpose and enable him to reach the gates of paradise, what did it matter if his flesh was sacrificed? In time, after the fires of Armageddon cleansed the earth, he knew that he would be reborn, perfect and incorruptible, to dwell among the Chosen for eternity.

His fellow agents would have laughed at him if he had tried to tell them how he felt, what he believed. No matter. *He* would have the last laugh, when the governments of men were swept away, replaced by the benevolent, all-knowing masters who had traveled countless light-years to bestow their seed and blessings on the planet Earth.

This morning—zero minus two and counting—he had been assigned to yet another sweep around the target zone. The Secret Service brass was never satisfied with the previous day's examination of the grounds, nor did they seem to trust the sensors, microphones and cameras they had installed themselves to make the place secure. There was a chance, however minuscule, that someone, somehow, had slipped past the various security devices, wormed his way onto the property and either planted booby traps or found a place to hide himself away, in ambush.

So, they searched each morning after breakfast using dogs, metal detectors and a special kind of infrared device that could differentiate between a man and lower forms of animal by body temperature. There was no levity among the searchers, but Apollo had to bite his tongue to keep from laughing when he thought about the wasted effort, all those hours spent in vain.

They didn't understand that when death came, it would be coming from the sky.

Of course, there had been preparations made for that contingency, as well. The property had several well-concealed antiaircraft batteries, each unit mounting twin Vulcan 20 mm Gatling guns, each capable of spewing armor-piercing high-explosive rounds at a cyclic rate of 6,000 per minute. If incoming hostiles managed to bypass the Vulcan emplacements, they would be met by Secret Service agents armed with FIM-92C Stinger missiles, equipped with advanced electro-optical seekers that were sensitive to both infrared and ultraviolet light. Each Stinger bore a three-kilo HE fragmentation warhead with a contact fuse, and while the payload sounded small, it was potent enough to bring down a Boeing 747 in flames.

The problem with those preparations being that they only worked with hostile aircraft when the gunners thought they had due cause to open fire. Again, it was Apollo's keen imagination that had found the chink in that protective armor, passing it along for what it might be worth. And so, the plan was finalized.

He wasn't current on the details, didn't need to be, although he knew enough from television to surmise what form the end would take. It was a gift of mercy, he decided, that the kill team would be using nukes. It would have been less tidy and less comfortable all around if they had come with sarin or some other CBW agent. Being vaporized, he thought, was infinitely preferable to thrashing on the ground, choking to death on your own bile and vomit.

Apollo would only strike if the first team failed somehow, and while he didn't expect that to happen, he was already prepared. The Smith & Wesson Model 1076 semiautomatic pistol on his hip, standard issue for the FBI since 1991, was loaded with ten Glaser Safety Slugs, each blue projectile containing pellets of No. 6 birdshot suspended in liquid Teflon. The safety slugs got their name by virtue of the fact that they exploded on impact with walls, doors and other inanimate objects, preventing lethal ricochets in combat situations. There was no such mercy for their human targets, though, since Glaser rounds also exploded after penetrating flesh, the resultant wound wholly internalized, with tissue damage equal to a close-range shotgun blast.

No man could take a Glaser round in the head or torso and survive. Between the loss of tissue, shock and hemorrhage, it simply wasn't possible. One Glaser slug anywhere between the hairline and the groin meant instant death.

Apollo would be packing ten rounds in his pistol, with another eighteen in spare magazines, hedging his bets against all odds.

He finished his portion of the standard morning search without discovering a trace of saboteurs or infiltrators on the grounds. It was a drag, but he made no complaint, preferring to appear devoted, dedicated to his mission.

Which, in fact, he was. The brass in charge were simply ignorant of what Apollo's mission *was*.

But they would find out soon enough.

Sometimes, he almost hoped the kill team *would* be stopped before it had a chance to fire their AGMs. He thought of how delightful it would be to glimpse the dazed expression on the faces of his various superiors when he produced his weapon and unloaded on the target, right before their startled eyes. There were long odds against that happening, he realized, but one could always dream.

Dreaming was free.

"What's funny?" someone asked him, and Apollo snapped back to the here and now, turning to face Walt Jesperson, another agent on the Bureau detail.

"Say again?"

"The way you're grinning," Jesperson explained. "Hear a new joke, or something?"

"Joke?" Apollo felt a sudden rush of panic, but he swallowed it and covered his mistake as smoothly as he could. "No, man," he said. "I've got a date tonight, is all. Hot little number I ran into at the Waffle House in town."

"You dog. I don't suppose she's got a friend?"

"You're married, Walt," Apollo said.

"Hey, I can dream," the G-man cheerfully reminded him.

To which Apollo silently replied amen.

"FOR SOMEONE KNOWN as Mercury, you're not too swift."

The hostage glared at Bolan, flicked his dark eyes briefly toward Bouchet and brought them back again to Bolan's face. He knew where danger lay, which one of them was holding the remainder of his life in none too gentle hands.

"I don't know you," he said at last. "I don't know what you want."

"That's easy," Bolan told him. "Information."

"Try the Yellow Pages," Mercury advised him, working on a sneer that wasn't convincing, somehow.

"You're a funny guy," Bolan said. "How about if I go first? Your name is Cornwell Cobb. That must have been great fun in school, right? You've got two or three old beefs on file—some B and E, a little grand theft auto—but there's nothing recent."

"Fuckin' ay, there isn't," Cobb shot back. "I know my rights! You can't just grab a person off the street without cause and take him—where the hell are we?"

"It's my home away from home," Bolan replied.

The warehouse off Industrial Boulevard was on loan from Brognola, maintained on the Q.T. by Justice for use at need in a variety of ongoing projects. The office where Cobb sat, while Bolan stood above him and Bouchet paced in the background, was a glassed-in cubicle located in a kind of loft that overlooked the warehouse storage area. Cobb's hands were cuffed behind his back, connected to a narrow chain around his waist that kept him seated. Otherwise, his legs were free.

"I know my fucking rights!" he said again. "You can't just hold me here!"

"That would be theoretically correct," Bolan replied, "if I was a policeman."

Cobb's face paled. "Who are you, then?"

"What difference does it make?"

Cobb took a shot at bluster, glancing once more toward Bouchet. "I know your girlfriend," he remarked. "Can't bring her name to mind, right now, but she remembers me. I see it in her face. You set me up, bitch!''

Bolan's open hand was cobra-quick, rocking Cobb's head back on his shoulders, while the sound of impact echoed like a pistol shot inside the little office cubicle.

''Is that supposed to hurt?'' he asked, blinking the tears away. Undaunted, Cobb craned to his left for a better view of Celeste, and went on talking to her.

''Your name'll come to me,'' he promised her. ''I mean your *real* name, girlie. And they'll find you. You can bet your worthless life on that. There's no place you can hide on Earth. No place in all the universe!''

''They found me twice already,'' she replied, meeting his twitchy gaze, ''but I'm still here.''

''Third time's the charm, babe. Cancel Christmas, if you get my drift.'' Cobb started giggling, but the sound died in his throat as Bolan shifted to obscure his view of Bouchet.

''You need to concentrate on what's important to you at the moment,'' Bolan said. ''Like getting out of here alive.''

''Nobody here gets out alive,'' Cobb said, his face split by a grin. When there was no response from Bolan or Bouchet, he made a pouting face. ''Hey, what's the matter? Nobody remembers poor Jim Morrison? The Doors, ya know?''

''Right now, the only doors you have to think about are those standing between you and the street,'' Bolan replied. ''It's up to you if you walk out of here today, or someone finds you when they come to dump the trash tomorrow."

Cobb blinked at him, considering the choice. At length, he said, "You haven't told me what you want yet. Information, yeah, I know. The question is, what kind?"

"I want to talk about The Path," Bolan replied.

"Some breakthrough," Cobb shot back. "I figured that one out the minute I saw *her*. You wanna narrow down the field a little bit, or should I try and guess?"

"You watch the news on television?" Bolan asked him.

"Not if I can help it," Cobb replied. "I want my MTV."

"Maybe you heard about a military plane that crashed in Arizona earlier today?"

"I might of heard something," Cobb said.

"You may have *seen* something," Bolan suggested, "when your friends picked up their vehicles."

It was a long shot, maybe, but he saw it hit the bull's-eye. Cobb blinked rapidly, just twice before he caught himself, then tried to bluff it out. "I don't know what you mean."

"I hope you're wrong," Bolan said.

"What the hell? She tell you I was in on that thing with the rockets? Huh?"

"Nobody mentioned rockets," Bolan said.

Cobb started blinking again. "I saw it on TV, just like you said."

"Nice try, but no cigar," Bolan replied. "The media was told about a missing payload, but the nature of the weapons wasn't specified."

"So what? I guessed, and I got lucky."

"You're all out of luck," Bolan informed his prisoner.

That said, he turned to face Bouchet and told her, "You should wait outside."

She hesitated, frowned at him, then nodded. "Right," she said, avoiding any glance at Cobb. "Okay."

"Hey, what is this?" the captive asked. "Where's she going?"

"She's in the way. You recognized her, right? There goes my edge. Besides," Bolan said and smiled, "she doesn't need to see the wet work."

"Hey, now—"

"Do you want to be a martyr?" Bolan asked him, leaning to meet the captive's gaze. "It's not a problem, if that's what you're after. It can be arranged."

"I'm not afraid of you," Cobb said, while clammy perspiration beaded on his face.

"Well, see, that's my mistake. Here I've gone and messed things up,"

"Say what?" Now Bolan's hostage was confused.

"I figured I was grabbing someone smart enough to know the score," he said. "You true-believer types, it's hard to tell sometimes. There's no way to be sure if you've lost contact with reality."

As Bolan spoke, he reached inside his nylon windbreaker and drew the sleek Beretta 93-R from its shoulder rig. The weapon's sound suppressor was custom-tailored for a combination of convenience and efficiency, unlike some of the heavy, foot-long cylinders that kept a semiautomatic pistol's slide from operating properly. Bolan had compromised by lightening the powder load on his 9 mm ammunition just a tad, without sacrificing any significant penetration. He changed the little muffler's baffles periodically, and it worked like a charm.

Cobb's eyes were locked on to the pistol as if he had never seen a gun before. "What's up with that?" he asked his captor, almost whispering.

"I don't like torture," Bolan told him. "Never have. The truth is, I don't have the stomach for it. Killing, well, that's something else. I figure, you don't want to talk, that's your business. I'll go find someone else. Try, try again, you know?"

He thumbed the pistol's hammer back with a metallic snapping sound. Cobb winced at that and tried to lean back in his chair, but there was nowhere left for him to go.

"Hey, wait a second, now—"

"You want to say a prayer or something?" Bolan asked him. "No, you're right. What sense would that make? This will only take a second, if you want to close your eyes."

"Don't shoot, for God's sake!"

"Look, guy—"

"I'll tell you what I know, all right?" Cobb said. "Just put that fucking thing away."

"Okay, then," Bolan answered. "If you're sure."

CHAPTER SEVEN

There is no airport in the capital of the United States. The sixty-nine square miles of Washington, D.C., have room for some three-quarters of a million people, an Air Force base, a U.S. Navy yard and Fort McNair, along with sundry public buildings, monuments and parks. However, incoming diplomats, lobbyists, tourists and terrorists who come to Washington by air touch down across the Potomac River, on the outskirts of Arlington, Virginia, and make their entry to the capital by land, across the historic George Mason Memorial Bridge.

Been there, done that, Apollo thought, and checked his wristwatch for the third time in eight minutes and eleven seconds. He was nervous, getting irritable, and he couldn't seem to will himself into a more relaxed and stable frame of mind. Deep breathing often did the trick, but not today, and there was no way on God's earth that he could strike a meditation pose while he was standing out there on the tarmac with a squad of fellow G-men, Secret Service agents and assorted fat cats from the presidential welcoming committee.

He would simply have to tough it out, let his experience and training take the lead, while dedication kept him ever on his toes. The action wasn't coming down this day—not here, not now—and that meant that, for all intents and purposes, he was precisely what he seemed to be: a bodyguard on station, waiting for his client to arrive.

This time, of course, the tension was exaggerated, due to the client's identity. Apollo's previous assignments to security had always dealt with Bureau brass, protected witnesses and such—the kind of people who, if somehow struck down despite his own best efforts, were expendable.

This day, it was a different ball game altogether.

They were waiting for the president of Russia to arrive.

It was the chief of state's first visit since his last election, when he had narrowly beaten back a new effort to resurrect communism—perhaps even Stalinism—via the ballot box. More to the point, this wasn't simply a vacation for the man from Moscow. He was visiting America in hopes of sitting, on neutral ground, with leaders of the Chechen separatists who had been giving Mother Russia hell the past eight years. No treaty was anticipated from the meeting, but a cease-fire would be nice. In any case, it was a start.

Or so the world believed, those mindless sheep who swallowed every sanitized, distorted morsel thrown to them by the corrupt news media. Large numbers of them certainly had never heard of Chechnya and didn't even know the Russian president was coming to America, much less why he was coming. They were self-made idiots who couldn't recognize this day as the beginning of the end.

So much the better. They would offer less resistance that way when it came their time to die.

The Russian plane was seven minutes and three seconds late when the announcement came, relayed through receivers that resembled hearing aids, worn by each agent on the pickup team. Transmission, if one of them had to broadcast in the direst of emergencies, would be achieved with microphones the size of tie clasps, clipped to each agent's lapel.

Apollo didn't actually see the 747 land. They had another team on that end of the deal, complete with pace cars and four snipers from the Bureau's Hostage Rescue Team, in case somebody tried to reach the aircraft as it taxied toward the terminal. It was unlikely, given the security in place, but you could never tell about those Chechen rebels, and it wouldn't suit Apollo's purposes if anything should happen to the target here and now.

With any other flight, the jetway would have been extended like some great umbilical cord, providing linkage with the terminal. In this case, though, the passengers would be deplaning on the tarmac under open sky and boarding limousines that waited for them in the shadow of the massive terminal. They wouldn't pass through customs, wouldn't show their passports and, above all, wouldn't mingle with the crowd inside. On the flip side, if any strangers showed up on the tarmac and attempted to approach the 747 or its passengers, the interloper would be treated to a night in jail…assuming he or she survived.

Apollo was alert now, focused on the job at hand with the intensity of an electron microscope. The safety of the Russian president meant more to him right now than to the other members of his team combined. The target would be worthless to him—to the Ancients—if it didn't reach the designated kill zone.

He watched the massive staircase rolling out to meet the aircraft, guided and propelled by a miniature tractor. The driver was a regular airport employee, triple-checked before he was allowed to take the gig, surrounded even now by men and women packing automatic weapons. One false move—a seeming bid to ram the plane, for instance—and he would be dead before he hit the pavement.

But for all their planning, nothing happened, which is just the way Apollo wanted it to go. The president and his small entourage deplaned, shook hands with several dickless wonders from the State Department and split up to give themselves some elbow room inside the limousines. Apollo would be riding in the tail car, bringing up the rear, with a companion from the FBI and two more from the Secret Service. Altogether, it made seven visitors, surrounded by three dozen guns.

The Russians might have been en route to prison, for the hardware that accompanied them. It was an all too necessary show of force these days, when anyone from mercenary terrorists to hopped-up car thieves posed a lethal threat to every motorist in Washington. They wouldn't be in town that long, however; they were simply passing through, not even stopping at the

White House on this first leg of their journey to the place where destiny awaited them.

The place where all of them would die, and in their dying, give the world new life.

HIS CHAT WITH COBB, a.k.a. Mercury, sent Bolan in a new direction, still uncertain whether it would be of any help, but he had to do something. At this point, anything at all seemed better than the inactivity that came from sitting on his hands.

His grudging source had provided Bolan with two names. The first, Antares, was the star name of a fellow cultist who had taken delivery on two Chevy Blazers from Mercury the day before the B-2 pilot pulled his disappearing act in Arizona with the AGMs. No matter how he squeezed the dealer, Bolan could get no more than the code name and a vague description of the man, Mercury swearing on his life—quite literally, in this case—that he had never seen the guy before. A call had come from someone in authority, close to The Two, instructing him to have a pair of four-wheel-drive vehicles ready on a certain date, and Mercury had done as he was told.

As far as a description of the Blazers went, they had been black and fairly new, the older of the two a 1997 model. Mercury had fitted them with stolen Arizona plates, but he didn't record the numbers. After all, as he told Bolan, "Why the hell should I? I'm not the fucking Motor Vehicle Department!"

The description wasn't much, and Bolan knew the Arizona plates—if not the vehicles themselves—had almost certainly been ditched by now, but he had passed the information on to Hal Brognola, just the same. From Washington, the big Fed could alert the FBI and state patrols, if he was so inclined, to see if they could stop the pickup team en route.

En route to where? That was the question that kept nagging Bolan, and his only hope of finding out lay in the second name he had received from Mercury. The name was Danny Pascoe, and its owner was another car thief, operating out of Amarillo, Texas. He wasn't a member of The Path, but Mercury had dealt with him from time to time, strictly on a cash-and-carry basis, and considered him the next thing to a friend. It obviously pained the cultist to betray Pascoe, but he had grudgingly confessed arranging for a pair of backup vehicles to be on standby when the pickup team rolled into Texas, just in case.

Bolan had kept that piece of information to himself when he was on the line with Brognola. Six hundred miles of open road lay in between the point where Mercury's compatriots picked up the AGMs and Amarillo, where they might—or might not—switch to different vehicles. Pushing the Blazers hard, with three or four pit stops along the way and no cops in the rearview mirror, it would still take eight or nine hours to cover that distance. If he could only beat their time...

The one thing Bolan couldn't do, in that case, was to stand around and wait. His phone call to Brognola had included a request that Jack Grimaldi meet them on the road outside of Kingman, Arizona, picking up Bolan, while Bouchet kept their wheels. Bolan had attempted to extract a promise that she would return to Phoenix and the Bide-a-Way Motel, wait for him there, but she had balked at staying on her own in Arizona, noting that The Path had members there who might be hunting them by now. Unable to enforce his will upon her from a distance, Bolan had reluctantly agreed with her suggestion that she keep on driving toward Amarillo, checking in with Hal Brognola periodically until there was some word. If she heard nothing by the time she got to Texas, she would find a place to stay in Amarillo, go to ground and wait.

Grimaldi picked them up on Highway 93, northwest of Kingman, passing by a small town with the cheery name of Chloride. He was flying a McDonnell Douglas AH-64 Apache helicopter this time, and the whirlybird was loaded for bear, with a 30 mm chain gun mounted in the nose, the wings mounting two 7-round rocket pods and two quad mounts for Hellfire tank-killing missiles. He made one pass above their vehicle, catching Bolan's attention, then moved out ahead and set down on a flat stretch of desert, away to the left.

"Remember," Bolan told Bouchet before he left her, "absolutely no contacts with any cultists on your own. Check in with Hal, and let it go at that."

"Yes, sir!" She snapped a mock salute, then made a pouting face. "I'm really not a total idiot, you know?"

"I noticed that," Bolan said, already retreating toward the chopper. "Just take care, all right?"

"You do the same," she called, still watching Bolan as he turned his back on her and ran for the Apache.

Grimaldi delayed the liftoff until Bolan had his safety harness fastened, nestled snug into the forward gunner's seat. The chopper ordinarily employed a two-man crew, though Jack could handle it alone if need be, still inflicting awesome damage on an enemy.

"Where to?" Grimaldi asked, when they were airborne, headed eastward.

"Amarillo," Bolan said. "I need to see a man about some wheels."

There was no doubt in Bolan's mind that Grimaldi could save him time, the Apache cruising at an average speed of some 180 miles per hour—versus seventy on the road if he was lucky—but he could never really make up for lost time. The pickup team had close to a six-hour lead when Bolan first learned of the AGM snatch, and his side trip from Phoenix to Las Vegas had given them all the time they needed to reach Amarillo, switch cars if they were going to, then continue on their way.

To where?

The fact that Mercury had placed them headed eastward didn't help a bit, as far as destinations were concerned. From Amarillo, they could strike off to the north, south, east or west, whichever they desired. Worse yet, they might split up and take the AGMs in opposite directions, bound for separate targets. And from there, God only knew what would become of the destructive warheads.

They would need some kind of aircraft fitted out for combat duty, if they meant to fire the missiles from the air, as AGMs were meant to be employed, but Bolan could already think of other options, each of them a nightmare in itself. Because you didn't have to fire the rocket; you could simply park them somewhere—in a truck or van, say—and then detonate the warhead with a timer. If that option didn't thrill you, and you knew what you were doing with the hardware, it was possible to crack open the warhead and remove the primary nuclear charge for more convenient transportation. Hook up a timer or a trigger to that, and you had yourself a nuke that would fit in a suitcase or backpack—smaller than the missile's warhead, to be sure, but still devastating enough to kill every living thing within a radius of six to eight city blocks.

That didn't sound like much of an explosion in the middle of the trackless desert, but it would be hell on Earth if detonated in the heart of New York City or Los Angeles, Chicago or Atlanta, Dallas or Miami. Hell, the possibilities were endless, doomsday multiplied by two.

And all he had to stop them, so far, was a lousy car thief's name.

ANTARES FOUND HIS CONTACT waiting at a highway rest stop east of Shamrock, Texas, five miles from the Oklahoma state line. They had exchanged the matching Blazers back in Amarillo for a GMC Suburban and a Chevy Astro cargo van, but he still felt as conspicuous as hell, one of the AGMs tucked in behind him, loosely covered by an Army-surplus blanket and a faded quilt. Poseidon drove the van and pulled off at the rest stop on a signal from Antares, riding in the shotgun seat. Behind them, captured in his mirror, the Suburban did likewise.

"Pull over by the rest rooms, there," he ordered, keeping one hand on the AR-15 rifle wedged between his right leg and the door. If they were being set up somehow, Antares reckoned he could swing the weapon into action easily enough—if not to save himself, at least to take some of the bastards with him.

A navy blue Mazda sedan was parked immediately to his right, the driver stepping out now, turning toward Antares with a crooked smile. Antares, startled, missed the inside door latch on his first try, fumbled with it, then came close to tripping on his weapon, as he stepped down from the van.

"Nobody told me *you* were coming," he remarked by way of greeting.

"No one was supposed to," Cerberus replied. "We're playing this one close. Too many losses lately. Too damned many accidents."

"We've done all right, so far," Antares said. He felt defensive, even though his team had been no part of the abortive operations that had wrought such havoc in the past few days. He couldn't make a move without remembering The Two, that they were counting on him to succeed, and sending Cerberus to meet them only drove the point home that much more emphatically.

"'So far,' is right," the top man in Thor's Hammer said. No sarcasm was audible, but it was hard to tell with Cerberus, sometimes. He was the kind of soldier who could smile at you and knife you in the gut while he was telling you a dirty joke.

"Is something wrong?" Antares didn't want to ask the question, but he couldn't help himself. They had been out of touch, no more than bits and pieces of the search relayed to them by radio, when they could pick up a commercial station in the middle of the goddamned desert.

"Not a thing," Cerberus said. "I plan to keep it that way."

"So, you're taking over?" Even as he spoke, Antares wasn't sure if he should feel relieved or disappointed, slighted in some way, as if The Two had suddenly begun to doubt him.

"Not unless you want me to," the field commander said. "I mean, you've got it covered, right?"

"Yes, sir," Antares replied, hoping it was the truth. "I just thought—"

"You'll continue as originally planned," Cerberus cut him off. "I'm just checking in to make sure everything's all right. I'll be around from time to time, between here and the depot…just in case you need me."

Meaning that he didn't trust him, Antares thought, but he kept from frowning at the sudden flash of anger—or believed he had, at least. The last thing that he wanted was to piss off Cerberus and give him any reason to relieve Antares of command. There would be no retrieving that kind of disaster, when so much was riding on the outcome of this mission.

"Thank you, sir," he said, and tried to sound appreciative. "I hope that won't be necessary."

"So do I," Cerberus responded. "The thing is, you never know."

"Yes, sir."

"You shook them up," the field commander said, and he was smiling now, apparently sincere. "They're looking high and low for Janus, not to mention his two party favors. He *is* with you, right?"

"Yes, sir." Antares cocked a thumb toward the Suburban, Janus seated in the back, the second AGM beside him like a rolled-up carpet, draped in blankets. "Everything went off without a hitch."

"I'll take him off your hands," Cerberus said. "The Two are anxious that he shouldn't be exposed to any more of this."

"Yes, sir. I understand, of course," Antares stated. Which was a crock of shit, because he didn't understand at all. How could the pilot who had dropped the missiles in their lap be any more exposed than he already was?

It hit Antares then, and he could feel his stomach twist into a knot. The Two were anxious, all right, but it didn't have a thing to do with keeping Janus safe. They were afraid that he could tie them to the missile theft if things went wrong, and Cerberus had been dispatched to silence him.

A sudden wave of doubt swept over Antares. If The Two were already hedging their bets, preparing for failure, what did it mean to him and his team? Should he be looking for a way out of the operation even now, to save himself? It felt like cowardice to even contemplate defeat. Antares felt the mixed embarrassment and anger warm his cheeks. He blinked at Cerberus, desperate for something to say.

"You want him now, sir?" was the best that he could do.

"Now is exactly right," Cerberus replied. "You can go on about your business, then, and be in Maryland on schedule."

"Yes, sir. I'll just fetch him, then."

"You do that."

Moving toward the Suburban, Antares imagined he could feel Cerberus staring at him, eyes boring into the back of his head. He knew that he was being paranoid. For one thing, he couldn't be absolutely positive The Two were getting rid of Janus. Maybe they had planned some kind of celebration for him, as a recognition of his contribution to the cause.

Yeah, right, Antares thought.

Even if his first guess was correct, though, why should it mean anything at all to him, or to the other members of his team? They still had work to do, a mission to perform. If Cerberus had any wicked plans for them, he wouldn't be alone. He would have come with men and guns to take them out—and what would be the point in that? Eliminating one team to replace it with another when the second group would have more guilty knowledge than the first made no damned sense at all.

Before Antares could relax, though, yet another nagging question came to mind. If they were safe right now, what would become of them when they had made delivery and passed the AGMs to other hands? Would Cerberus or someone else be waiting for them later on, in Maryland, to clip another bundle of loose ends?

Antares had already pledged himself to die, if need be, for the Ancients and their holy cause—redemption of the planet Earth—but he had no intention of submitting to a double cross from his own people, when he had performed his duty faithfully and followed orders to the letter. If The Two had no more faith in him than that, why did he still have faith in them?

Slow down, he told himself, aware that he was leaping over bridges that might not exist outside his own imagination. For the moment, all he had to do was keep on driving with the AGMs, and see them to their destination.

After he got rid of Janus, right.

The pilot frowned, apparently confused, when he received the change of plans. "I thought I was supposed to go with you."

"What can I tell you? Orders change," Antares said.

"You got that right," Janus replied, shrugging off his first reaction. "Hey, I should be used to that by now."

"You did all right," Antares said, and shook the pilot's hand before the man turned away and went to join Cerberus, standing by the Mazda. Antares walked back to the van and climbed into the shotgun seat.

"What's going on?" Poseidon asked him, once the door was shut.

"You're asking me?" Antares said. "I just work here."

"Yeah, but—"

"Let's roll, all right? We've got a schedule here."

Driving away, he watched Janus and Cerberus until

they dwindled into fly specks in the mirror, and were gone. Antares guessed that he had seen the last of Janus in this world, no matter what was going on. And if he never saw the smiling face of Cerberus again, he thought, it just might be too soon.

THE WHEELS WERE EASY, once they got to Amarillo. Brognola had called ahead, and the FBI resident agent had set up a rental, charged to the Justice Department. Grimaldi, grounded, waited at the local airstrip while Bolan dropped the G-man at his office and went to keep his date with Danny Pascoe.

The rental's radio was crooning "Amarillo by Morning" when he parked downrange from a house that had seen better days, on the outskirts of town. He double-checked the address, wondering why a successful car thief would reside in such a dump, then decided maybe Pascoe had been faithful to his roots.

Whatever.

It was twilight, merging into darkness, as he left the rental car and cut across the nearest yard to reach the porch of Danny Pascoe's shabby residence. A quick scan of the street showed no one close enough to memorize his face, and while he couldn't swear he wasn't being watched from half a dozen windows up and down the block, at that point Bolan didn't care. With any luck at all, whichever way it went, he would be out of there before an anxious neighbor could decide to call the law.

The front rooms of the run-down house were dark, but he could see lights burning in the back, from the direction of what Bolan guessed would be the kitchen and/or dining room. He stepped off the porch and walked around the west side of the house, grass ankle-high and swishing against his feet with every step. If there had been a dog on guard, it should have sounded off by now, but Bolan kept one hand on the Beretta in his shoulder holster just in case.

The lawn out back had gone to seed, with large dead patches where the dirt was showing through, and long-necked beer bottles littered the yard. The back porch passed for storage, with an old refrigerator standing at one side of the door, cardboard boxes, plastic milk crates and assorted bits of unpacked junk taking up most of the remaining space.

He mounted three steps to the porch and edged toward the door. Some kind of gauzy curtain hung across the upper half, which was a pane of glass. The kitchen, just within, was larger than he would have guessed. Two men were seated at an old, Formica-topped card table, spooning something that resembled stew from plastic bowls. More long-necked bottles stood between them, three or four already drained, two more well on their way. A moment longer, and he saw both men were carrying blue-steel revolvers tucked into the waistbands of their faded jeans.

He drew his weapon, tried the doorknob with his free hand and was pleasantly surprised to find the door unlocked. That made the next step easy, but it could still go to hell in a heartbeat. Bolan didn't know if the two were alone inside the house, or which of them—if either—would be Danny Pascoe. He would have to play it by ear, and at the moment, all that he had going for him was the sweet advantage of surprise.

He caught them gaping as he stepped into the kitchen, gun in hand, and gently closed the door behind him. "Evening, gents," he said, striding toward them.

"So who the fuck are you?" the man on his left demanded.

"Hey," the other one put in, "if Ray Aguirre sent you, this is bullshit, man! He told me I could have until next week before I paid that money back!"

"I need those wheel guns on the floor," Bolan instructed them. "Two fingers when you take them out, then kick them over here."

"So who the fuck *are* you?" the first man inquired.

Bolan squeezed off a silent round that smashed a couple of the bottles, spraying both of them with beer and slivered glass. Revolvers hit the deck an instant later, scuffed boots hastily propelling them across the worn linoleum.

"Now, which of you is Danny Pascoe?" Bolan asked.

They sat and blinked at him like cornered rodents. He could almost hear them thinking, it was so predictable. Both of them guessing Danny was about to take a dirt nap, one of them—the selfsame Danny—wishing he had risked a quick-draw with his .38, instead of giving it away. The next step was to stall him, but he didn't have the time for games.

"It must be you," he said, and took a long step closer to the loser on his left, raising the sleek Beretta, sighting on the young man's face.

"No way!" the guy cried, half rising from his chair before he caught himself, thought better of it and sat again. He aimed a finger at his erstwhile friend, and Bolan saw that it was trembling. "He's Danny, right there!"

"That so?" he asked. But the young man had no answer for him. He was busy glaring daggers at his comrade.

"You piece a shit!" Danny snarled.

"So who are *you?*" Bolan asked the first guy, turning it around.

"Me? Hey, I'm nobody. You don't want me."

"I guess that's right," the Executioner replied and rapped the Beretta against the guy's forehead, knocking him to the floor unconscious.

"Holy shit!"

Pascoe was on his feet, anger and fear overriding common sense, when Bolan sidestepped, grabbed one of the long-necked bottles in his free left hand and swung it like a sap. Your average beer bottle wouldn't shatter on first impact with a human skull, as special props do in the movies, and the bottle made a satisfying clunk on impact, spilling Danny Pascoe back into his chair, which promptly toppled over with a crash and dumped him on the floor.

Bolan was kneeling on his chest when Danny's eyes blinked into focus, one orb swimming in the blood that drizzled from a gash along his hairline.

"Jesus, man!" the car thief blurted. "What do you want?"

"I want information, and I want it straight the first

time," Bolan said. "Try dicking me around, and I'll go somewhere else. You won't be going anywhere."

"I hear ya, man! It's not a problem, really. Shit, I'll tell you anything you wanna know!"

"You got a call, sometime within the past few days," Bolan said, "from a contact in Las Vegas. The guy calls himself Mercury, but his real name is Cornwell Cobb."

"Cornwell?" It almost brought a smile to Pascoe's blood-streaked face. "That fuckin' guy. I knew there must be something wrong with him."

"He wanted vehicles," Bolan went on. "I'm guessing two, both big enough for midsize cargo hauling."

"That's a fact," Pascoe replied. "I fixed him up, too, right on time. I got him a Suburban and a Chevy Astro. That's the cargo van."

"Describe them for me."

Pascoe did, Bolan recording details in his mind. Predictably, the thief had made no effort to recall the numbers on the stolen Texas plates he had affixed to either car.

"Just license plates, you know?" he said.

"I know," Bolan said, rising from his crouch.

"So, we're all square, then?" Pascoe sounded hopeful.

"We're all square," the Executioner replied, and whipped out the plastic cuffs. Two minutes later the men were trussed and waiting for the Justice Department agents who would pick them up following Bolan's call to Brognola.

CHAPTER EIGHT

The motel room was small, but clean, with a door that stood ajar, connecting her with Michael Blake's adjacent room. Celeste Bouchet wasn't an eavesdropper, per se, but it was hard not to pick up Blake's side of the terse conversation.

"I know.... Smart money says they're headed east.... It's all I have, right now.... I know.... And when was that?"

Frustration was in his voice, edging toward anger, and she knew exactly how he felt. Granted, she wasn't being paid to save the world, watching the operation slip between her fingers, but she still felt like the cause of it somehow, no matter how she told herself the feeling was irrational. Blake and his people had been dealing with The Path for several weeks, while it was going on three years since she had tried to break away and leave the cult behind. At first the group had been resistant to her leaving. When cajoling shifted to harassment, turning into threats, Bouchet had gone for payback, cyberstalking them, letting the goons see how it felt, but then the game had backfired. She had learned too much, stirred up a deadly hornets' nest, and by the time she found a former lawman with connections who didn't think she was crazy, well, Andy Morrell had paid for that decision with his life, and they were still a long, long way from any kind of cease-fire, much less an assurance that the cult had been defanged and rendered harmless.

That would take a miracle, she thought, and she was long past praying, long past trusting anyone or anything she couldn't see and feel.

Still, maybe there was something she could do.

She had her laptop plugged into the phone jack in her room, running the backdoor sequence that, with any luck, would place her back inside The Path's virtual brain. She held her breath at the last instant, certain that they had to have found her secret door by this time, but a moment later, she was in without a hitch.

Too easy?

Even as her fingers flew across the keys, she wondered. Last time she had logged on, back in Colorado, they were waiting for her. Shooters had responded, and Bouchet had very nearly lost her life. There was a chance, she realized, that they were letting her inside deliberately to spring another trap, but she had run her plan past Blake beforehand, and he had encouraged her to go ahead.

Whatever happened, there was no denying that she felt much safer, knowing he was right next door, prepared to deal with any danger that resulted from her little fishing expedition.

Thinking of him, hearing him next door, drew her

thoughts back to their intimate encounter in Phoenix. There had been no time for a repeat performance, no room for endearments as they rushed about, pursuing maniacs and stolen missiles, but she found herself— again, she thought, irrationally—wondering if what the two of them had done meant any more to Blake than a release of tension, a delicious kind of therapy.

Stop that! she silently demanded of herself. This was real life, not some romantic fairy tale. She had lost track of all the people who had died since she and Michael Blake first met, a good number of them by his hand. The only thing that mattered now was heading off the grand disaster that The Two had planned and orchestrated as their key to sparking Armageddon. Countless lives were hanging in the balance, and Bouchet could ill afford to let her mind wander through fields of daffodils, chasing a phantom prince.

She still had no clear grasp of how the stolen missiles, even with their vast destructive capability, played into a design for bringing on the Final Days. Needless to say, a nuclear explosion anywhere in the United States—much less in one of her great cities— would be an apocalyptic tragedy for all concerned, but most of those concerned would be Americans. By definition, Armageddon was the final conflict waged between vast powers, nations clashing in their death throes, and a tragedy of any size in the United States was still light-years away from sparking World War III.

Unless...

She grabbed for the remote control and flicked on

the television. It was preset for CNN, but she had missed the headline updates by perhaps five minutes. They were rolling into economic news, some gibberish about Wall Street. It made no difference. She switched off the set, turned back to the laptop, trying hard to swallow, but her mouth had suddenly gone dry.

She knew where they were going now, but it was hardly good enough. Guarding the target might be adequate, if they were dealing with a sniper, even with a small hit team, but this was very different. With a stolen nuke or two, the plotters didn't have to show themselves at all. They could reach out from miles away, perhaps by telephone, call in their lethal message from the far side of the world, and it would have the same result.

The only way to head off Armageddon was to prevent the warheads from arriving at their target, and Bouchet knew that she might already be too late.

Still, she would have to try. She didn't have it in her makeup to sit back, surrender, let it go. She had already come too far and risked too much for her to simply quit. There might be nothing she could do, no final reservoir of information she could tap, but she would never know for sure unless she tried.

Once she had made her way inside the system, it was relatively simple. She had learned the ropes from Ingrid Walsh, known to the cult as "Star," who had designed the network utilized by Millennial Truth and its commercial arm, Stargate Enterprises. Of course, there were certain tricks to digging out the goodies, contacts and connections that were meant to be concealed from all but the select few at the top. Practice made perfect, though, and she had learned a few tricks of her own along the way.

The target, she was reasonably certain now, would be somewhere in Washington, D.C. That narrowed the primary search zone to Maryland, Virginia, and perhaps a piece of Delaware. A name, an address, something...

Suddenly, two lines of data leaped out at her from the laptop's monitor, and sent her vaulting from her chair.

THE FARM WAS in Prince Georges County, something like a mile southwest of Cedarville. They came in from the south, on Highway 301, crossing the Potomac on a toll bridge, north of Morgantown. It was the closest they would come to Washington, and even here, some fifteen miles out from the capital, Antares still felt hinky, half expecting SWAT teams to appear as if by magic, from the very earth itself, and bring them under fire.

"Looks good," Poseidon said, as if to mock his fears.

"We'll see," Antares answered, keeping one hand wrapped around the barrel of his AR-15.

The farm was nothing special—which, of course, would make it perfect—but a quick scan showed a multitude of hiding places: in the old, ramshackle house, the barn that looked like something from *Tobacco Road,* even among the trees that screened a portion of the property from nosy passersby. There was an ancient pickup sitting in the yard, impossible to say if it still ran, or if it was allowed to stand there as some kind of monument to rust. Antares reckoned there could be a hundred guns aimed at his head right now, and he would never see a one of them until they opened fire.

"Looks fine to me," Poseidon said in that mumbling way of his that sometimes made Antares want to snap at him, tell him to speak the hell up for a change, if he had something on his mind.

Instead of snapping, though, he simply said, "Let's check it out."

They pulled into the yard, Antares keeping the white-knuckled grip on his weapon, flicking a glance at his mirror, making sure that the Suburban was behind them. It might have been a wiser move to have the second vehicle hang back, stay safely out of range until he found out if the setup *was* a trap, but it was too damned late to change the orders now.

Whatever happened next, Antares thought, it would damn well happening to all of them.

He didn't recognize the man who stepped out on the porch, but then again, there was no reason why he should. Appropriately dressed in black, with buzz-cut hair, the stranger had the proper look, but even that could be a ruse, Antares thought. The Feds and everybody else were on their case by now, no doubt had files and all kinds of surveillance videos to work from. It would be no challenge for an ATF or FBI man to put on a baggy shirt, black pants and running shoes. Most of them had short hair already.

To be sure, Antares realized, he would be forced

to face the stranger, speak to him up close and personal. It was the only way.

"Stop here," he said, and took the rifle with him as he stepped out of the van. Another glance in the direction of the barn revealed no movement there, and that was good, he told himself. Both vehicles were stopped now, and he had a weapon showing. If the law was waiting for them, they would surely have revealed themselves by now.

He walked around behind the van, giving a heads-up signal to the occupants of the Suburban as he circled toward the farmhouse. On the porch, the one-man welcoming committee hadn't moved. He stood there, waiting, with a half smile on his face, hands empty, hanging at his sides.

So far, so good.

"You made good time," the stranger said before Antares had a chance to speak. "I thought you might not be here for another hour, yet."

"We did all right," Antares said. "What do you hear from Cerberus?"

It was the best he could do, as far as testing the stranger. No pass words had been worked out in advance, The Two apparently believing nothing could go wrong.

"He hasn't called," the stranger said. "Were you expecting word?"

Antares shrugged. "Just checking."

"I'm Juno. You must be Antares."

"Yes."

Instead of offering his right hand, Juno raised it to his chest, fist clenched, the first and third fingers extended in a greeting sign. Antares switched the rifle to his left hand and returned the greeting, feeling better now. If there was trouble, they would surely be surrounded by guns and uniforms by now.

"You might as well park in the barn," Juno said, nodding toward the drab, decrepit structure situated fifty paces from the house. "It's empty. You've got ample room."

Antares turned back toward the vehicles and pointed, waving them on. Poseidon led the way, with the Suburban closely following. Another moment, and both cars were out of sight. Antares knew they were completely hidden from the road. A prowler would be forced to cross the open ground on foot and peer inside to see them, and he meant to have a guard on duty around the clock, from now until they made their final move.

"What happens now?" he asked Juno. His orders ended with delivery of the AGMs to Maryland. No one had bothered telling him what was supposed to happen next, how one or both missiles would be delivered to the target.

"You don't know?" Juno sounded surprised.

Antares was embarrassed. Admitting ignorance made him feel vulnerable once again, just when he thought he was on top of things. He pictured Cerberus once more, with Janus, standing at the rest stop back in Texas, and he couldn't help but wonder if the pilot had survived.

If they were cutting links, destroying evidence, he thought, what difference would it make to Cerberus, eliminating one brother or five? Antares made his mind up then and there that he wouldn't be sacrificed for nothing, executed like a traitor, without so much as a hearing from The Two. If it came down to that, and he suspected for a moment that he had been set up for a killing, then he would resist with every means at his disposal.

And the others on his team could look out for themselves.

"Have you got anything to eat?" he asked Juno.

"The basics," Juno said. "Come on inside."

The others were emerging from the barn, no problem there. Antares turned and trailed Juno into the house.

"A TEXAS RANGER FOUND the Blazers near some little burg called Dumas," Hal Brognola said. "That's thirty miles or so due north of Amarillo. They were doused with kerosene and torched. We can forget about trace evidence and latent prints."

There was no point in asking if the stolen missiles had been found inside the burned-out vehicles. The big Fed wouldn't keep that kind of news a secret, and it would have been too easy. Bolan had already given up on quick solutions to the hunt.

"We still assume they're eastbound?" Bolan asked.

"I would. It makes no sense to drive that far, then turn around and double back. There's nothing to the south unless they want to take out an oil field, and I don't see them being dumb enough to ditch the Blazers in the same direction they were headed."

"No." Again, that would have been too easy, leaving them a pointer on the trail. But east from northern Texas still left roughly half of the United States at risk. The missiles could be going anywhere.

"I'm thinking maybe we should look at this another way," Brognola said. "Instead of chasing shadows, maybe we should think in terms of targets, try anticipating them and head the bastards off."

It had occurred to Bolan, too—a basic piece of strategy, in fact—but he was at a striking disadvantage when it came to thinking like a spaced-out lunatic. Despite his time spent with the cult as one of them, he only knew the basics: namely, they were bent on touching off the final war for planet Earth, but how? Even with live nukes up their sleeves, how would The Two attempt to pull it off?

"Did you come up with anything?" he asked Brognola.

"Nothing but the obvious, so far. We know they've got the punch to take out several million people if they hit a major population center—say Chicago or New York, for instance—but I still think something's missing."

"Right. The Armageddon link."

No matter how he turned the problem over in his mind, it still came out the same. His enemies could wreak mass murder and destruction in a thousand different places—anywhere, in fact, from sea to shining sea—but how would any of it push Earth closer to a global conflict? Maybe, Bolan thought, if it was set up so that some aggressor nation seemed responsible for the attack, even claimed credit for the blast, but would that trigger the desired response?

Offhand, he didn't think so. In the old days, maybe, when the evil empire ruled from Moscow had been pulling strings from Cuba to Hanoi and parts of Africa, a first strike from the hinterlands, if blamed on Russia, could have done the trick. Today, though, it was known to one and all that Mother Russia had no client states, could barely hold herself together, while the Red Chinese were wrapped up in their own emergence from the days of Mao Zedong. If Chechen rebels, say, or someone from the Middle East, set off a nuke in the United States, retaliation would be swift and vicious, but it would come nowhere close to World War III.

More like a wounded giant stepping on a bug.

The old alliances that would have triggered something like a global flameout in the wake of an attack on U.S. soil had mostly been dismantled or were slowly fading in the wake of the dismantling of the old USSR. The Warsaw Pact was dead and gone, as were the Soviet alliances with puppet governments throughout the vast Third World. Moscow might bluff and bluster if enraged that America lashed out at someone else.

Unless, of course, the Russians were themselves somehow involved.

But that would mean...

Something was clicking in the back of Bolan's mind. He didn't have it yet, but he was getting there.

"What is it?" Hal Brognola asked. After so many years, he was adept at reading Bolan's silences, his shifting moods. "You onto something there, or what?"

"Could be. Try this. Smart money says they're headed east, agreed?"

"Sounds right," Brognola said. "They took the Blazers north, or paid somebody off to do it for them, hoping it would throw us off."

"And Washington is east of Texas, more or less."

"So is roughly half of the United States," Brognola protested. "We've covered this."

"I know," Bolan replied, "but if you're looking for a target that will light a fuse halfway around the world, you don't go hunting for it in Chicago or in Boston. Even in Miami, no one cares that much about Fidel these days."

"There's still New York. Don't be forgetting the United Nations."

"It's too much," the Executioner replied. "Too many countries, Hal. No matter how they tried to frame a statement taking credit for the job, it wouldn't gibe with casualties unless one of the countries was involved, and they were tipped off in advance to pull their people out."

"But Locke and Braun don't *have* foreign connections," Brognola reminded him. "Not that kind, anyway."

"That's right," Bolan agreed. "They need a target whose elimination, in and of itself, will get the party rolling."

"And," Brognola prodded, "that would be…?"

"You've got a special visitor in town today, I understand."

"That's true enough," Brognola said. "We had to

loan out some agents from the Bureau, beef up security.''

"And what if something happened to him all the same?''

"You're thinking something nuclear?''

"That's right,'' Bolan said.

"Well, the chances are *I* wouldn't be around to see it, come what may,'' Brognola said. "I'd say it all depends, though, on what happened, who turned out to be responsible.''

"Your visitor has problems back at home.''

"And then some,'' Brognola agreed. "He's got rebellions going on in three or four so-called republics, most of which have armies, not to mention nukes left over from the bad old days.''

"And agents overseas.''

"Absolutely. When the KGB got overhauled, some of the old hard-liners took their talents elsewhere. They've been showing up all over, working for the highest bidder.''

"And they've used assassination in the past, destabilizing governments,'' Bolan said.

"Well,'' Brognola said, "who hasn't, when you think about it?'' But it clicked with him, a heartbeat later, and his last words were a muffled curse. "Oh, shit.''

"Exactly. Someone could lay the whammy on your visitor, take out as many of the home team as the hardware would allow—confusion only helps this kind of play—and claim the strike for someone in the commonwealth. It wouldn't have to make much sense. I'm guessing the investigation would be superficial, with retaliation way up on the list of top priorities.''

''Assuming anyone was left to pull it off.''

''There's always someone,'' Bolan replied. ''It only takes one finger on the button.''

''Jesus Christ!'' Hal groaned. ''I'd better get right on—''

Celeste Bouchet burst in on Bolan just then, through the connecting doorway to her room. Her eyes were fever-bright, most of the color leeched out of her face.

''It's Washington!'' she blurted. ''The Russian president!''

''We think so, too,'' Bolan said. ''Just hang on a sec—''

''We haven't got a second,'' she replied, still moving toward him. ''I believe I've found the missiles.''

LISTENING, BOLAN AGREED she might be on to something. It made sense, and the logistics fit. A strike from Maryland, nearly within the suburbs of the capital itself, would mean a short trip with the warheads on their final leg—and maybe only one of them, at that, if those involved were feeling cocky, or if they planned on holding something in reserve against the need to stage a second strike.

Brognola listened from his office, both men interjecting questions while Bouchet ran down the train of thought that had delivered her to what she felt was the solution to their mystery, both why and where, rolled into one.

Bolan could only hope she was correct.

"It was a news report about the Russian president that got me thinking," Bouchet said, "but you're ahead of me on that, I guess."

"Go on," Bolan prompted, echoed by Brognola.

"I'm thinking, what could make a better target, everything considered, than the president of Russia in the heart of Washington, D.C.? It's like..." She hesitated, groping for a simile. "Like knocking down a thousand birds with one stone, right? So, anyway, I guessed that having ditched the stolen bomber, they might not have access to another military plane."

"Jesus, I hope not," Brognola chimed in.

"And it would take some major work to launch them from your average civilian plane, yes?"

"Difficult, but not impossible," Bolan told her.

"Anyway, I'm thinking it's more likely they would drive it in or something, like we talked about before. And even with the barricades they've got around the White House now, what difference would it make? I mean, it's not your ordinary car bomb, right?"

"Not even close," the Executioner replied.

"So, what I started looking for, once I hacked in, was something close enough so they wouldn't have to drive all day or night to reach the target. That was basically Virginia, Maryland, or maybe Delaware. Aside from some commercial action in New York, through Stargate, it turns out The Path is mostly concentrated in the western half of the United States. You knew that, too."

"The answer being...?"

"Maryland!" she said, smiling despite the general mood. "In fact, the only property the cult has any firm connection to, within five hundred miles of Washington, turns out to be a farm fifteen or twenty miles outside the capital. Prince Georges County.''

"Give me coordinates," Brognola said, "and I can have some people there in half an hour, give or take.''

"Let's table that, for now," Bolan suggested. "When's the ceremony with your visitor tomorrow?''

"Ah, I'd have to ask around, but things like that, they usually set it up within an hour before or after lunch. Best guess off the top of my head, sometime between eleven and one o'clock.''

There was no need for Bolan to consult his watch. "No sweat," he said. "I get with Jack ASAP, and I can be there well before midnight.''

Brognola clearly didn't like the sound of that. "Why wait?" he asked. "We don't know what their schedule is, or what they're doing with those warheads, even as we speak. Installing timers, triggers— hell, who knows? We've got no head count, no idea how many guns are waiting for you. If you get right down to it, we can't be positive they're even there.''

"I'm positive," Bouchet stated.

"With all respect—''

"If no one's there," Bolan said, interrupting his old friend, "then all I've done is kill some time, which, otherwise, I would have spent right here waiting for bad news on the telephone. The only thing we're losing is some helicopter fuel. Meanwhile, you've got an Army checking other options, right?''

"Uh-huh." Brognola didn't like where this was going, but he saw the logic of his old friend's argument.

"Still, what's the harm in calling up some reinforcements?"

"Like you said," Bolan replied, "we don't know what they've done or may be doing with the warheads. Say they've already installed some kind of trigger. One glimpse of your reinforcements hanging out on the perimeter, they might get nervous, and Prince Georges County goes up in a mushroom cloud."

"The folks I had in mind don't come equipped with neon signs," the big Fed said. "And they don't telegraph their moves."

"Mistakes happen," Bolan said. "If this was just a couple truckloads of C-4, I'd say go for it. But we're talking two nukes, with a yield of forty kilotons. It won't be Armageddon if they go off in the suburbs, but you're still looking at one hellacious loss of life—plus all that fallout, with the White House and the Congress barely fifteen miles away."

"Goddammit!" Brognola knew when to argue, push his luck; he also knew when he was on the losing end. "Are you in touch with Jack?"

"I've got his number," Bolan said. "Say ten or fifteen minutes for him to retrieve the chopper, and about the same to pick me up. I'll have coordinates by then, and we'll communicate when airborne. With any luck at all, I should be on the ground again in four, five hours, tops."

"Around 11:30 our time, then," Brognola said.

"Or sooner, if we catch a tailwind."

"Just don't get your tail shot off, all right?" Brognola groused. "And when you give me those coorinates, I *will* be sending backup, but they'll be discreet, hang back a couple miles."

"We'll need a hazmat team," Bolan said, running down the checklist in his mind. He pictured bulky recon suits, the hazardous matter retrieval squad lumbering across somebody's yard, beneath the glare of floodlights.

"They're already standing by. Nobody has been counting on much sleep tonight."

"With any luck, we can all catch a nap tomorrow," Bolan stated. "I'm out of here."

"Good luck," the big Fed said, before the link was broken.

Celeste Bouchet was waiting for him, as Bolan stood from the bed. "I want to go," she told him.

"No can do," he replied. "The chopper's a two-seater."

"Shit!"

"Such language," Bolan said, and smiled at her. "I've got another call to make, but maybe later when I'm done..."

"Be careful," she said, stepping close to kiss him lightly on one corner of his mouth. "Anything you say may be held against you."

"I'm counting on it," Bolan said, already lifting the receiver, tapping out another number on the telephone.

CHAPTER NINE

Approaching from the south-southwest, the AH-64 Apache followed Highway 301 past White Plains and St. Charles, veered off between Waldorf and Beantown, homing on coordinates that had been worked out in the air, en route from Texas to Prince Georges County, Maryland. The district passing underneath the chopper really didn't qualify as any kind of suburb, separated as it was from Washington by fifteen miles or more, but in the pitch-black of a moonless night, cruising around one thousand feet, the nation's capital was clearly visible, its distant lights resembling a bed of white-hot coals.

The image failed to bolster Bolan's confidence as they approached the target zone. He concentrated on a last check of his gear, preparing for insertion into unfamiliar territory, knowing that whatever happened in the next half hour or so involved more pressing concerns than his own survival.

"I still say it wouldn't hurt to spark these suckers from the air," Grimaldi said. "It can't hurt, with the warheads on those AGMs."

"Unless they've tinkered with the mechanism,"

Bolan replied. "By now, they could have rigged some kind of makeshift triggering device."

"All the more reason we should blitz them out. If you go in shooting, and it turns out they've got numbers on their side, it only takes one guy to reach the nukes and set them off."

"That's why I left the marching band at home," Bolan stated, and flashed a quick grin at his friend.

"So, you have all the fun again," Grimaldi groused, not meaning it. Bolan could hear the worry in his pilot's voice and knew what his friend was thinking. They had been around this block before, as recently as Bolan's operation in New Mexico. The Stony Man pilot always grumbled about Bolan taking chances, but he also never failed to do his job, follow instructions, playing it by Bolan's rules.

"What can I say?" the Executioner came back at him. "It's in my contract. I get all the close-ups."

"You and Kevin Costner," Grimaldi said. "Coming up on it, I think."

"One circle, high and wide," Bolan reminded him.

"You got it, bro."

Grimaldi took the chopper up to fifteen hundred feet and circled wide around the target zone. The yard between a rundown house and barn was lit by a single floodlight mounted on a power pole, a glimpse of softer light through tiny windows at the west end of the house. The only vehicle in evidence appeared to be a pickup truck. There was no other sign of life around the property.

Returning southward, Grimaldi was busy checking out the dark terrain below. When they were some three-quarters of a mile beyond the farm, he cocked his head and pointed toward the earth.

"Those trees look like the best cover we're going to find," he said.

"Let's do it, then," Bolan told him, resting one hand on the buckle of his safety harness, while the other gripped his combination CAR-15/M-203.

There was no bailing out of an Apache in midair. He had to wait for touchdown, which Grimaldi managed in a fallow field behind the screen of weeping willows. Bolan kept his fingers crossed that darkness, distance and the trees would cover them from being seen or heard by any sentries on patrol around the target zone.

Grimaldi cut the engine, sprang the door and placed a hand on Bolan's shoulder as the Executioner released his harness. "I'll be listening," he said and tapped the headset that he wore, for emphasis. "You want these assholes dusted in a hurry, give a shout. I'll be there inside sixty seconds, guaranteed."

"I hear you," Bolan said and slapped Grimaldi's open palm as he went EVA.

It felt good, moving through the darkness, slipping in between the willows with their long tendrils brushing his face and shoulders. In another moment, he was past the trees and homing on the light that marked the farmyard, moving at a brisk pace over ground that had been cultivated once, but not within the past few years. The weeds and wildflowers had taken over, Mother Nature reasserting her supremacy where man relaxed his grip.

If any living thing was watching, it made no attempt to hinder Bolan on his way. He crossed the dark ground like a shadow and was gone.

ANTARES COULDN'T SLEEP. He didn't know if it was nerves or the six cups of coffee he had polished off since their arrival at the farm. Whatever, he was wired, and lying in the darkness with the top flap of a sleeping bag pulled up beneath his chin did nothing to relax or lull him into sleep.

He thought a smoke would help and rolled out of the sleeping bag, stepping around Poseidon and Columba as he headed for the door. Pictor was out on watch, the second shift, and two hours remained before Columba was supposed to spell him. In the silence of the open countryside, it almost seemed ridiculous to even post a sentry, but they were taking turns regardless. With the way he felt, his nerves on edge, Antares wouldn't even think of letting down his guard.

Outside, the night was cool, but nothing that he couldn't tolerate in shirtsleeves. Lighting a cigarette, he scanned the yard looking for Pictor, but his man was nowhere to be seen.

No sweat. The orders were to roam and stay alert for any sign of trouble. It was only common sense to stay out of the light, which spoiled night vision at the same time it revealed a sentry to potential enemies. From his position on the porch, concealed in shadow, there was still a sense of being watched that made Antares clench his teeth, the short hairs rising on his nape.

He ordered himself to relax. If anyone was watching, it had to be Pictor.

Right. Their contacts weren't expected until morning, sometime shortly after dawn. Who else would have the first clue where they were?

Antares wanted to call out to Pictor, but he stopped himself and felt like a moron standing there, his mouth half open. He would only wake the others if he started shouting in the yard, and all for what? His nerves were working on him, that was all. He should go back inside and just forget about the whole damned thing, blank his mind until he drifted off to sleep.

He took a last drag on his cigarette, was just about to flick the butt across the yard, when suddenly he froze. There had been something, like a furtive movement, at the corner of his vision. Something moving in the barn? Or was it some*one* moving, stealthy as a hunting cat, trying his best not to reveal himself?

Pictor?

It was the only answer that made sense. Pictor was checking out the barn, working his beat, and what was wrong with that?

Still…

Something didn't feel right, and Antares wished he had his rifle, still back in the bedroom, where three sleeping bags were stretched out on the hardwood floor. He was unarmed, and almost went back for the weapon—briefly thought of waking up the others, raising an alarm—before he stopped himself, eyes fixed upon the barn, its door ajar, pitch-dark within.

If he ignored what he had seen, or thought that he

had seen, Antares knew that he would never get to sleep. The night was nearly half gone as it was, and he would need a clear head in the morning when the others came, and they prepared the doomsday message for their enemies.

Antares knew what he had to do, and still he hesitated, up until the moment when the cigarette burned down enough for embers to reach his fingers, and the sharp pain snapped him out of it. If he retreated, even went back for his rifle now, it would mean feeling like a coward, and it made no difference that he was alone, that no one else would ever have to know.

He stepped down off the porch and moved across the lighted yard, feeling the same way that he used to during adolescence, when he sometimes dreamed of walking into school stark naked. Clenching angry fists against the fear that taunted him, Antares moved with long strides toward the barn. He kept his mouth shut, stubbornly refusing to announce himself, despite the nagging thought that anyone within a hundred yards could plainly see him, draw a bead and cut him down if they were any kind of shot at all.

It was a toss-up, whether anger or defiance of his own fear kept him going, but he reached the barn alive and paused outside the open door. Having adapted to the light, he now rebelled at leaving it behind and plunging into darkness, where he would be blind until his eyes could readjust.

"Pictor?"

The voice that issued from his throat didn't sound like his own. Antares realized that he was whispering, torn between fear that no one would answer and the dread that someone might. It made him feel like some damned eunuch, standing there. Disgusted with himself, Antares shoved the ancient wooden door aside, wincing as rusty hinges squealed.

He stepped inside.

"Pictor?" A little louder, this time, though the darkness of the barn seemed to swallow his voice, like a black hole in space. "Answer, for Christ's sake!"

The scuffling sound behind him was so faint, it could have been a mouse in transit, maybe even his imagination. Even so, he tensed, was turning toward the sound, prepared to rip his soldier up one side and down the other, if the idiot was playing games.

Antares never saw the hand that clamped across his mouth, but he could feel the power of the arm behind it, jerking back his head so that his throat was taut, exposed. The blade that pierced his flesh was either white-hot or ice-cold; Antares couldn't tell, for sure.

And in another heartbeat, he no longer cared.

BOLAN DEPOSITED the second body with the first, two corpses slumped together in a corner with some rusty shovels, rakes and hoes. The second man appeared to be unarmed, and Bolan didn't bother with the first one's weapons, knowing they were useless in dead hands.

He had already checked out the Suburban and the Chevy Astro van, using the needle-thin beam of a penlight, satisfied that he had found the missing AGMs beneath those tarps and blanket, "hidden" in the back of each vehicle.

That had been step one, followed immediately by step two—elimination of what seemed to be the only guard assigned to watch the property while others slept inside the house. The second man's arrival had briefly distracted Bolan, but it clearly didn't indicate a trend toward wandering insomniacs.

He didn't try to reach the AGMs. There was no immediate way of telling whether the two vehicles were fitted with alarms or booby traps, and if he had to wake up the others, he had a better way in mind to do it. Turning from the dead men, he unslung his heavy carbine and moved back into the open doorway of the barn.

This was the time when he could raise Grimaldi on the radio, give him a piece of it, and watch in safety while the old farmhouse was torn apart by rockets from two hundred yards away. More than security, there would be grim poetic justice in it, even though the rending blasts that woke them in the instant of their own destruction wouldn't taint their lacerated flesh with radiation, leaving them to die a slow and agonizing death by inches, praying for the end.

He could have called the Stony Man pilot, but he didn't. Rather, Bolan thumbed an HE round into the M-203's open breech and snapped it shut. He tucked the weapon's short stock underneath his armpit, aiming it as much by feel and long experience as anything, before he stroked the trigger.

In his military days, the 40 mm launchers had been nicknamed "bloop guns" for the muted sound they made when they were fired. Still, there was nothing quiet on the other end, as Bolan's HE canister crashed through a window, detonated with a boom that shook the house to its foundation and lit the shattered room with leaping flames.

He slipped another HE round into the stubby weapon, turned slightly to his left and let it fly. There was no brittle crash this time, since all the window glass had been shattered by the first explosion, but the second boom was every bit as satisfying as the one before it.

Was he imagining those voices, emanating from somewhere inside the house? His ears weren't immune to shock waves from the dual explosions, but he didn't think that they were playing tricks on him. Both rooms that he had taken out with HE rounds had faced the barn, which placed them in the front part of the house. If it was anything like most homes, Bolan thought, the bedrooms would be somewhere toward the back, or on one side.

Which meant that he had several adversaries still alive.

"I'm coming," Bolan told the night, and went to hunt them down.

THE FIRST EXPLOSION yanked Poseidon from the warm midst of a sexy dream and brought him to his feet instinctively, before he knew he was awake. A second blast ripped through the house an instant later, almost knocking him down again, but he was deft enough to keep his balance, use the motion as he dropped into a crouch and grabbed his submachine gun from the floor beside his sleeping bag.

Columba staggered past him, tripped over Antares

or his sleeping bag and went down with a thud. He came up cursing, but the fact that there was no sound from Antares told Poseidon that their team leader was up and out of there ahead of them.

And still he had no clue to what was happening.

His first thought, as he shrugged off the remaining wisps of sleep, was that the warheads had to have detonated somehow. That was crazy, though, he realized. If either of the AGMs had blown, he would have been incinerated in his sleeping bag, nothing as large as ashes left for the shock wave to blow away.

What, then?

He reached the bedroom doorway, stuck his head out cautiously into the hall and spotted flames off to his right in the direction of the front porch and the sitting room. Whatever else had happened, then, the damned house was on fire, and from the looks of it, the way it smelled so musty, he couldn't imagine that it would be long before flames raced the full length of the structure and the roof came down around his ears.

He spied a figure, lurching toward him through the smoke and swirling dust, almost unleashed a burst of automatic fire before recognized that it was Juno, walking with a limp and one arm out to brace himself against the wall, a shotgun dangling from his other hand. The left side of his face was smeared with something, maybe blood, but he was up and moving, which was really all that mattered at the moment.

That and getting out.

"This way!" Poseidon barked at Juno and Columba, taking charge despite the overwhelming urge he felt to run away and hide, since neither of the others seemed to have their full wits about them. Turning to his left, the fire behind him now, he led them through the combination kitchen-dining room and out the back door, to the cluttered porch and open yard beyond.

Clear of the burning house, Poseidon knew they still weren't safe. Not yet, until he found out what had triggered the explosions and the fire, tracked down the others—Pictor and Antares—and determined whether they were really under siege. A city boy himself, for all he knew, a rundown place like this out in the sticks, they could have blown an ancient propane tank. Some redneck long departed might have stashed a cache of dynamite under the porch and then forgotten all about it, leaving it to age and sweat a pool of nitroglycerine, just waiting for a careless mouse to scuttle past and set it off.

They were circling toward the front of the house, the smoke bringing unwanted tears to Poseidon's eyes, when he saw the enemy. Even without a clear view of his face, there was no question of it being Pictor or Antares. This man was too tall, too muscular, dressed all in black and wearing combat gear Poseidon hadn't seen since he had done his two years in the Army, being all that he could be. The weapon that he carried was some stubby variation of an M-16; the launcher mounted underneath its barrel told Poseidon everything he had to know about the blasts that had awakened him from his best dream in years.

He didn't waste time on a warning to the others, squeezing off a short burst from his submachine gun in the general direction of the target, simultaneously breaking to his left, in the direction of the farmhouse. It wouldn't provide much cover, but the smoke was thicker there, and he hoped he could go to ground and get a clean shot at his adversary from a different angle.

Poseidon had barely taken two long strides before all hell broke loose around him. His companions fired on the stranger, Juno with his shotgun and Columba with a Ruger Mini-14 semiautomatic rifle, while the man in black returned full-automatic fire. There was a cry of pain behind him—Juno?—and he kept running toward the house, hell-bent to save himself, if he accomplished nothing else.

But save himself from what?

Poseidon didn't even know how many adversaries might be circling him in the dark. He couldn't focus on a thought that complicated at the moment, when his full attention was consumed with things like picking up one foot and putting it before the other, trying not to lose it.

He was almost to the house when something rattled past him and the world exploded in his face.

WHEN BOLAN SAW the three bewildered-looking gunners coming toward him, through a drifting pall of smoke, his first thought was, that couldn't be all of them.

It seemed impossible—insane—to detail such a tiny squad for the appropriation of two Air Force AGMs and transportation of the stolen nukes across eight states. Was one of them the missing B-2 bomber pilot? Were there more inside the burning house, or maybe coming up behind him in the darkness, somewhere on the grounds?

There was no time to think about it, as the pointman spotted him and stopped dead in his tracks. Bolan expected the man to warn the others, who were plodding forward with their heads down, like a pair of worn-out runners bringing up the rear end of a marathon, but the lead man wasn't about to waste his precious time on words. Instead, he cut loose with a compact submachine gun, firing from the hip, his haste and shaky hands enough to send the bullets winging off ten feet or more to Bolan's left.

The shooter broke formation, dodging toward the house, as his companions pulled up short, eyes locked on Bolan for the first time since they came into his field of vision. One of them, on Bolan's right, was limping, and his face was streaked with blood. Whatever injury he might have suffered, though, it didn't slow him appreciably as he raised a shotgun to his shoulder, sighting down the stubby barrel. To the wounded gunner's right, his partner braced a semiautomatic rifle tight against his hip and opened up in rapid fire.

There was no time to aim, as Bolan hit them with a blazing figure eight, his 5.56 mm tumblers ripping into the shotgunner's chest, slamming him back and downward even as he triggered off a charge of buckshot, pellets scattering safely over Bolan's head. He never had the chance to pump and fire another round before he touched down in a boneless sprawl.

The rifleman was quicker, but again, haste and anxiety conspired to spoil his aim. A bullet tugged at Bolan's sleeve, while several others whispered past him in the smoky darkness. The remainder of his looping burst slashed through the gunner's torso, just above the waist, and spun the semiauto rifle from his dying fingers.

Bolan didn't watch him fall, already spinning toward the third man—still uncertain if he was the last man—only knowing that he couldn't let one of them escape. Instinctively, his left hand found the M-203's trigger, and he launched an HE canister to meet the runner, as he sprinted toward the house.

One moment, Bolan's target almost seemed to have a chance; the next, he was enveloped in a boiling cloud of smoke and fire, the echo of the blast eclipsing any sound he might have uttered as his life was snatched away. A broken, blistered thing lay steaming on the grass, and the Executioner passed it by, skirting the other corpses as he made his way around the house.

Inside, the fire was spreading rapidly, already flaring room-to-room and gnawing at the eaves. He moved as close to the inferno as he could, peering through windows that provided him a glimpse of hell, perhaps a blast furnace at work. Before he made it all the way around, he was convinced that nothing human had survived the fire, and he was also certain that there were no living men outside.

Withdrawing from the funeral pyre, he took the compact walkie-talkie from his belt and thumbed the button down. "I'm finished here," he said. "You want to give the backup team a shout?"

"Will do," Grimaldi said. "I'm on my way."

CHAPTER TEN

Apollo got the call at 3:18 a.m. He was in bed alone at home, and consequently answered with his Earth name.

"Marx."

"We've had some difficulties," the familiar voice informed him, speaking calmly even in the face of what could only be disaster. "It will have to be Plan B."

The sudden chill that raced along Apollo's spine could have been fear, excitement or a wicked blend of both. "I understand," he said, and fumbled the receiver back into its cradle on the nightstand.

He was wide awake now, and the hour made no difference to him. He switched on the bedside lamp, blinking in the sudden glare that lanced his eyes, rose and went to the kitchen, where he put on the coffee. It would be ready by the time he finished his shower, alternately scalding hot and icy cold to clear the final cobwebs from his brain.

Plan B.

The very fact that backup plans existed meant they might be used, but it had always seemed improbable somehow. Plan A, the first-string operation, had been worked out to the last detail, and it had seemed to go without a hitch, right through the ditching of the bomber and retrieval of the AGMs. There had been nothing on the news about a foul-up when he went to bed at eleven o'clock, but something clearly had gone wrong in the meantime.

Emerging from the shower, pale flesh pebbled with goosebumps, Apollo rubbed himself briskly with a rough terry towel, then left it draped across one corner of the bathroom door and padded toward the kitchen. Halfway there, he picked up the remote control and switched on his television. It was still set on the all-news channel, and he knew that he had found what he was looking for the moment he saw Live from Maryland emblazoned at the lower left-hand corner of the screen.

The bird's-eye picture taken from a helicopter seemed to be some kind of rural setting, something like an old barn in the upper right-hand corner of the shot, a smoking, burned-out patch of rubble in the center. All around the battleground were squad cars, fire trucks and meat wagons, their multicolored lights giving the scene an eerie, psychedelic feel. A pair of EMTs in white were loading what appeared to be a sheet-draped corpse into their ambulance, while the airborne reporter raised his voice to make it audible above the chopper's engine noise.

"Again, for those just tuning in, we're on the scene of what appears to be a major firefight in Prince Georges County, Maryland, some fifteen miles southeast of Washington, D.C. We don't have confirmation yet, but unofficially, we have been told that federal agents have recovered two cruise missiles stolen earlier this week in Arizona, following the crash of a B-2 Stealth bomber. You may recall the weapons officer in that aircraft was killed—apparently shot at close range before the plane crashed—and the pilot was missing, along with the payload of two air-to-ground cruise missiles, each equipped with a twenty-kiloton nuclear warhead.''

"Shit!" Apollo nudged the volume higher, even though he could already hear the bitter news too well.

"We're seeing bodies now," the newsman said, "being removed from what appears to be a farm. The house, apparently, has been destroyed by fire sometime within the past few hours. We've been told that several persons have been killed, apparently in an exchange of gunfire with a raiding party from the FBI and ATF—that's the Bureau of Alcohol, Tobacco and Firearms. No officers were injured in the battle, if our early information is correct. None of the dead has been identified by name, or by any group affiliation that would indicate specific terrorist involvement in the missile theft. We have no word, so far, as to whether missing Air Force Captain Earl Stant is among those found dead here tonight. Once again, for those viewers just tuning in—"

Apollo switched off the television, unconsciously squeezing the remote control in his fist until he heard the plastic crack. Enraged, he flung it toward the nearest wall and watched it shatter, various components littering the floor.

So what? He wouldn't need the damned thing anymore, now that The Two had called Plan B.

Incredibly, Apollo wasn't frightened by the prospect of what lay ahead for him that day. He felt a certain agitation, nerves on edge, but that was only natural. How many men were privileged to know the future, not just making plans and trusting luck, but knowing to the minute when and how he was supposed to die?

It was an honor, certainly, to be selected for the fallback plan, picked out to save the day when all else failed. He spent five minutes roaming through the small apartment where he lived, relieved when he was finished with the tour to note that there was nothing he would miss, no object that he had become attached to, as some hopeless humans did.

The mirror stopped him momentarily, Apollo wondering if he would find his next form—his eternal body—half as pleasing as this one had been. If he had any single failing, it was vanity, verging on narcissism, but he was committed to the cause and course of action he had chosen, and he wouldn't waver now.

The blue-tipped Glaser rounds in his Smith & Wesson automatic would be useful to him, after all.

Returning to the kitchen, still dressed only in a towel, Apollo fixed himself a hearty breakfast: two eggs over easy, half a dozen strips of bacon, hash browns, toast and marmalade, with more hot coffee, black and strong. He cleaned his plate and left it on the table. Someone else could pick up after him this time, if there was anyone around to bother, once he lit the fuse to Armageddon's doomsday charge.

It was too bad about his brothers down in Maryland, but they had earned their place in paradise, and he would see them soon enough, reborn in glory without stain or blemish. He hadn't known any of them personally, so Apollo guessed it wouldn't matter if their new forms were the same as those they wore in earthly life or not.

He dawdled over getting dressed, and it was 5:30 a.m. before he slipped on his jacket and prepared to leave his digs for what he knew was the last time. Before he left, though, there was still one duty to perform.

He made the phone call from his kitchen, tapped out the number from memory and waited for a sleepy voice to answer after half a dozen rings.

"Plan B," he said without preamble. And, when there was no immediate reply: "You heard?"

"Um…yes."

"Plan B," Apollo said once more for emphasis, insuring there was no mistake, before he lowered the receiver and walked out to meet his destiny.

FOR THE FIRST TIME since assuming office, the elected president of Russia actually felt relaxed. It was ironic, since the feeling only came to him once he had left his homeland and the people who—however grudgingly and with whatever second thoughts in mind— had chosen him to rule at least a portion of their lives.

All things considered, though, it should have come as no surprise that he felt more at ease—and safer; yes, that too—in the United States than in his own homeland. There were so many troubles plaguing

Mother Russia at the moment that he barely knew where to begin the listing of them, much less any kind of meaningful solutions. The economy was first and foremost on his mind, of course: inflation, unemployment, shortages of food and clothes and nearly all consumer goods, compounded by a black market the state had thus far been unable to eradicate. Which brought him to the plague of crime, both organized and random, that had made his native land a laughingstock of sorts these past ten years, since communism's fall. Of course, there had been smugglers, killers, thieves and every manner of corruption long *before* the USSR was dissolved, but it had seemed much easier to hide the problem then...or crush specific obstacles, if they created too much trouble for the party's taste. These days, it seemed, there was no end to tales of homicide, drug-dealing, bribery, embezzlement—and that was all before you got to random crimes by individuals, who ranged from desperate or dishonest businessmen to prowling gangs of neo-Nazi thugs.

Beyond economy and crime, there were the diehard Communists to deal with, still unable to believe their system could have failed and been rejected by the people. There were right-wing nationalist groups who plotted territorial expansion and considered a return to czarist rule, religious fanatics by the carload, and sputtering rebellion in several smaller states of the Russian Federation, verging at times upon outright civil war.

All that, and in his "spare time," the elected president of Russia was required to deal with various petitions for his own removal, based on sundry claims that he was physically unfit to serve, he was corrupt—allegedly for selling out to the Americans, the Japanese, the Chechen Mafia—that his election had been rigged somehow, or, in his favorite petition of the lot, filed by a small religious sect in the Ukraine, that he wasn't even Russian, but rather the misplaced son of a Greek diplomat, whose infant was switched at birth with another some sixty years before in the confusion of a Moscow maternity ward.

Most days, since his election to the presidency, he would have been quite content to be a Greek, or any other nationality at all except the one that he was saddled with. What madness had possessed him to pursue the game of politics in the first place? There were times when he told himself, if he could only roll back the clock, that he would do something—*any-thing*—else with his life, abandon the charade of "public service," which for most, himself included, was in truth a path to personal success, wealth, power, recognition—whatever the individual statesman had craved since his youth. Those who hung on and played the game successfully reaped their rewards over time, but there were also dues to pay, and no one warned new players about the fine-print clauses, which explained how the job—the campaign—would absorb and finally become your life, crowding loved ones and everything else into subordinate positions. Even the heady rush that came with winning an election didn't last, in the end. Inevitably, the perpetual candidate simply felt...exhausted.

His trip to the United States, therefore, was a combination of business and pleasure, although the second part had been kept strictly to himself. Of course, he had no plan to ditch his escorts, lose himself in Western decadence, or anything like that. It was enough, for now, that he was simply out of Russia, several thousand miles removed from his most pressing problems in the flesh, no matter how they dogged his thoughts. He could relax, enjoy a walk around the park perhaps, without the Moscow press corps speculating on his motives for the stroll.

And, even more important, there was the possibility that his discussions with the President of the United States would help to solve some of the problems waiting for him back home. The FBI was already cooperating with police in Russia on their problem with the so-called Mafias—although, from what he saw on television, leaders of the Bureau had some major difficulties of their own on tap, ranging from accusations of brutality and murder to negligence and corruption in their world-famous crime lab. As a man who spent his life on the receiving end of just such scrutiny, the Russian president could only sympathize with their predicament.

The mob aside, he also had great hopes for certain talks on economic aid and opening new avenues of trade. At home, he made no secret of the fact that he would welcome Western goods and corporations into Russia, if and when the individuals behind them thought the time was right—meaning the times were stable enough—for massive infusions of capital. His visit to the States was scheduled to include some talks with various captains of industry, in the hope that he could sell them on the image of a new Russia, a nation slowly but surely leaving its troubles behind.

Outside the lavish room where he was nearly finished dressing, he could hear his bodyguards preparing for their day. He scarcely needed them, with all the Secret Service men and FBI agents assigned to keep him safe and sound on U.S. soil, but he was saddled with them, all the same. Still, after keeping him alive so long, he reckoned *they* deserved a break, as well.

"Mr. President?" Alexi's voice was muffled by the door between them, but still recognizable. "The time, sir."

"Yes, I'm coming."

In the great suite's central room, Alexi and six other men stood waiting for him. With the exception of Mikhail, his private secretary, all of them were armed with pistols, at least two of them with compact submachine guns worn beneath their jackets. At least two of them were on guard around the clock, but all of them went with him when he left the suite. They formed the inner circle of his bodyguard, while FBI and Secret Service agents hovered all around and offered constant reassurances that nothing had been left to chance.

The president could only take them at their word, since the Americans had—until very recently, at least—had more experience with lunatics and terrorists than any other nation of their size.

"All ready, then?" he asked the group that stood before him. To a man they responded with a courteous affirmative. "Well, then," the president of Russia said, "by all means, let us go."

"PLAN B."

Those simple words had come as no surprise to Icarus. He had left word with those on duty at the base to let him know, regardless of the hour, if there was any word about the missing AGMs. It had been shortly after two o'clock that morning when the message reached him, and he thanked the caller with what sounded like a cheerful voice, seeming relieved, although his guts were seething at the prospect of another failure, this time on a project of his own creation, which had occupied his every waking hour for months on end.

He still had no idea what had gone wrong. The details presently eluded him, but it made no real difference to the end result. *His* tracks were covered, had been from day one, now that the middleman had been eliminated. Cerberus had seen to that, as a precaution, but it hardly seemed to matter now.

Plan B.

At best, the fallback option was a pallid shadow of the plan he had devised. Instead of taking out both heads of state *and* wreaking mass destruction in the nation's capital, they would be forced to settle for a relatively crude—albeit simple and presumably effective—scheme. It should go off without a hitch, but then again, he would have said the same about his own plan, once they had the AGMs safely in hand. Apollo had the backup story in place, his legend nailed down with documents, bank records, everything the Feds would need to prove conspiracy. Of course, it wouldn't be the *real* conspiracy, but what the hell? By the time anyone figured out that wrinkle, it would damn well be too late to call the missiles back.

Icarus knew it shouldn't matter to him which plan did the trick, as long as they succeeded in their grand design to bring the Ancients back, but he couldn't suppress an urge to punish someone for intruding on his plan and bringing it to ruin. He would never have the chance to do that now, assuming it was even possible to learn the names of those responsible. The game was too advanced, moving too swiftly now, for any kind of private action on the side. But it was something he could think about, savor the mental images, while he was waiting for the other shoe to drop.

He had no part in the festivities that morning, hadn't been invited to the White House for the Russian visitation. Why should anyone have asked a mere lieutenant colonel in the Air Force to observe the nation's so-called leader fawning over one who, until several years ago, had been a member of the dreaded Evil Empire? Icarus had grown up hating Russians, fearing Russians—it was really all the same—and even now, when he had seen the interstellar light and knew the truth about humankind, its origins and destiny, old habits still died hard. He wished that it would be *his* plan that took the Russian out, along with those in Washington who had forgotten all the lessons of their recent history.

Too late.

His plan was history, and if he never knew exactly

who to blame for that, what earthly difference did it make? Before much longer, all his enemies would be wiped out, eliminated, vaporized. It made no difference that the stolen AGMs had been retrieved before their white-hot fire could light the doomsday fuse. There would be other missiles, by the hundreds, blanketing the world with death for unbelievers of the human race, once word got back to Mother Russia of her chosen leader's fate in decadent America.

It couldn't miss.

Unless, of course, something should happen to Apollo.

Granted, the idea of yet another failure seemed improbable, even bizarre. Whose luck could be that bad? And yet, it was a possibility that Icarus had forced himself to contemplate. Too much had gone awry the past few weeks for him to simply shrug it off and blame coincidence. He meant to be prepared for anything that happened at the crucial, final moment.

And to that end, Icarus had hit upon Plan C.

To guarantee the utmost in security, he kept it absolutely to himself. No other living soul knew of his plan—even The Two were ignorant of what he had in mind, although it smacked of sacrilege—and thus would Icarus insure that he succeeded, should all others fail.

Or he would die in the attempt.

Whichever way it went, as far as true believers and the Ancients were concerned, he came off smelling like a whole bouquet of roses. Who could fault him for displaying some initiative, if all else failed? Should something happen to Apollo and Plan B, the man who grasped that fallen torch and carried it to final victory would be a hero for the ages. And if *he* should somehow drop the ball, if he was cut down in the face of overwhelming odds...well, then, he wound up as a hero and a martyr, one who freely sacrificed his life to aid the cause.

It was a win-win situation, though he naturally preferred the first scenario, in which he managed to survive. There was no harm in thinking positively, after all.

According to the duty roster, Icarus was off that day, but he was going in regardless. It was doubtful anyone would question him about his presence in the office—only half a dozen officers at Bolling Air Force Base had rank enough to question him, in any case—and if they did, he would explain that he had slipped up on some paperwork and had to sort things out. The story would ring false with anyone who knew his record for efficiency, but that was nit-picking. He knew no one would question him or doubt his motives for appearing on the base. Why should they?

He was true-blue all the way, the perfect patriot.

And that was how he knew Plan C would work, if all else failed.

But first, it was Apollo's turn to shine. Icarus could respect the G-man's dedication and his willingness to sacrifice. It was commendable, although no less than any true believer of The Path would do, if circumstances were reversed. Knowing the truth about the Ancients and the Final Days meant giving up all obsolete perceptions of the future, scrapping mundane hopes and dreams, to focus on a cosmic paradise that was beyond the contemplation of most Homo sapiens.

The Chosen would be few and far between, and that was fine with Icarus. He could relate to feeling special, one of the elect, the blessed. In fact, he had convinced himself it was his destiny. It wasn't vanity or arrogance, he told himself, but rather simple confidence in what he knew to be the truth.

He finished dressing, double-checked the load on the Beretta hidden in his briefcase and walked out the door at 8:13 a.m. Something about the sunshine told him it was going to be a glorious day.

BOLAN AND GRIMALDI waited for the hazmat team to show before they cleared out of the way, against the microscopic odds that someone else might come along and try to grab the AGMs. That threat was over now, at least, and it was someone else's worry.

"We finished now?" Grimaldi asked.

"Not yet," Bolan replied.

"Okay. What's next?"

In fact, Bolan couldn't be sure. They had defeated one more effort by The Path to bring disaster down upon the heads of unsuspecting innocents, and while the effort had been crushed beyond a shadow of a doubt, he also knew it wouldn't be the last. As long as Galen "Hermes" Locke and Helen "Circe" Braun were still alive and free to move among their acolytes, they wouldn't rest or give up on their twisted psychopathic dream of lifting Armageddon from the realm of myth and bringing it to brutal, cataclysmic life. Before Bolan could stop them, though, he had to find them, and so far they had ranked among the most elusive adversaries he had ever faced. It could have been embarrassing—or even humorous, depending on your view of life, its ironies—but Bolan had no time for frivolous concerns. He had to find The Two and put an end to them, by one means or another. It was absolutely top priority.

Except that something else was nagging at him now, demanding his attention, and he couldn't say for sure exactly what it was. A still-small voice was telling him—

"We go to Washington," he said.

Sometimes, in cryptic conversations, he and Brognola referred to it as Wonderland, not for the awesome some people felt the first time they were privileged to see the nation's capital, but for the sense of unreality that often traveled hand-in-hand with government affairs—the compromises, deals and sellouts, crazy logic, sometimes verging on insanity, that often seemed to power national affairs. This day, as far as Bolan could determine, though, the capital was no enchanted or deluded place.

It was a target.

"Something wrong?" Grimaldi asked him, frowning.

"I'm not sure yet," Bolan replied. "Call it a hunch."

"That's good enough for me."

Bolan hadn't expected arguments from his friend. They had been down too many hellfire trails together in their time, survived too many close encounters with the Reaper, for Grimaldi to start doubting Bolan's hunches now. Of course, the very concept of a hunch demanded some specific notion of a problem, and the sense of danger the soldier had right now was still too vague to qualify. It was a feeling, more than anything, that he had dropped a stitch somewhere, failed to account for something that he didn't recognize, some mortal threat that lay in wait for him, prepared to bite him on the ass unless he watched his step.

The nukes were out of it; that much was definite. Whatever else The Two were holding back, prepared to throw at him, he only hoped the weapons would be more conventional, less geared for mass annihilation. Murder on a smaller, less dramatic scale, perhaps.

The Russian president was still a tempting target. Bolan guessed that after other recent failures in their cosmic terrorist campaign, The Two wouldn't give up so easily and risk him slipping through their fingers. If and when they tried again, he meant to be there, waiting for them, once again to block their minions from succeeding.

And the hunt could wait, he told himself. Although disabling The Two was crucial to defeating their believers, it was still a secondary problem at the moment, when the cult had come so close to pulling off their latest scheme. He meant to be on hand and ready if they tried to run a backup plan.

The first thing he would need, Bolan thought, was a change of clothes. The second was an invitation to the White House. In the circumstances, with no time at all to spare, both items would depend upon Brognola's pull, his skill at slashing through red tape.

Grimaldi aimed the helicopter north and cranked the throttle open, speeding them along at treetop height.

Toward Wonderland.

CHAPTER ELEVEN

"Say, Luther, how's it going?"

Turning at the sound of a familiar voice, Apollo cracked a smile with no connection to his soul and gave the answer that this earthling unbeliever would expect: "I'm fine, Pete. How about yourself?"

"I can't complain," Pete Dickson of the U.S. Secret Service replied. "Or, if I did, it wouldn't help."

"I hear that," Apollo said, keeping up the smile. "Some crowd today."

"A frigging pain, is what they are," Dickson replied, thus proving that he could, in fact, complain. "Most of them newsies, as per usual, but we've got senators and congressmen thrown in, some corporate bigwigs hoping for a shot to make their pitch, a little bit of everything."

Apollo scanned the crowd, looking for three familiar faces. When he spotted them, it felt as if a weight had lifted from his shoulders. He had been prepared to run Plan B alone, if necessary, but the chances of success would have been markedly reduced. This way, at least there would be cover, a certain margin for error.

"Yo, Earth to Luther!"

Flushing with embarrassment, Apollo turned to face the Secret Service man. "I'm sorry. What was that, again?"

"You single guys," Dickson said, grinning to himself. "You never get the sleep you need. Hell, I should have such problems. What I asked you was, how'd you get stuck with this detail?"

Apollo used the lie he had rehearsed. "Us single guys, just like you said. My SAC worked out the overtime this job was going to involve and asked for 'volunteers' who didn't have a wife at home to nag their asses off."

"Fat lot of good the wife does me on missing overtime," Dickson replied. "I swear, you Feebs are sounding more like bankers all the time. Next thing, you'll be on strike for extra holidays."

"It's not a bad idea," Apollo said, forcing a laugh at Dickson's "wit" and hoping that it sounded natural. He was acutely conscious of the Smith & Wesson on his belt, mere inches from his hand. He wondered where the others had concealed their weapons, what they would be carrying. Some kind of compact automatics, probably, the little "room brooms" that were more renowned for cyclic rate of fire than pinpoint accuracy. Not that it would matter, since they were primarily on board as a diversion, anyway; something to draw the Secret Service and his fellow Bureau agents off, giving Apollo room to work.

It was the best part of an hour yet before the Russian president, his White House hosts and various escorts were scheduled to arrive. Apollo had considered trying to reach his targets before the press conference, when security would—at least in theory—be somewhat reduced in private quarters, but he had backed off the plan for two reasons. First and foremost, the killing needed to be public for shock value and to maximize the later stages of the plot that would be orchestrated by The Two. A secondary concern had been the impossibility of diversions or backup in the private milieu, which would have complicated Apollo's mission, even as he sought to simplify it.

The Kevlar bulletproof vest beneath his shirt and jacket was a new addition to his wardrobe, something less than comfortable, but he was satisfied that no one knew he had it on. Apollo hadn't worn it in the hope that he would somehow walk away from what would follow, but rather as a precaution, to keep himself from being shot down before he could finish his job. The Secret Service agents were well trained, almost automatons when it came to the point of risking their own lives to save the chief executive, and Apollo harbored no doubts that they would fire on him the moment he revealed himself as an enemy of their charge. Some of them—like Dickson—knew him fairly well, perhaps considered him a friend, but it would make no difference when the guns went off. To that end, he had taken out insurance; just enough, perhaps, to let him see the mission through before he fell.

But if he was presented with an opportunity to complete the job *and* slip away…why not?

It gave Apollo something to consider, as he settled in and waited for his target, killing time.

THE SUIT WAS NEW, a hasty fit, and while the pants were riding up on Bolan at the inseam, he was more concerned about the jacket being loose enough to hide the shoulder rig he wore, with the Beretta 93-R slung beneath his left arm, two spare magazines in pouches underneath the right. The lightweight Kevlar vest had been a late addition, courtesy of Jack Grimaldi, who reminded him—unnecessarily, in fact—that even though Hal Brognola was supposed to tip the Secret Service detail at the White House, things were bound to be a little hectic if his hunch proved right and bullets started flying in the rose garden. Accustomed as he was to wearing body armor in his military days, through drenching rain and jungle heat, the Kevlar didn't cramp his style at all.

Of course, it only shielded Bolan from his shoulders to his waist, excluding arms and armpits, which left any number of potential targets for a skilled—or lucky—marksman to score fatal hits.

As he approached the milling crowd, Bolan drew greater comfort from the pin on his lapel that marked him as a Secret Service agent, plus the small earpiece that let him hear commands from those in charge of the security detail. It was entirely possible that he would miss a gunman in the crowd—assuming there were any gunmen present—but another set of eyes might pick him out in time, and thereby give the Executioner a shot.

Bolan cherished no illusions about the nature of his mission here. He was acting on a gut instinct, the least scientific of motives, hunting in territory known primarily from TV clips and hasty sketches Hal Brognola had prepared from memory within the past half hour. He was operating in the midst of an unarmed, civilian crowd that could be counted on to scatter in a panic at the first sign of a weapon. Add the cameras, microphones and some two dozen federal guards who didn't know the Executioner from Adam, and the risks were multiplied a hundredfold. Some of the guards might fire on him if there was trouble, and he had to watch his own rounds in the same event, to spare civilian flesh. Put it together, and it had to be one of the most uncomfortable missions he had ever undertaken, with a snafu quotient that was through the roof. The slightest error would by echoed and compounded in a mob scene, and the job could go to hell like that, before he even felt it slipping out of line.

As if those worries weren't enough, Bolan was also conscious of the fact that time was racing past him, while he dawdled in the White House rose garden. If he was wrong about the feeling in his gut, he would have given Locke and Braun an extra half day to refine whatever scheme they had in mind to top the bungled action with the AGMs. If it didn't involve the Russian president—or more specifically, his public outing at the White House—Bolan's detour could well allow his enemies the precious time they needed to make sure they didn't fail next time.

And he would have to live with it.

Experience had taught him to short-circuit morbid trains of thought and concentrate on something positive—the next thing he should do, alternatives, logistics, layouts, memorizing faces and positions in the crowd. There was no end of things to see and hear, but all of it reminded Bolan that he was, in essence, flying blind. Assuming any shooters from the cult were present, Bolan didn't have a clue who he was looking for or how to pick them out before they opened fire. He noticed that the White House press credentials many members of the crowd were wearing didn't feature photographs, a fact which made him wonder if a wily terrorist could gain entry that way, faking a pass, or simply lifting one from a reporter who no longer needed it because he had stopped breathing unexpectedly. Such action would require a measure of finesse, he realized; only a brain-dead shooter would impersonate Sam Donaldson, for instance, but with better than two hundred news people present, he could surely find a man—or woman—who would not be missed immediately, who wasn't well-known enough for a new face to sound alarms.

The prospect brought a scowl to Bolan's face, meaning that he would have to watch the press, as well as those unmarked civilian hangers-on whose purpose at the moment was, apparently, to stand around and shmooze. People without a day job, he imagined; or more probably, those who were so successful, so damned rich already, that they simply had to make a call and get invited to a little shindig at the White House. If they were "working" at the moment, Bolan calculated that a troop of narcoleptic monkeys could have done their jobs and never dropped a stitch.

There was no calculated pattern to his movements, as he paced around the area that had been set aside for the reception. No one stopped him, which he took to be a hopeful sign, Brognola's warning and the small lapel pin kicking in. He hadn't drawn a gun yet, though, and that, as Bolan knew from past experience, made all the difference in the world.

Perhaps this time the gun wouldn't be necessary.

Maybe he was wrong. It happened, and the Executioner had never claimed his hunches were infallible.

Maybe he was wrong, Bolan thought again, and almost hoped that it were true.

But the Executioner kept on prowling, just in case.

THE RUSSIAN PRESIDENT spoke English fluently, along with French and German, but he still felt some concern about meeting the press. Americans were often rash, impetuous, and there was no predicting—or preventing—what he might be asked, once he had microphones and cameras thrust into his face, nowhere to run and hide.

The press at home was picking up on Western style, regrettably. So many years of censorship and bland official press releases had prevented journalistic feeding frenzies while the old regime was in control. If there was anything the Russian president still missed about the bad old days—aside from job security, of course—it was the safely silent press.

How simple it had been to cover up an "accident" in those days. There had been no fear of crime, to speak of, in the old USSR, because *Pravda* and other organs of the state denied that crime existed. How could there be any lawbreakers in paradise? So what if the militia took three years to catch a psycho killer operating on the Moscow subway? No one but his victims and their families knew that the man existed, and once he was caught, he went directly to the Lubyanka lockup, where he soon ceased to exist. The Mafia? *What* Mafia? Reports of syndicated crime were foul disinformation tactics, manufactured in the West and circulated by the CIA or MI-6. How could police and statesmen in the perfect socialist Utopia be deemed corrupt?

Life had been so much simpler in those days.

The President of the United States had been his usual charming self at breakfast, telling jokes and laughing at the quips his chief guest offered in return. It was a far cry from the days when men who held their two respective offices had spoken only to impart dire threats or warnings of potential war, a holocaust that would have, quite possibly, destroyed all human life on Earth. The Russian president had been a child when it began, the long cold war, but he remembered old Nikita Khrushchev pounding on a lectern with his shoe and telling the Americans, "We will bury you!" He could remember Josef Stalin if he really put his mind to it, but what would be the point?

Times changed, and people who refused to change become a danger to themselves and others. With any luck at all, the bulk of them became street-corner preachers, borderline fanatics constantly predicting doomsday if the tide of history didn't reverse its course and roll back to an era they remembered fondly as the best of times. A handful would seek more dramatic means of self-expression—suicide, perhaps; or a career in politics—and some of those would strike off down the warpath, calling plagues of fire upon a new world they could never truly hope to understand.

The president of Russia understood new times, all right. He simply wasn't certain that he could survive in them.

"How long?" he asked Alexi, speaking English out of habit, now that they were in the White House proper and surrounded by Americans.

"Ten minutes," Alexi replied in Russian. He had no imagination, that one—which was why he made the perfect bullet catcher. Having once accepted the assignment, he would do whatever might be necessary to preserve his client from all harm, no matter what the danger to himself.

Exactly as it should be, thought the Russian president.

Ten minutes. Suddenly, from out of nowhere, he was conscious of an urgent need to use the rest room. Lowering his voice and lapsing into Russian, he stepped closer to Alexi and explained his problem briefly, moving toward the corridor to his left, where they had passed a men's room coming in. Behind him, at Alexi's signal, two members of the Russian security detail fell into step with the president, trailed by another pair of Secret Service agents.

Inside the men's room, which was empty, he veered in the direction of a toilet stall and closed the metal door behind him, latching it.

His escorts might be paid to listen, thought the president, but he wasn't about to let them watch.

SATURN WAS PROUD of having drawn the White House gig. Why not? Years back, he had been one of The Path's earliest recruits, and while he had been willing to make the ultimate sacrifice then, giving up his job and bank account, walking away from all that he had known, The Two had looked into his future and decreed that he would have a more important duty somewhere down the line. Meanwhile, they said, his work in television news, with frequent coverage of Congress and the White House, might be used to benefit The Path in other ways.

And so it had for years on end, Saturn alerting The Two of any pending legislation that affected "fringe" religions in the slightest, keeping his ear to the ground around Justice for rumors of investigations, raids, arrests. Along the way, he had been able to advance the cause from time to time, putting a subtle twist on "silly season" news reports that covered UFOs and similar phenomenon, or casting doubt on some federal action that displeased The Two.

This day, though, was the moment Saturn had been waiting for, the moment he was born for. He had a chance to serve the Ancients openly, dramatically, and if it cost his earth-bound shell to pull it off, so what? After the cleansing, all that he had lost and more would be restored to him, perfect next time, without the smallest flaw.

It was too bad about his normal cameramen, of course, but they were unbelievers anyway, thus doomed to ultimate destruction. Saturn had advanced their schedule, fudged their finish line a little closer to the starting blocks, but it would make no difference to them in the end. If anything, he reckoned that the quick death they were meted out, one bullet to the back of each man's head, was merciful compared to what they may have faced if they had lived to see the Final Days.

Because the plastic press tags bore no photographs, and since his face was well-known to the Secret Service detail at the White House, Saturn had no problem walking his two soldiers past the rank of bodyguards. He had imagined doing such a thing on more than one occasion in the past, and it never ceased to amuse him, thinking of how easy it would be to blitz a White House press conference. For all their high-tech gear, the Secret Service was basically just another over-worked security detail, prevented by the very nature of their client's business from enjoying full success.

These little get-togethers in the White House garden, for example. There was "screening" of reporters, in the sense that each one present had to show credentials that were previously issued to a bona fide media unit, but once you had the plastic tag—begged, borrowed, stolen or forged—your problems were basically over. By definition, reporters coming to the White House were expected to bring along cases of gear the average person on the street would never recognize, much less identify, and there was no examination whatsoever to find out if minicam no. 0137428 contained a hidden automatic weapon, say, or if those battery packs belted around the cameraman's waist were loaded with plastic explosives. The visiting reporters themselves weren't even searched or scanned; how could they be, when they came bearing all those cameras, tape recorders, cellular phones and pagers?

It was a shooter's paradise and a nightmare for security.

He had spotted Apollo up on the dais, but no signal passed between them, nothing that could possibly give them away. The Secret Service might be overworked and sometimes careless, but its men weren't idiots, and Saturn wouldn't risk his one big shot at glory through an act of stupid negligence. It was enough, right now, for him and his companions to be in their places and waiting for the main event.

Centaurus and Triton were going through the motions, setting up the camera gear. They had rehearsed it at the station, after hours, so they wouldn't be too awkward. Even though they weren't really taping anything today, it wouldn't do for them to fumble with the equipment, draw attention to themselves from other camera crews, perhaps even the presidential bodyguards.

"All set?" Saturn asked.

"Just about," Triton replied.

"Okay. We'll do the lead-in afterward." As Saturn spoke, he raised his voice enough for anyone close by to hear him, just another normal setup for the crew from Channel 17. Five nights a week, the drones and couch potatoes tuned in by the thousands, saw his smiling face, immediately followed by some thirty seconds of inane bullshit, and then forgot what they had learned almost immediately.

Whenever colleagues sat around discussing problems of the day, Saturn would listen quietly, keeping his own opinions to himself. The truth was, though, that he knew what had happened to America across the past three decades. It wasn't an economic thing, or rising crime rates, not even the breakup of the family that threatened to destroy the old U.S. of A. On the contrary, the real problem was that so damned many of her people were lazy and stupid.

Each year, American high schools churned out thousands of "graduates" who couldn't find the index in a book, much less explain its purpose. Many of them couldn't read or write a simple declarative sentence. Forget about punctuation. If you asked one of them to describe the function of a period, nine times out of ten the response would be a stupid giggle, à la Bevis and Butthead. As for math, history, current events, science, the arts—they were all a lost cause.

But all that was about to change.

A stirring in the crowd told Saturn that his targets had arrived, and he was ready for them. America's hopeless couch spuds were about to witness the beginning of a miracle, broadcast live or on tape-delay from every station *except* Channel 17.

Because two of Channel 17's former employees were dead, and the third had his hands full with more important matters.

He was about to change the world.

APOLLO WAS READY when the two heads of state cleared the White House proper, stepping into sunshine behind an advance team of three security guards. Two of those were Secret Service, while the third was a stranger to Apollo, wearing some kind of blue-and-white tag on his lapel that marked him as a member of the Russian delegation. He was squarely built, solid, hard-faced, with a bulge beneath his coat that might have been a submachine gun or a really serious pistol.

Apollo stood his ground and waited for them. It wasn't time yet. He wanted cameras rolling and microphones live, broadcasting everything that happened to the nation and the world at large. What was the point in pulling off the coup of the millennium unless you had a global audience?

His jacket was unbuttoned, normally a violation of the Bureau dress code, but allowed in situations such as this one, where security was paramount, and instant access to a firearm was desirable. Intensely conscious of the Smith & Wesson on his hip, Apollo felt the fingers of his right hand twitching slightly, eager to receive the pistol's weight and swing it into target acquisition, absorbing the recoil as he opened fire.

Soon, now.

The presidents were on the dais, grinning back and forth at each other, while the guards around them concentrated on the crowd. No trouble was expected, but the security team was still on alert, watching everyone except the other members of their team.

A critical mistake.

Apollo had been cleared for White House duty on the basis of his spotless service record with the FBI. The Bureau, in its turn, had done a background check when he enlisted, but the rest of it, as far as keeping tabs on what he might have done since then, was all a fairy tale. Without complaints, some reason to suspect an agent's honesty, the FBI didn't routinely mount surveillance on its own employees. No one in the Bureau was aware that he had joined The Path, much less the rest of it, from leaking confidential files to plotting the assassination of two presidents—one Russian, one American.

There would be crimson faces back at FBI headquarters when the smoke cleared, but Apollo, in all probability, wouldn't be around to enjoy the show. His moment was coming, any second now.

The President of the United States was speaking, introducing his guest of honor, when all hell broke loose in the audience. There was a startled cry of "Gun!" before the shooting started, two or three loud pops at first, before an automatic weapon kicked in like a string of firecrackers.

On stage, Secret Service agents were rushing the two heads of state, prepared to tackle them and take them down, surround them with a human shield and sweep them back inside the White House. Guns leaped into waiting hands. Apollo had *his* gun out, now, and he was moving toward the stage.

In front of him, Pete Dickson was in midair, vaulting toward the dais, when Apollo shot him in the ass. The Glaser round took out his right hip and turned his leap into a wobbling somersault that dumped him in a twisted heap on stage. Passing the wounded G-man, he glanced down and saw a dazed expression of disbelief in Dickson's eyes, and answered with a fierce, bright smile.

Apollo raised his pistol, sighting down the slide at destiny.

CHAPTER TWELVE

Bolan had his back turned to the shooters when the cry of "Gun!" went up, immediately followed by the popping sound of semiautomatic pistol fire. He had the Beretta out and ready, turning toward the source of gunfire, when an automatic weapon joined the chorus, ripping like a chainsaw through the sound of shouts and screams.

Still, Bolan couldn't see the gunners right away. For one thing, he was on the wrong side of the crowd with some two hundred people in his way, a fair percentage of them on their feet with bulky cameras shouldered, sweeping from the dais toward the center of the unexpected action. Worse yet, most of those who had turned out to cover the assignment were now scrambling for their lives, careening into one another, stumbling over metal folding chairs, some of them going down and tripping others as they fell.

And some of them were wounded, maybe dying. He could tell that from the different quality of cries that sprang from pain, instead of simple fear.

Plunging into the crowd and bulling through by sheer brute strength, there was no doubt in Bolan's mind as to the group responsible for the attack. If it wasn't The Path, then it defied the wildest limits of coincidence that some completely different group of terrorists would strike precisely here and now, so soon after the stolen AGMs had been recovered barely fifteen miles away. And if his hunch was wrong, by one chance in a million, it made no substantive difference. He was duty-bound to intervene, in any case.

More shooting now, and from the number of weapons involved, he knew that members of the presidential bodyguard had joined the firefight. Secret Service agents would be hesitant to fire in the confusion, but they couldn't simply let the shooters blast away at anything that moved. The risk of friendly fire at that point seemed less fearsome than the danger posed by letting unknown gunners blast away at will.

Bolan picked out one of the shooters through the shifting bodies that surrounded him, and he was lining up a quick shot, when a woman suddenly collided with Bolan, throwing him off balance. Neither one of them went down, but it was close, and when she saw the gun in Bolan's hand, the woman—Bolan thought he recognized her as a weekend network anchor—took off screaming in a new direction, plunging blindly through the crowd.

By that time, Bolan's shot had come and gone. He mouthed an angry curse and kept moving, dodging panicked runners who had found themselves with nowhere to go. A ring of suits and guns had closed off access to the White House rose garden, preventing any of the suspects from escaping, even if they couldn't be immediately stopped from squeezing off rounds in the crush.

Distortion of acoustics made the sounds of gunfire seem to come from everywhere at once. It almost sounded as if someone was firing from the dais, off to Bolan's left, but when he glanced in that direction, there was nothing to be seen. He knew that agents of the FBI and Secret Service would have thrown a ring around the presidents before they did another thing, and Bolan left them to it, concentrating on the hit team that apparently had reached the killing ground disguised as newsmen.

Time enough to think about that later, Bolan told himself, and it was someone else's headache, working out how the fiasco was allowed to happen in the first place. His first and only job was to eliminate as many of the shooters as he could before they ran up a greater body count.

One of the cameramen in front of him saw Bolan coming, marked the weapon in his hand, while overlooking his lapel pin, and decided it was time to be a hero. He charged at Bolan, brandishing the not-so-minicamera above his head like some demented caveman.

Bolan feinted to his left, then sidestepped to the right and drove the rigid fingers of his free hand deep into the hero's solar plexus, stopping short of lethal force. The would-be Tarzan doubled over, retching, and his camera hit the ground with an expensive-sounding crash.

The Executioner moved on, stepped over what appeared to be a dead or dying man, blood welling from a ragged head wound. He was closer now, a few more paces, and—

A shot rang out in front of him, no more than ten feet distant, and he saw a woman go down screaming, clutching at her side. Beyond her, facing Bolan, was a young man in a navy blazer, khaki trousers, with a plastic press badge dangling from a clip on his lapel, the pistol in his hand pointed at Bolan's chest.

Their guns went off together in the midst of chaos, blasting back and forth at point-blank range.

SATURN SQUEEZED OFF another short burst from his Ingram M-11 submachine gun, the compact .380-caliber weapon producing a sound like the ripping of sailcloth. He had deliberately neglected to attach the foot-long Sionics suppressor, both to conserve space for spare magazines in the already crowded camera case, and to create more pandemonium among his targets, letting noise as well as flying bullets amplify their terror.

Behind him, Centaurus and Triton were banging away with their pistols, choosing targets at random, enjoying themselves. So far none of their bullets had come close to either of the presidents on stage, nor had they been expected to. The point of a diversion, after all, was to divert, and from the rush of Secret Service agents closing on them now, Saturn could see they had achieved their goal.

The rest was all up to Apollo. If he failed, their sacrifice would be in vain, but it was too late now for second thoughts in any case.

Saturn picked out a pair of Feds, approaching on

his right. He swung around to meet them with his Ingram, heedless of the so-called innocent civilians in his path, as he unleashed a withering barrage of automatic fire. The Ingram's cyclic rate approached 1,200 rounds per minute, making any effort at pinpoint-precision fire a hopeless waste of time, but it was bloody murder at close range, particularly in a crowd.

He held down the trigger and swung his weapon like the nozzle of a hose from left to right and back again. Before he emptied the magazine, he watched the stream of bullets chop down two reporters, one of them a woman, then rip into the Feds. He couldn't tell if they were wearing vests or not, but with the Teflon-coated bullets he was using, Kevlar wouldn't help. The Secret Service men went down before they had a chance to fire a shot, and Saturn dropped his empty magazine, reloading swiftly with a fresh one he had taken from the camera case.

He flashed back to the final moments of *The Wild Bunch,* one of only two or three films that he had ever felt compelled to watch repeatedly. It was the scene where William Holden and three cronies found themselves surrounded by a company of several hundred soldiers, in a hopeless confrontation that resulted in bloody death for nearly all concerned. The movie outlaws had died laughing, each one gunning down a dozen men for every bullet he absorbed, leaving the dead stacked like a cord of wood on the smoky battlefield. Before the credits rolled on his first viewing of the movie, Saturn knew how he would like to die when it was time, assuming that he had a choice.

And now the choice was his.

He fired at random, laughing as his bullets toppled men and women, smashed expensive camera gear, and sent the walking wounded lurching in desperate search of cover. Some of them, he saw, had run into the famous White House rose bushes now, sharp thorns adding pain to their panic, ripping flesh and fabric of the media elite.

He wished the top network anchors were here to enjoy his performance and taste the excitement first-hand. Tom Brokaw, Peter Jennings, Dan Rather: the Big Three would have loved it, but he guessed they didn't get out much these days.

"What's the frequency, Kenneth?" he shouted, squeezing off another burst into the mad stampede.

He caught Triton blinking at him, seemingly confused, and bellowed at his soldier, "What's the matter with you?"

Triton went back to work, twin pistols blazing, and Saturn left him to it. Another pair of presidential bodyguards were closing on him from the general direction of the dais, and he wondered if Apollo had already made his move. If not, it was his own damned fault, since Saturn's men were holding up their end.

He went to meet the Feds, ducking behind a pudgy cameraman when one of them squeezed off a shot. The bullet meant for Saturn passed him by and drew a squeal from someone in the crowd behind him, making Saturn laugh again. He threw an arm around the hefty newsman's neck and fired beneath his up-raised arm, wielding the Ingram one-handed. It was tricky, holding down the little subgun's muzzle on full-auto fire, but he had practiced in advance, and he did well enough.

His bullets cut a zigzag pattern on the nearer agent's chest and punched him backward, knocking off his mirrored aviator's glasses, revealing eyes bugged with shock and sudden pain. The dead man's partner tried to duck and dodge, but no one could outrun a bullet, much less ten or fifteen of them, and the miniblizzard of .380 manglers nearly hacked his right arm from his body at the shoulder. He might live, if ambulance attendants reached him soon enough to quell the bleeding, but as far as posing any threat to Saturn or his soldiers, the Fed was history.

So far, so good.

The thought had barely taken shape, when Saturn felt a solid slap against his thigh, an inch or so below his left buttock. At once, his balance vanished, and he felt himself begin to topple, firing even as he fell, intent on taking out as many of the grubby bastards as he could before he died.

And he wasn't dead yet, by any means. It would take more than one shot in the ass to put him down.

Sprawled on the blood-flecked grass, supported on one elbow, Saturn still found strength to ditch the Ingram's empty magazine and slap a fresh one home.

"Come and get me!" he cried out to enemies he couldn't see. "Come on, you bastards! I'm not going anywhere!"

IN RETROSPECT, Apollo would consider shooting Dickson in the ass his first mistake. While the man apparently had no idea who shot him, there were others on or near the dais who had unobstructed views and who reacted swiftly to the shot.

"Luther, you bastard!" one of them—another Secret Service agent—shouted, as he veered off course to intercept Apollo. "What the fu—"

He never finished asking the question, because a Glaser slug took him in the face and nearly ripped off his lower jaw, in a splash of crimson that immediately drowned his words. The dead man twirled on tiptoe, spinning from the impact of the shot, Apollo brushing past him as he fell.

Where were the presidents? He felt a sudden rush of panic, realizing that in the time he had required to shoot two men, his targets had been overtaken and surrounded by a wall of human flesh. The guards were already rushing toward the nearest White House entrance, flankers covering their progress as they rushed their principals to safety.

No!

Apollo swung in that direction, tracking with his Smith & Wesson, but one of the flankers saw him, never even hesitated as he milked a short burst from the mini-Uzi he was carrying. Apollo dodged the bullets, heard a scream somewhere behind him as at least one of the wasted rounds met flesh, and he was ready to return fire when a body slammed into him from the left and took him down.

It was a hasty tackle, but it seemed to do the job. He went down underneath the agent who had struck him, gasping as the breath was driven from his lungs, but all his training—at the FBI Academy *and* with

The Path—prevented him from giving up, surrendering to what another might have called relief.

The man on top of him was cursing, hammering a fist into his ribs, his free hand clutching at Apollo's gun. Apollo suddenly went limp, as if deciding that resistance was a waste of time, but that response lasted no longer than it took for him to feel his enemy reacting, taking victory for granted.

"All right, give me that," the agent said, still leaning toward his gun, "you miserable piece of—"

When Apollo fired, he wasn't aiming; at that range, it was unnecessary to select a mark. He simply cocked his wrist and squeezed the Smith & Wesson's trigger, felt the Glaser round singe his face in passing, heard it strike the man who lay on top of him.

It was a shoulder wound, and crippling, though the Secret Service agent still might have survived in other circumstances. As it was, the shock of impact slammed him over backward, freeing Apollo. The cultist caught a glimpse of other agents, the protection detail, vanishing inside the White House.

He had missed his chance. Both targets were beyond his reach.

Enraged, he turned upon the agent who had tackled him, and for the first time recognized a "brother" agent of the FBI, Paul Grammage, whom he knew from headquarters. Both of them had been assigned to guard the Russian president, but only one had been wholeheartedly committed to the job.

And still was, from the look of it. Paul Grammage tried to sit and, failing that, prevented by the shock and pain, he reached across his body with his one good arm and fumbled for the pistol on his belt.

"Too late," Apollo said and shot him in the face. It still wasn't enough, somehow, and so he stepped closer, bending down, and fired another round point-blank into the dead man's shattered skull.

Somewhere beyond the dais, gunfire sputtered on, the suicide diversion still in play. On stage, Apollo was aware of several agents staring at him, closing in on him, and knew he had to do something very quickly if he was to have a prayer of breaking out.

Escape hadn't been factored into the original design, of course, but as a thorough man, Apollo tried to cover all his options. He had known there was a chance that he might miss his targets, and while some regarded death as the appropriate apology for failure in such instances, Apollo viewed it as a symptom of weakness. Being killed in the attempt was one thing, but a wretched suicide on top of failure seemed to him the furthest thing from honorable death.

But what to do?

"Throw down the gun!" one of the Secret Service men called out.

"Don't move!" another ordered.

"Get down on the ground!" a third commanded.

"Freeze!"

The senator came out of nowhere, slipping past the agents somehow, stumbling as he mounted low steps to the dais. His was a familiar face, though blood-smeared now from what appeared to be a bullet graze along the hairline. While Apollo couldn't come up with a name to match the bloody face, it made no difference. He moved with catlike grace, before the Secret Service men could fire, and clamped one arm around the senator's throat, jamming the Smith & Wesson tight against his skull.

"Must get away from here," the legislator mumbled.

"That's a plan," Apollo said and started edging toward the northwest corner of the stage.

A HUNDRED DIFFERENT questions clamored in his mind, demanding answers, but the Russian president was speechless. It was a rare condition for a politician, and the fact that he was fluent in four languages made his stunned silence even more incongruous.

What could he say? What was the point of saying anything?

He knew the sound of gunfire when he heard it, and there was no second-guessing what had nearly happened in the White House rose garden. Assassins had been waiting for them, even with the so-called tight security surrounding the event, and at the moment, it appeared to make no difference whether they were gunning for the U.S. President, or for himself.

What mattered, first and foremost, was that he had managed to survive—escape unharmed, in fact. He quickly counted noses and discovered that his men were also present and accounted for, all seemingly intact. His presidential host, likewise, had come through the fray without a scratch.

What more could anyone expect?

Some in Russia, this president among them, might once have suspected an FBI-CIA plot behind such an incident as this, but he had seen the American President's face as the first shots were fired, the shock and fright mingled with outrage that registered there. Long-term survival in politics, regardless of nationality, required a fair ability to judge character, and he couldn't believe his present host had any warning whatsoever of the violence that had cut short their meeting with the press.

"What happens now?" he asked of no one in particular.

"We're safe here," said his host, who frowned and turned immediately to the nearest Secret Service agent. "We *are* safe here, right?"

"Yes, sir," the stone-faced agent said, his Uzi submachine gun pointed at the nearest door.

They hadn't lingered in the foyer fronting the White House rose garden, but had retreated well inside the building, down two flights of stairs to reach a sparsely furnished basement chamber. It was some kind of shelter, he imagined, though it clearly wasn't deep enough to shield the President from any kind of air strike, if it came to that.

He forced himself to put that thought out of his mind. It was a simple shooting, and a bungled one at that. It came as a surprise to him that anyone could smuggle guns onto the White House grounds, but he would let that problem rest with the Americans. His first concern, now, was that what had happened in the rose garden might somehow sabotage his mission, keep him from discussing certain urgent matters with the U.S. President, as he had planned to do. Could that, indeed, have been the purpose of the foiled attack? To demonstrate, perhaps, that dealing with a Russian leader—any Russian leader—was a risk best left alone?

"Well, I don't know about the rest of you," his host was saying now, "but I could damn well use a drink."

"Yes, please," the Russian president replied.

"Vodka?"

"Just now," he said, "I think I would prefer a double Scotch."

"I believe I've got some single malt that might be what the doctor ordered. Stuart?" the U.S. President said.

"Yes, sir?" a young, blond bodyguard replied.

"Why don't you go upstairs and have a look around. Bring back a bottle of Glenlivet, while you're at it, and a couple glasses." Turning back to face his guest, the President went on, "We might as well relax. I'll have to make some kind of statement once they get this mess cleaned up, then I suggest we head to Camp David. You and I have lots to talk about."

"Yes, sir," the Russian president replied. "We do, indeed."

And for the first time since the shooting started, he remembered how to smile.

THE SLUG HIT Bolan's vest, off center. The impact shoved him backward, made him grimace from the bruising pain, but it was too late to prevent his own slug drilling home on target, through the shooter's face. One moment, he was standing there; the next, he wasn't, and the weapon in his hand was silent.

Bolan scooped it up in passing to prevent somebody else from grabbing it, regardless of the motive. The soldier's enemies were well enough armed as it was, and he didn't need any amateur commandos "helping" the professionals to bring them down.

Thus doubly armed, he moved out toward the sounds of gunfire that continued sputtering some ten or fifteen yards in front of him. The crowd was thinning there, flight and attrition winnowing the ranks between him and his enemies.

As far as he could see, two members of the hit team were alive and still unloading on the crowd, holding their own against attempted flanking movements by the FBI and Secret Service agents on the scene. Neither had noticed Bolan, yet, but that was pure dumb luck. Another moment and they might—

As if in tune with Bolan's thoughts, the nearest shooter turned to face him, leveling a semiauto pistol in each hand. Bolan let go with both of his at once, firing on instinct, and he saw the rounds slap home with stunning force. The shooter went down, firing as he fell, his wild rounds snapping over Bolan's head.

Beyond his crumpling target, number three was turning toward the latest sound of gunfire, leveling a stubby Ingram SMG. Bolan squeezed off a snap shot with the Browning automatic he had lifted from his first kill, biting off a curse as it went low and to the left. Still, it wasn't a total waste, his adversary's leg collapsing as the bullet took him in the hip and brought him down.

He gave the shooter points for toughness, rattling off the last rounds from his Ingram's magazine before he hit the deck, reloading smoothly, even though he had to have been in pain, shock setting in. That kind of staying power told him that the guy had either been well trained, was a fanatic for his chosen cause—or both.

And he was propped up on one elbow, squeezing off another burst, as Bolan threw himself aside, dodging the line of fire. It was another near-miss, but some of those behind him weren't so lucky, if the screams were any indication.

Bolan landed on his belly, both arms out in front of him, his pistols sighted on the wounded gunner. Rapid-firing without any visible delay, he saw the Browning's slide lock open on an empty chamber after two more rounds, while three from the Beretta 93-R also found their mark and pitched the human target backward, like a sack of dirty clothes.

He ditched the empty Browning, bolted to his feet and was already turning toward the dais when he heard more shots from that direction.

On stage, a man he didn't recognize had seized another stranger, this one with a bloody face, and had a pistol jammed against his skull, using the hostage as a human shield. Encircled by no less than half a dozen FBI and Secret Service agents, it appeared that he had nowhere left to go, Bolan relaxing slightly as he drifted toward the stage. Whoever this guy was, apparently some adjunct to the hit team, he was clearly running out of time.

Or so it seemed, before his left hand swung back, out of sight, then reappeared a heartbeat later, lobbing what appeared to be a small green soup can toward the center of the stage. Bolan had recognized the canister before it hit, bounced once, and started spewing thick, white smoke in blinding clouds, obscuring the gunman and his hapless prisoner in seconds flat.

Another shot rang out, the agents rushing forward, heedless of the danger, as their quarry bolted. Bolan didn't follow, knowing there were agents all over the grounds, and anything he tried to do on their behalf would only further complicate what should turn out to be a fairly simple search.

But he was wrong. Ten minutes later, when the smoke had cleared and he was standing on the dais with another body stretched out at his feet, one of the Secret Service agents came to stand beside him, scowling at the corpse.

"This is the shits," he said. "A senator, for Christ's sake. Maryland, I think."

"The shooter?" Bolan asked him.

With another glance at the lapel pin Bolan wore, the agent loosened up a bit. "We lost the bastard," he replied. "Won't matter, though. The Bureau has a fix on him."

"Oh, yeah?"

"They damn well should," the agent told him, bitterly. "He's one of theirs. Can you believe it? Fucking Special Agent Luther Marx."

CHAPTER THIRTEEN

The presidential retreat at Camp David lies barely ten miles southeast of the White House in Prince Georges County, Maryland. A security fence encloses 125 acres of hilly terrain, the cottages and meeting facilities screened from outside view by a thick growth of oak, poplar, hickory, maple and ash. Arrival, for the most part, is by air. Once on the ground, transport within the camp itself is limited to golf carts, bicycles and foot traffic. The several cottages are situated so that no one has to see his neighbor outside working hours, if he isn't so inclined. The cottages themselves are named for different trees, a folksy touch in lieu of simple numbering.

The Russian president had all this information at his fingertips before the helicopter designated as Marine One lifted off from Washington, a stout phalanx of FBI and Secret Service agents keeping the reporters well back from the White House helipad. For once, the lawmen had an excellent excuse to play rough with the media, if any of the talking heads or camera crews stepped out of line, and none of those who lined the curb on Pennsylvania Avenue, as they took off, had seemed inclined to press his luck.

"I feel I must apologize again," the President of the United States was saying, grim-faced as he spoke, but otherwise apparently relaxed "A thing like this...I just don't know."

"My friend," the Russian president replied, "you are no more responsible for the behavior of fanatics in your country than I am for those who would return to Stalinism and the purges in my own. Alas, we cannot always choose our countrymen."

"It's kind of you to say," his host replied. "Still, the security—"

"Was excellent, I think. We are alive still, yes? I must commend your Secret Service. They had been well prepared."

"I'm told three were killed, and three more were wounded," said the U.S. President. "Once everything gets sorted out, I'll have to call their families."

"Please add my heartfelt thanks to all of them," the Russian said.

"Thank you. I will." His host glanced out the window, and one corner of his mouth twitched slightly, trying for a smile before he caught himself. "We're almost there."

The Russian president knew more about Camp David than the site's location and the layout of accommodations on the grounds. In fact, he knew things he wasn't supposed to know about this piece of real estate where peace treaties had been negotiated and the leaders of the modern world had come to argue points that sometimes changed the course of history.

He knew, for instance, that security around Camp David was not limited, by any means, to the encircling fence. The Secret Service had an operational headquarters on the site, and while there were no land mines or explosive booby traps, the retreat had been fully renovated, fitted out with state-of-the-art security devices to detect and repel intruders. Camp David was guarded and patrolled at all times, but with the president en route—and word of the attack in Washington still dominating every television channel in the land—extra security would be imposed, more agents and hardware deployed, to rule out any repetition of the morning's ugliness.

They had been tracked by radar since departing from the White House, a special transponder in the helicopter's nose identifying Marine One for the ground crew at Camp David. Even so, if the pilot hadn't responded correctly to particular prompts from ground control, Marine One would have touched down on a helipad ringed with automatic weapons, surrounded with nowhere to go. Aircraft approaching Camp David without the special transponder, meanwhile, got one warning to alter their course. Failure to comply with that directive could result in Stinger missiles being unleashed from the ground, although such drastic means had yet to be employed outside of special training exercises for the White House bodyguards.

At night, he had been told, the agents who patrolled Camp David wore special kinds of goggles, infrared or something, that enabled them to hunt men in the dark. Their weapons had been outfitted with laser ights; if they could point, it was supposedly impossible to miss.

He raised a silent toast to the technology of death.

It was among the reasons for his visit to the States, of course, this business with "deactivated" warheads stockpiled in the vaults of several former Soviet republics. Rumor had it that the nukes—or some of them, at any rate—were for sale and going to the highest bidders, with perfect disregard for political ideology or mental stability. Officially, the Russian president denied that the traffic existed; privately, he recognized it as a fact of life that gave him nightmares.

With any luck at all, perhaps some help from the United States...

"Welcome to Camp David," the pilot said over the intercom, as they gently touched down. "Please watch your step and mind your head as you exit the aircraft."

The Secret Service men went first, even here, where they presumably controlled the ground and air. His host was next, the Russian president following, with his own men bringing up the rear. It was a brilliant day outside, the sky an azure miracle. The nearest town, he knew, was a hamlet called Parker's Corner—its coordinates once a primary target for Soviet ICBMs—but you would never know such things as towns existed, much less teeming cities, if you gave yourself up to the beauty of the place.

He was reminded of the dacha north of Moscow that he rarely had time to visit these days, and which he could barely afford to maintain in a post-

Communist economy. Perhaps, if he was lucky here and struck the proper note, those hard times might be ending soon.

"I love it here," his host was saying. "If you want to know the truth, sometimes I feel like I should hide out here and not go back."

"I have such days, as well," the Russian president agreed.

This time, his host made no attempt to hide the smile. "Let's get you settled in, first thing. You're in the dogwood cottage, if I'm not mistaken. That would be this way."

"THE JOKER with the Ingram," Hal Brognola said, "was Philip Sikes. You might've recognized him if you hung around the D.C. area for any length of time. He was a weekend anchor, more or less, with ABC's affiliate in Arlington."

"A TV man?" Celeste Bouchet could only shake her head in wonderment. "They're everywhere."

"The others?" Bolan prodded him. He felt exposed there, strolling on the Mall like tourists, as if a sniper's crosshairs were centered on his back.

"Still working on it," the big Fed replied. "Nothing from AFIS, so I guess they kept their noses clean, no military service records we can check."

The FBI's automated fingerprint identification system—AFIS for short—was fully computerized, designed to scan millions of prints in record time, seeking points of identity with fingerprints lifted from crime scenes—or as in this case, from unidentified corpses. The print index had been J. Edgar Hoover's pride and joy, including not only the fingerprint records of convicted criminals, but also those of U.S. military personnel and various professionals throughout the country—such as teachers and security guards in a number of states—whose occupations required fingerprinting for a criminal background check.

"Speaking of the Bureau," Bolan said.

"God, don't remind me." There was no concealing Brognola's disgust on this one. "Special Agent Luther Andrew Marx. They're already calling him the FBI's Aldrich Ames. Your guess on how the cult recruited him would be as good as mine, but I'm inclined to think we'll never really know."

"There's still no sign of him, I take it," Bolan stated.

"Oh, we've got signs all right," Brognola said. "Unfortunately, they all read Dead End. It's like the son of a bitch evaporated—pardon my language."

"I've heard the term before," Bouchet reminded him, "and used it on occasion."

"So, what *do* we know about him?" Bolan asked.

"The basics," Brognola replied. "This is—or was—his twelfth year on the job. Clean record, with a commendation three years back for taking down one of the Ten Most Wanted fugitives. Marx saw this guy at a Bethesda shopping mall and recognized him, made the collar on his own. That was about eight months after the Bureau transferred him to headquarters, in Washington. He lived across the line in Chevy Chase, but HRT's already trashed his house. If there's a lead to where he might hide out, they haven't found it yet. His car's at headquarters in the garage downstairs. No traffic on his credit cards to indicate he planned a getaway.''

"Because he hadn't," Bolan said. That much was obvious. The rogue G-man couldn't have planned on living through his mission at the White House, even though he came prepared with smoke grenades in case the game went south on him.

"I was thinking that myself. But if the guy's a kamikaze, why would he take off like that? I mean, the thing to do is stick around and try to raise the butcher's bill.''

"He isn't finished," Bolan said. And he was guessing now, but it felt right. "He didn't do the job he was assigned to do. It's fifty-fifty now, if he'll come back to try again, or else present himself for discipline to Locke and Braun.''

"He can forget about the rematch," Brognola said. "That ship sailed without him, big time. His prospective targets are already at Camp David, and the Secret Service guys are all on Defcon One. They're hoping that he will try. Frankly, I am, too.''

"But if he's running, maybe we can use him," Bolan said.

"You're thinking track him back to fruitcake central?" Brognola inquired. "That's not a bad idea— except we have to find the bastard, first. I don't expect much good from tracking something we can't see.''

"Nothing at all on how he got away?" Bouchet inquired.

"Oh, sure," Brognola said. "We know he commandeered a car on Pennsylvania Avenue and ditched it out in Glen Mar Park. That's Maryland again, northwest of Washington. Cops found it at a strip mall, but we don't know where he went from there. He might have had a car stashed, or he could have bagged another one. They're checking GTA reports, but it's a semiresidential area, some people out of town, whatever. Hell, it could be weeks before we find out what he drove, much less which way he drove it.''

"Where's Camp David?" Bouchet asked. "In reference to Washington, I mean."

"Southeast," Brognola said.

"Okay, then. If he's headed there—and we're agreed that it's a long shot, then he has to double back. My guess would be he'd go the long way around, avoiding Washington."

"That's Highway 95," Brognola said, "or any of a hundred different ways if he decides to take his time. We've covered what we can, considering that no one knows what kind of vehicle we're looking for, or whether Marx has people helping him."

"All right," Bouchet went on. "And if he's headed for a meeting with The Two, he must be going west."

"We still don't know where they are, either," Brognola reminded them. "You say he's 'going west' from Washington. That still leaves something like four-fifths of the United States, plus most of Canada and Mexico."

"You know," Bolan remarked, prepared to drop the bomb he had been hoping to avoid, "Marx might not be the one we really need to think about right now."

"Meaning the cult could have another backup plan," Brognola said.

"It's possible," the Executioner agreed.

"Here I was hoping they put all their eggs in one big basket with the AGMs, and now we're looking at more backup plans than Nixon's plumbers had the month before election day," Brognola groused.

"It's not for sure," Bolan reminded him, "but somebody should be prepared."

"You mean Camp David? That's a lock. They've more than doubled up on Secret Service personnel, and they've got hardware up the— What I mean to say is, they're prepared."

"Like at the White House?" Bolan asked.

"I really hate it when you ask those kinds of questions," Brognola said. "Everybody's thinking Marx must be a fluke. I mean, how many infiltrators could they have in sensitive positions?"

"That's the question," Bolan said. "How many would it take?"

"Depends," Hal said. "If they had someone with his finger on the button who could bypass fail-safe, they could nuke the whole damned planet."

"On a realistic scale," the Executioner replied.

"What's realistic in this freaking mess?" the big Fed asked him, raising empty hands only to let them drop again. "You got me, guy. Worst-case scenario, they could have someone at Camp David, but I'm thinking we'd have heard about it."

"Second worst?" Bouchet inquired.

"Someone outside," Brognola answered, frowning, "but still close enough to be a trusted aide, with access to the President. That gets him through security, gives him his shot.''

''And if he's not invited in, he has to take the place by storm,'' Bolan said.

''Either that,'' Brognola said, ''or just kick back and bide his time, let things cool down and roll the dice another day.''

''No good,'' Bolan replied. ''They need the Russian president to make it international. It's wasted effort if they let him get away. No hit on U.S. soil, no global incident.''

''I hate it when you're right,'' Brognola said. ''Suppose they wait until the meeting wraps, and try to take him on his way back to the airport?''

''It's a possibility,'' Bolan agreed, ''but any hunter who's concerned about results will take the stationary target every time.''

''That makes it easy, then,'' Bouchet put in. ''They'll have to come to you.''

Brognola scowled and said, ''Oh, great. I'm feeling *so* much better, now.''

In GLEN MAR PARK, Apollo—better known to those now hunting him as Special Agent Luther Marx—had bagged another set of wheels with no great difficulty. Understanding that his stolen ride from Washington would soon be found—within a day at most, and sooner if his luck was wearing thin—he didn't choose to lift another vehicle in circumstances where the theft would be reported right away. That ruled out taking one from any local parking lot or residential street, where it might soon be missed and then reported to police.

It meant that he would have to take the driver with him, to insure that there was no report.

Apollo dawdled in the parking lot outside a shopping center two blocks from the one where he had ditched the stolen car, giving himself a quarter hour to pick out a likely mark, before he absolutely had to move and try another stand. In fact, it only took eight minutes, an old man emerging from the hardware store with plastic shopping bag in hand, proceeding toward a Mitsubishi Diamante LS four-door parked well back from spotty traffic passing on the street. Apollo came up on the old man's blind side, waiting for him to unlock the door before he badged him and requested his assistance with an urgent matter of supreme importance.

Blinking at Apollo, astounded by the notion of excitement gracing his pedestrian existence, the old guy had asked what he could do to help the FBI. Apollo glanced around, as if afraid spies might be eavesdropping—in fact, to check for pesky witnesses— then sucker-punched the old man in his flabby gut, a short jab backed by desperation and a fierce will to survive. The old man doubled over, retching, and Apollo grabbed him in a headlock, twisting sharply, holding up his deadweight as the guy went limp.

It was a little awkward, shoving him across the driver's seat and down onto the floorboards on the other side, a life-sized rag doll, but he got it done. The old man's keys had hit the pavement when Apollo slugged him, and a moment later he was rolling, putting Washington behind him, picking up the George Washington Memorial Parkway to cross the Potomac on Interstate 495. From there, the Beltway took him south to Highway 66, and he was westbound well past Fairfax, looking for a place to dump the old man's body by the time the all-news channel named him as a fugitive.

Camp David was a washout. He could save all kinds of time and simply shoot himself if all he wanted was to die. It might still come to that—indeed, Apollo knew his life was almost certainly the price that he would have to pay for failure—but at least he could keep faith, present himself and let The Two decide his punishment.

Or he could simply run away.

It was an option he hadn't ignored, although the odds of a successful getaway lay somewhere on the scale of slim to none. If he wasn't already on the Bureau's Ten Most Wanted list, he would be by the time the sun went down. He was the sole surviving shooter from what several talking heads had dubbed the White House Massacre, which meant the bland, unsmiling photo from his FBI credentials would be on TV by now, beamed all around the world by satellite. By suppertime, he would be staring out from the front page of half the newspapers in America, and the rest would serve him for breakfast.

The Bureau would be pulling out all stops to get him, to clean up their own mess in the glare of national publicity before some local yokels did it for them. There had been enough embarrassment since Hoover died, from the COINTELPRO revelations to

Waco, Mark Putnam and the spying cases, Ruby Ridge and Richard Jewel. This had to be the capper, and Apollo could expect no mercy from the "brother" Feds he had humiliated with that morning's handiwork.

Not that he had been very handy, when he got down to it. He had gone in gunning for two presidents, fully expecting to be killed in the exchange of gunfire, but had wound up bagging two G-men, a half-assed senator and running for his life. The compact smoke grenade, lifted from HRT at headquarters, had been a last-minute addition to his gear, selected on a whim, and it had wound up saving him. Was that predestination or a stroke of pure dumb luck?

More to the point, what frigging difference did it make?

The bottom line was failure. He was on his way to face The Two and tell them what by now, they had to already know: that he had let them down, just like the others who had screwed up careful plans in recent days. They would decide what should become of him, and he would passively submit. Confession and submission were his last, best hope of salvaging his place in paradise, and if he had believed his cause was hopeless, there would have been nothing to prevent him swerving into lethal impact with the nearest vehicle.

Without hope, why survive?

In order to present himself before The Two, however, he would have to wriggle through the net that was already cast for him, flung far and wide across the continent. He had to make contact with Cerberus and take it from there.

Whatever happened after that would be determined by the Ancients and the stars.

"I TAKE RESPONSIBILITY, of course." The words were bitter, actually tasted bad to Cerberus, but what else could he say? Except to add: "I still don't know what happened, what went wrong, but it's my ultimate responsibility."

He stood before The Two, uncertain whether he would still be breathing in another ten or fifteen minutes. He had come to tell them of the Washington snafu in person, hoping he could beat the media reports and do some spin control, but CNN was there ahead of him with live shots from the White House followed by a vigil mounted just outside, on Pennsylvania Avenue.

The silence was oppressive, seeming almost to deprive the room of air. Cerberus had begun to think The Two would never speak, might be intent on staring him to death, when Hermes broke the ice.

"You seem to think," his leader said, "that we are more concerned with placing blame than with attempting to repair the damage that's been done."

"No, sir. I—"

Hermes went ahead as if Cerberus hadn't spoken, interrupting him. "This project was—*is*—critical to everything we've worked for through the years. I thought you understood that, Cerberus."

"Yes, sir. But—"

"Now we find the plans, *your* plans, have been deficient. Not once, mind you. *Twice.*"

That wasn't fair, of course. They weren't his plans at all, but rather had originated from The Two, presumably with Ares smoothing out the details, back when he was still alive. Same thing with all the other operations that had blown up in their faces during recent days. The only part of this fiasco Cerberus had managed on his own had been eliminating Janus, and that part of it had gone without a hitch.

"I understand your feelings, sir," he said between clenched teeth.

"Do you?" Circe replied. Her tone was ripe with mockery. "Are *you* descended from the Ancients, Cerberus? Have you been waiting all these ages for reunion with your own kind, trapped among the remnants of a failed experiment?"

He was about to say he thought they all were, all believers, but he still hoped to survive the meeting, so he kept that observation to himself. "No, ma'am."

"It's essential," Hermes said, "that we shouldn't allow this opportunity to slip away. Who knows how long we might be forced to wait before we have another chance like this? How many of us will be left by then?"

"Sir, I—"

"Did you take care of Janus, as you were instructed?" Circe asked him.

"Yes, ma'am. As you ordered."

He had dropped the pilot's body down an old abandoned well in Oklahoma, on a dried-up farm outside a tiny town with the peculiar name of Slapout. If and when it was discovered, all authorities would have to work on was the cause of death, two perfectly anonymous 9 mm bullets in the cocky bastard's brain.

"Thank heavens for small favors." Circe sighed and turned her face away from him, oblivious to the angry color staining his cheeks.

"The media is trying to assist us," Hermes said. "We know the presidents were taken to Camp David after the fiasco at the White House. Every effort must be made to reach them there while they are still together. We can save this, yet, if we apply sufficient ingenuity and effort."

Cerberus was forced to bite his tongue to keep from laughing right out loud. Save this? he thought. Attack Camp David? For the first time since he found The Path and took its message as his own, he wondered if The Two might be insane. Oddly, the thought that maybe they were losing it, after so many years of butting heads with an oppressive system, didn't lead him to suspect their basic teachings might be false. That would have been too great a leap for Cerberus, calling his own life and his own mind into question.

"Sir," he said, attempting to be tactful, "I'm afraid we don't have the equipment or the personnel for that kind of procedure."

"Ah," Hermes said with a sidelong glance at Circe, "but I think we do."

"With all respect, sir, the security around Camp David makes the White House look like Kmart in the middle of a back-to-school sale. For one thing, it's not even on most maps, and—"

"We know where it is," Circe informed him. "We know many things."

"Yes, ma'am," he said, feeling his cheeks on fire. "Then you must know they have all kinds of hardware on the site that they could never use in downtown Washington. Five minutes' notice, and they've got jet fighters in the air from Bolling Air Force Base, or paratroops and helicopter gunships out of Fort McNair."

"Ah, so you *do* know where Camp David is?" There was a gleam in Circe's eye that made the short hairs bristle on his nape.

"Yes, ma'am, but I—"

"You'll be relieved to learn," Hermes said, interrupting him once more, "that you will not be held responsible for what must now be done. Through communion with the Ancients, we anticipated that a backup plan might be required, despite the months of planning we invested in the first two operations."

"Sir?" He didn't like the sound of that at all. It had the makings of a brush-off, possibly demotion. Still, Cerberus thought, it could have been much worse.

"You've done your best, we realize," Hermes said. "But—and I say this with deep regret—it simply isn't good enough."

"Sir, if I may—"

"No, you may not!" For such a slender woman, Circe had a voice that lashed like a whip when she was angry.

"The decision has been made," Hermes said, "and it's final."

"Very final," Circe added. And the worst part was that she was smiling now.

"I understand," he told them, trying to be reasonable, "if you both think I should be replaced." What else had he expected, after all?

"Replaced?" Hermes pronounced the word as if it was entirely new to him. "Replaced! Now there's a thought."

Too late, Cerberus saw the pistol in his master's hand. Where had it come from? Tucked behind his back, perhaps, under the loose tail of his baggy shirt. Cerberus thought of running, but his traitor feet ignored the silent order. Glancing down at them in scorn, he understood at last why this room had a vinyl floor instead of carpeting. A few swipes with a mop and there would be no trace of him.

Resigned, he closed his eyes and waited in the dark.

CHAPTER FOURTEEN

Although he knew it was disloyal, in some respects—might even jeopardize his entry into paradise—Icarus felt a smile of secret satisfaction coming on when he discovered that the White House operation had gone south. It wasn't that he wished Apollo ill; far from it. At the same time, though, he still couldn't help feeling that the job was his, by rights. He had arranged for the delivery of two cruise missiles for the execution of Plan A, and it wasn't his fault, in any sense, that federal agents had retrieved the AGMs before they could be utilized.

The failure wasn't his, by any means, and yet he still felt driven to complete the job that he had volunteered for in the first place. Icarus still felt the burden of responsibility—and, yes, he'd admit it, a frustrated craving for the glory that would lie in store for the person who helped the Ancients find their way back home.

Ironically, it all came down to him now, and he found that knowledge both invigorating and unsettling. He was looking forward to the challenge in the same way he had once looked forward to his bombing runs in Vietnam and Laos; a chance to show what he was made of and destroy some of the little yellow bastards who were threatening America, his sacred way of life. He had learned many things since Nam, but there was still that old, familiar eve-of-battle tingling in his groin, the surge of energy that came with knowing everything depended on him and no one else.

His apprehension, on the other hand, derived from wondering if it was already too late. He knew enough about Camp David to respect the presidential hideaway's defenses, even as he realized that they hadn't been planned with him in mind. The place was covered, right, but no one in logistics with the Secret Service had considered that a modern, high-tech military aircraft might come gunning for the President on U.S. soil. It was preposterous, in fact. If international relations had degenerated to that point, the President wouldn't be lounging at Camp David, and the hostile fliers would be met somewhere in mid-Atlantic, where a flameout was the same thing as a burial at sea.

So, they weren't really prepared to deal with a determined aerial assault. More to the point, they weren't expecting Icarus—Earth name, Lieutenant Colonel Nathan Holt, USAF.

He had been tempted to put on his full-dress uniform, medals and all, but at the final moment, when he had it laid out on his bed, a small, familiar voice inside had asked, What for? What difference did it make?

No difference, Icarus decided, opting for the one-piece flight suit that would be more comfortable in the cockpit, while attracting less attention en route to the aircraft he had chosen for his mission. If they shot him down—which, he admitted to himself, was still a possibility—his silver star and campaign ribbons would be nothing more than deadweight as he plunged to earth in flames.

His personal equipment for the mission was a pack of Wrigley's Spearmint gum, a Ka-bar fighting knife and an old Colt .45 that he preferred to the Berettas now in standard use as U.S. military side arms. He enjoyed the automatic's reassuring weight beneath his arm, and knew that he could generally hit what he was aiming at within a range of thirty feet or so.

The gum was for his ears, to keep them clear once he was in the air.

There could be trouble when he tried to board the aircraft. No, scratch that: there *would* be trouble. That was why he had the Ka-bar fighting knife, in hopes that he could keep the trouble quiet, leave confusion in his wake to stall pursuit.

And if he couldn't keep it quiet, there was still the .45.

No matter what it took, he meant to be airborne within the next half hour, winging toward his rendezvous with destiny. Whatever happened next, he would confront each obstacle as it appeared and deal with it decisively. Saving the main punch for his target at the other end, of course.

He cast a final glance at his reflection in the mirror, knowing that he might not see himself again, this side of the reflecting pools in paradise, and checked his watch. It was a birthday gift, the last his wife had given him before she died of cancer nine years earlier. Holt wondered how she would feel about what he was doing, then as quickly decided the question was pointless. The Ancients were clear on that point, in the voice of their prophet, recorded as scripture:

The dead know not anything.

So much for heaven and hell, loved ones writhing in torment or dawdling on clouds, watching while their survivors went bumbling on with their lives. What a peculiar myth the self-appointed "holy men" of humankind had fashioned to delude their followers and keep them docile, looking forward to a magic payoff in the by-and-by, if they would only say their prayers and keep those fat donations rolling in.

Icarus blinked at his reflection, almost tempted for the barest fraction of a second to ask himself if *he* wasn't the one deluded by a fantasy. Suppose *his* firmly held belief was wrong, in fact, while those whom he dismissed as mindless sheep were—

No!

The difference between himself and them, the herd, was that *he* knew the truth. He had been chosen by the Ancients, granted the ability to see what most benighted members of his species never understood.

Icarus knew his role in cosmic history, and there could be no turning back. The Ancients and his brothers in The Path were all depending on him now. He wouldn't let them down.

His bachelor quarters on the base were the equivalent of a cheap one-bedroom apartment in town, nothing Icarus would miss in leaving, save for memories that always seemed to bring more pain than pleasure.

Departing from his life, he switched the lights off room by room, and then went out to set the world on fire.

APOLLO LEFT the Mitsubishi's former owner at a highway rest stop outside Chambersville, Virginia. There was no one else to see him, as he pulled up to the cinder-block facilities, parking as close as possible against the north end of the building where a faded wooden sign read men. He got out, walked around the car and checked for witnesses once more, before he dragged the old man's corpse out of the car and carried it into the men's room.

There, he found four empty toilet stalls and lugged his burden to the last one, farthest from the door. Inside the stall, he propped the old man on the commode, waited awhile to satisfy himself the body was secure, then closed and latched the door behind him. It was awkward scrambling over the partition into the adjacent stall, but G-men had to stay in shape. The worst part, other than some minor bruising to his ribs, was when he hung suspended, both feet flailing in the air, and almost kicked the old man off his throne.

Outside the stall, he made a final check. The old man's feet were visible if someone stooped to look, and that was fine. It was a rule of civilized society that one didn't attempt to strike up conversation with a stranger in a rest room when his mind was on his bowels. Some small talk at the sink was fine, but crap-per chat was definitely not approved.

A happy bonus was the rancid odor in the men's room, which assured Apollo that his erstwhile trav-eling companion might remain in peace for days be-fore the stench at last moved someone to find out if anything was wrong inside stall number four. Feeling relieved, Apollo washed his hands, dried them on gritty paper towels and walked back to the car.

The interstate required a long run south from Win-chester to Lexington, but it was better than pursuing some misguided shortcut into backwoods West Vir-ginia, maybe winding up in some hillbilly's yard, mis-taken for a "revenuer." He filled the Mitsubishi's tank in Lexington and picked up Highway 64, which ultimately wound its way to Charleston, then to Huntington and across the border to Kentucky. By the time he got that far, even the all-news channel had moved on to other stories, only breaking in for White House updates on the hour, to remind its listeners that Special Agent Luther Marx was still at large, consid-ered armed and dangerous.

They had that right, he thought, and grinned at his reflection in the rearview mirror—surprised to see the flashing lights behind him, closing fast from some-thing like a quarter mile.

"Goddammit!"

He was somewhere west of Cannonsburg, the last town he had passed on Highway 64. A glance at the speedometer showed him that he was doing close to seventy, distracted by the radio and his relief at hav-ing come this far from Washington without a hitch.

And now, Apollo realized, he was in deep trouble.

The car he drove was registered to God knew who—a dead man sitting on a toilet in Virginia—and it didn't even matter if the cop ignored that little problem, since his driver's license and his FBI ID card were emblazoned with the name of the most-wanted fugitive in the U.S. of A. What were the odds that a Kentucky traffic cop was out of touch with the late-breaking news from Washington?

Not nearly good enough.

Apollo eased up on the speed. No way in hell was he about to run for it and bring a dozen squad cars screaming after him. The situation hadn't gotten out of hand so far. He knew what he had to do, and if he kept his wits about him, he still had a chance to pull it off.

A road sign up ahead showed him the turnoff for a town called Princess, but he passed it by, still braking, pulling over to the shoulder of the highway, maybe sixty yards beyond the sign. The black-and-white rolled up behind him, lights still flashing amber, blue and white. The driver, in his Smoky Bear hat, spent a moment talking on the radio before he stepped out and approached Apollo's vehicle.

The check-in was routine, Apollo knew. So many violent incidents erupted out of traffic stops that most departments now required their officers to radio a license number and description of the car before initiating contact with the driver, then to check back in once they were finished handing out the ticket. That way, if the stop went fatally awry, at least dispatchers could identify the shooter's car. The weak spot in their plan, Apollo knew, would always be the call-back, since you never knew how long a traffic stop would take. A thousand different things could happen, dragging out the conversation, the patrolman making up his mind to issue a citation or a warning, finishing the paperwork in either case. Ten minutes was about the average, nationwide, but the dispatcher probably wouldn't get worried under twenty-five or thirty minutes, after which there would be ten more minutes wasted, minimum, attempting to make contact with the officer. Figure another ten or fifteen, anyway, before a backup could be summoned to the scene.

An hour, then, at the outside, if he was lucky.

He was ready with the window down, the Smith & Wesson in his hand, as the trooper approached the Mitsubishi on the driver's side.

"Guess I was speeding, there," Apollo said.

"Yes, sir, you were. I'll need to see your license and—"

The first shot hit him in the chest and knocked him backward, the Glaser slug splattering against his Kevlar vest. Apollo didn't give the trooper time to catch his breath or reach the pistol on his hip. He cleared the driver's door and fired a second round into the trooper's face.

That finished it, but there was still the task of cleaning up. He checked the highway, east and west, with no sign of approaching vehicles. That done, he found the trooper's hat and skimmed it like a flying disk toward the nearby woods. Apollo quickly jogged to the squad car, leaned in to switch off the flashers, then he returned and grabbed the dead man by his ankles.

He dragged him far enough off the road that any passing motorist would need an eagle eye to spot the corpse.

That left the black-and-white, which was a little trickier. He got behind the wheel, turned on the engine, and sped down the highway for a hundred yards or so, until he spied a rough break in the tree line. Swerving sharply off the road, he rushed forward at forty miles per hour, plowing through the undergrowth for twenty yards or so, until the squad car nosed into a dry streambed. Apollo couldn't see the highway when he checked the rearview mirror, and assumed the squad car would be likewise unseen from the road.

He hiked back to the Mitsubishi through the woods, remaining hidden from the road and any passing vehicles until he came within a dozen paces of the car. Emerging from the forest then, he could have been a simple traveler who had stopped to take a leak. In fact, no one passed by before he got behind the wheel, put the vehicle back in motion and headed west.

His fingerprints would ultimately be recovered from the black-and-white, but then, what difference would it make? He was already wanted by the FBI for killing federal officers and trying to assassinate the President of the United States. The murder of some careless blue-suit in Kentucky was the least of his concerns.

Apollo focused on his task of making contact with The Two. It was the only thing that really mattered to him at the moment, and because it mattered, he would be more conscientious in his driving, try to hold his speed to a legal fifty-five.

THE U.S. AIR FORCE, while best known for high-tech spy planes, fighter planes and bombers, also had its share of helicopters standing by, as did the Army, Navy, Coast Guard and Marines. In theory, Air Force helicopters were primarily reserved for minor cargo hauls and rescue missions, but it shouldn't be presumed that they were simply beasts of burden.

Some of them could rock and roll.

The Bell AH-1S Cobra sought by Icarus that afternoon had been specifically designed as an attack helicopter for antiarmor missions: an airborne tank killer. It normally flew with a pilot and gunner, but one skilled operator could handle the show by himself, if he wasn't outnumbered by fast, attack aircraft. And even if he was, the Cobra could wreak bloody havoc on the ground before they knocked him from the sky.

The Cobra carried 259 gallons of fuel to power its single Avco Lycoming T53-L-703 turboshaft engine, with a maximum speed of 140 miles per hour, a range of 315 miles and a ceiling of 12,200 feet. The gunship's payload was a trifle over 1,500 pounds of sudden death, with varied armament to choose from. Icarus had called ahead to specify the load he wanted, starting with the standard M-197 three-barreled 20 mm Gatling gun in a nose turret mount, linked feed, with a rate of fire approaching 750 rounds per minute. Four stubby wing pylons mounted two LAU-61A/A rocket pods, each with nineteen 2.75-inch antipersonnel rockets, and two quad launchers for

Hughes BMG-71 TOW antitank missiles. An onboard IRCM jammer was supposed to let the Cobra dodge incoming rockets, like the Stinger missiles used by Secret Service agents to protect the President of the United States from aerial attack. Before the sun went down, Icarus would find out how well the jammer worked—or if it worked at all.

His first and most demanding trick, though, would be simply taking off.

The call ahead was easy. A lieutenant colonel had the rank to get himself a chopper almost any time he needed one, assuming that his order wasn't overruled by someone higher up. In this case, since his order was unknown to his superiors, and no one with a lower rank was likely to be double-checking his authority, the coast was clear...at least, until he reached the helipad.

The officer in charge of final clearance was a first lieutenant with the fresh face of a college student and a deferential attitude that suited Icarus just fine, until the youngster understood that he was flying on his own. While not strictly forbidden, neither was a solo outing in the Cobra highly recommended, most especially when it was loaded with weapons. The young lieutenant checked his clipboard, looked perturbed and checked the board again.

"No weapons officer today, sir?" he inquired.

"That's negative," Icarus replied. "I'm going up alone to log some air time, pot some targets on the range. I like to keep my hand in."

"Yes, sir." He glanced at the knife and pistol Icarus had before he ducked his head and gave the clipboard one more scan. "Um, sir, we don't have any exercises scheduled for this afternoon."

Icarus smiled. "I know that, son. I couldn't very well be checking out a Cobra if you did, now, could I?"

"No, sir. I was just wondering…" No matter how he tried, the young man couldn't seem to shake his frown.

"Don't keep me in suspense, Lieutenant. What exactly are you wondering?"

"Well, sir…that is, I always get a call when we're flying this much hardware, even for a practice run."

"You got a call, Lieutenant." Icarus was tired of playing games, now, and the new note of impatience in his voice was clearly audible. "*I* called down with the order, as you may recall."

"Yes, sir. I have that here, sir." Far from wilting under pressure, the lieutenant seemed intent on sticking to his guns. He would have made a decent officer, Icarus thought, if he had lived. "It's confirmation that I don't have yet, sir. You're familiar with the rule, of course, sir."

One more *sir* from the young pup, and Icarus believed he might just lose it right there on the helipad. Instead, he hung on to his cool with something close to superhuman effort and replied, "I am, indeed, familiar with the rule, Lieutenant. It appears that someone dropped the ball. Now, I suppose you'll need to call it in?"

"That is correct, sir. It should only take a minute."

"Well, let's get it done."

He trailed the youngster toward a nearby hangar,

presently deserted, and they stepped into an office cubicle that would have felt like a sardine can if a third man had arrived.

"I'll just call through, sir," the lieutenant told him, as he turned his back on Icarus and leaned across the desk to reach the telephone.

"You do that," Icarus replied, and shot him once behind the ear, at point-blank range. Explosive impact pitched the young man forward, right across the desk and off the other side. The telephone went crashing down with him, and Icarus could hear the dial tone humming as he moved around the desk to tidy up.

It took him all of thirty seconds, manhandling the body out of sight beneath the desk and shoving in the swivel chair to hide it from a cursory inspection. He replaced the telephone, shifted some paperwork to hide a splash of blood across the desktop and retraced his steps to reach the helipad.

So much for clearance.

Icarus couldn't begin to guess how much time he would have before they found the body. Minutes, hours—it was all the same to him. He hadn't only burned his bridges, now, but also ground the ashes underfoot and flushed them down the toilet. There could be no going back, short of a court-martial that had to end with life imprisonment or maybe an appointment with a firing squad.

But, then, the thought of turning back had never crossed his mind.

Lieutenant Colonel Nathan Holt was on his way to strike a blow that would insure the future for a chosen few, and nothing short of death could stop him now.

JUST WHEN BROGNOLA thought that he had seen the worst of it, that no more rotten news could fit into a single day, an urgent phone call from a contact in the Pentagon corrected that mistake. He listened silently, his free hand clenching on the desktop, knuckled blanched bone-white, then willed his muscles to relax before they went into an agonizing cramp.

"Okay," he said at last, "I've got it. Thanks for calling... Right... I'll see what I can do... You'll let me know if— Sure, okay. Goodbye."

He cradled the receiver gently, as if worried that it might explode beneath his hand. But, then, the news he had received was explosive enough on its own— and perhaps literally, at that. Brognola squinted at the wall clock, calling up a number from his memory before he lifted the receiver once again and tapped out seven digits. It rang twice before Mack Bolan picked up on the other end, in his motel room.

"Yes?"

"You sitting down?" Brognola asked him.

"What's the word?"

"You won't believe it."

"Try me."

"I just got a call regarding Bolling Air Force Base," Brognola said.

"And?"

"And a certain officer just murdered a lieutenant over there and took off in a Cobra gunship loaded to the gills. Rockets, the whole nine yards."

"Someone we know?" Bolan inquired.

"I never heard of him," Brognola said. "Lieutenant Colonel Nathan Holt. A lifer, spotless record, combat missions over Vietnam, assigned to Bolling for the past few years. They're shitting bricks. Nobody has a clue what's going on."

"But you do," Bolan said.

"I've got a hunch. I pray to God I'm wrong."

He didn't need to spell it out, as Bolan asked, "How long ago was this?"

"An hour, give or take. Could be as much as ninety minutes," Brognola replied.

"That's way too long."

Brognola knew what Bolan meant. Skimming along at half its best air speed, the Cobra could have flown from Bolling to Camp David in ten to twelve minutes. So where was the damned thing, already?

"They're looking," he told Bolan, "but it's like they don't know where to start. They're used to tracking crash sites, but apparently they've never had a chopper stolen off the pad before. I have to say, they don't sound hopeful."

"Understood," the Executioner replied. "I'll get hold of Jack and see what we can do."

Brognola knew he should have felt relieved, and yet he didn't. "Right," he said. "I'll let you go. Oh, wait. One thing. When you find this joker?"

"Yeah?"

"Feel free to smoke his ass."

"Affirmative," Bolan said and the line went dead.

CHAPTER FIFTEEN

It would have been too simple—too predictable—for Icarus to fly directly toward his target. Several airmen on the ground had seen him lift off in the Cobra, flying in a southerly direction toward Prince Georges County, and he had indeed kept on that way till he was clear of Washington, past Glassmanor and Forest Heights, but that was where his keen strategic mind kicked in.

When he had first conceived the plan some weeks ago, he had considered flying straight from Bolling to Camp David and blitzing everyone in sight, to hell with risk, but logic and experience in airborne combat quickly changed his mind. There were, he realized, too many things that might go wrong and doom his plan.

For one thing, he had managed to complete a fair map of his target, over time, by hanging out with personnel who knew the layout. Icarus had learned that cottages were scattered all around 125 hilly, wooded acres, and picking out the two he needed was a virtual impossibility without some kind of homing beacon to identify his prey. At the same time, given the past two days' events, he reasoned that the missing Cobra would be instantly reported to the Secret Service, just to play it safe. He had been seen by several members of the Bolling ground crew when he lifted off. There was no way to determine how much time would pass before they found the young lieutenant's body, but in any case, an unexpected military gunship closing on Camp David now, less than six hours after the assault staged at the White House, would be met with a concerted opposition that gravely reduced his chances for success.

Icarus knew this might be his last flight, but he didn't intend to simply throw away his life. And that explained why he had literally bought the farm.

It was a small and long-abandoned place across the river in Virginia, east of Groveton, in Prince William County. It was less than forty acres and would never yield a profit from the soil, but what did he care? Icarus had taken one look at the rundown house, measured the entrance to the weather-beaten barn and knew that he had found what he was looking for. The name he used was false, but he had paid in cash, so no one had to check his references.

He worked around the place when he had days off from the base, mostly installing brand-new locks on house and barn against the outside chance that local kids or homeless trash might try to use the place while he wasn't around. His nearest neighbor was three-quarters of a mile due north, and Icarus didn't stop by to introduce himself.

That afternoon he flew the Cobra south in Prince Georges County, staying low to beat the radar out of

Bolling AFB, then turned due west across the river, entering Virginia like a smuggler, homing on his farm. An easy touchdown in the yard and moments later he had locked the stolen helicopter inside his barn, where it would remain until he judged the time was right.

Away eastward at Camp David, they should all be sitting to dinner now, his quarry gathered underneath a single roof. He knew the placement of the dining hall. Once he invaded presidential air space, all he had to do was lock on to the target and let go with everything he had. Kill 'em all, like the poster suggested, and let God sort 'em out.

By now, he knew, the body in the hangar had to have been discovered, and he reasoned that the search should already have passed him by. Depending on the time of the discovery, a simple calculation based on the Cobra's cruising speed and range of travel would establish search parameters. When he didn't show up on radar, and they didn't spot him on the ground, no helpful tips from eagle-eyed civilians, those who hunted him would start to puzzle over the alternatives.

A crash in the Potomac was improbable. More likely, given the scenario enacted with the recent theft of AGMs in Arizona, was the prospect of a waiting pickup team, perhaps equipped with something like an eighteen-wheeler that would let them hide the Cobra, while they carried it away. Beyond the Cobra's 315-mile range, the search would clearly be grounded, since they knew the gunship couldn't pull into a filling station and refuel.

Of course, it didn't need to.

After flying barely ten miles from the base, it still had fuel enough to shuttle back and forth between the hideout and Camp David twenty-five to thirty times, but no such weird maneuvers would be necessary. Whatever happened on the next flight, the most that Icarus demanded of the Cobra would be one round-trip.

He hoped he would be able to return, drop off the chopper, then retrieve the change of clothes and Harley-Davidson motorcycle that he had waiting in the barn to make his getaway, but that was secondary, looking farther down the road than he could comfortably see.

Icarus stepped out of the farmhouse in his flight suit, checked the sky above and was relieved to find no observation choppers hovering. So far, it seemed that he was in the clear. Ten minutes more would see him airborne, and the rest of it...well, he would have to wait and see what happened.

He was whistling as he stepped off the porch and headed for the barn.

"YOU'RE SURE ABOUT THIS?" Jack Grimaldi's voice came through the earphones sounding small, vaguely mechanical, as if they were conversing on a trans-atlantic phone line in the middle of a storm.

"I told you, I'm not sure of anything," Bolan replied. "Holt could have lost his marbles. Maybe he's gone Dr. Strangelove on us, and they'll find him strafing Newark."

"Right," Grimaldi said. "But you don't think so."

"No," the Executioner admitted.

They were back in the Apache, southbound from the rendezvous at Fort McNair, with Bolan in the forward gunner's seat. He had refreshed his memory on the controls that would enable him to fire the M-230 chain gun mounted in a belly turret just below him, loaded with 1,200 30 mm rounds—enough for some two minutes of sustained full-automatic fire. Besides the cannon, Bolan had his finger on the trigger that would launch thirty-eight 2.75-inch rockets and four FIM-92 Stinger air-to-air missiles. Whether they found the Cobra on the ground or in the air, he was prepared to take it out.

Unless, of course, it found them first.

"He should have hit by now," Grimaldi said, skimming the chopper over Hillcrest Heights a hundred feet above the rooftops. "What the hell's he doing all this time?"

"Maybe thinking," Bolan said, "or hiding out somewhere to let the hunt pass by. I doubt we'll get a chance to ask him."

"One clear shot," Grimaldi said. "That's all I want."

With emphasis on clear, Bolan thought, but he didn't have to speak the words aloud. Grimaldi would have thought about the danger to civilians below if they engaged the Cobra in a dogfight while they overflew a residential area or business district. The pilot was smart enough to watch it, and the Executioner knew when to hold his fire, but would their adversary—if and when they found him—give a damn about bystanders on the ground?

Fat chance.

If this Lieutenant Colonel Nathan Holt turned out to be another closet member of The Path, as Bolan was anticipating him to be, they could expect the same who-gives-a-damn-about-tomorrow attitude displayed in previous attacks that were specifically designed to generate mass body counts. The truck bomb bound for Vegas, sarin nerve gas in L.A., the AGMs addressed to Washington—all of it indicated a monumental contempt for human life. That made it easy for the Executioner when he was looking toward solutions for the problem, but the odds were skewed against him where his adversaries mingled with a crowd—or, in this case, hovered above a populated area.

One problem at a time, he told himself. They hadn't found the Cobra yet, and there was still a possibility they might not find it. Even if the missing Air Force officer was a disciple of The Path, Bolan still had no guarantee that Holt would try to score a hit on the same targets as his predecessors from the White House raid. In fact, the smartest thing Holt could have done was choose another mark—the Pentagon, for instance, or the Justice building—but there were at least two reasons Bolan was convinced that he would try Camp David, hoping he could bag two presidents for the price of one.

First, if he was shooting for a mark in downtown Washington, D.C., he should have done his thing by now, before the federal offices shut down at five o'clock and sent most of their workers home.

And second, nothing he could do in Washington, including strikes against some foreign embassy, would have the same potential to ignite a doomsday fuse as taking out the Russian president, wherever he had gone to ground. The cult still had a chance to save the play, release whatever half-baked "terrorist" announcement they had planned to cover the attack, and even with the first two fizzles, there was still a chance that they could pull it off.

By this time, Bolan knew, Brognola would have spoken to the Man, who would in turn have briefed his Russian guest on what was happening. The odds were excellent that calls had been relayed to Moscow, just in case, advising any trigger-happy ministers and generals there that this wasn't a plot by the United States or by some Baltic breakaway from the former Soviet bloc. Whether the men in Moscow would accept the story was another problem, beyond Bolan's reach or ability to intervene.

He had his plate full, as it was, pursuing one man with enough munitions at his fingertips to take out several blocks of real estate and turn them into smoking rubble. What he didn't need right now were doubts and second thoughts.

"The Secret Service is expecting us, you said?" Grimaldi's tone told Bolan that he wasn't looking forward to the prospect of a Stinger rising up to meet them in midair.

"Hal called ahead," Bolan confirmed. If there was no sign of the Cobra when they got there, Bolan was prepared to wait awhile, hang out and play his hunch, see where it led. They had no better prospects, anyway.

And then it hit him.

Brognola had called ahead. The Secret Service was expecting them.

Which meant they would be waiting for a helicopter. Were they trained to differentiate between the AH-64 Apache and the smaller, lighter Cobra at a glance?

"Dammit!"

"What's up?" Grimaldi asked.

"Nothing, I hope," Bolan replied. "Is this as fast as we can go?"

THE WARNING HAD BEEN telephoned from Washington at half-past five o'clock. The President of the United States informed his guest of what was going on and added his assurance that the matter would be handled expeditiously.

Somehow that didn't put the Russian president at ease.

He had expected some excitement over his visit to America—the White House and Camp David, sorting out his country's problems with the help of the United States, perhaps some frivolous sight-seeing on the side—but this was something else again. He most emphatically had not expected to be hunted like an animal by maniacs who took their cue from flying saucers and desired to start World War III.

He understood religious zealots, from Rasputin to the Castrators—a cult in czarist Russia whose male members were required to sacrifice their manhood on admission to the sect. In modern Russia, now that atheistic communism had been brushed aside, the zealots were returning, crawling out from under rocks that sheltered creeds ranging from spiritualism to black magic. Still, none of them—so far, at least—appeared to be intent on touching off a global holocaust.

Leave it to the Americans. What would be their next craze?

The Russian president could only hope that he would be alive to see it.

After the excitement at the White House, it had been agreed that any meaningful discussions would be put on hold until the following day, when both parties could start fresh, with all their wits about them. It was hard work, running for your life from violent lunatics, and he was looking forward to a good night's sleep.

But first, he realized that he was hungry. It was another twenty minutes until they were scheduled to meet for dinner in the rustic-looking dining hall. His stomach grumbled over the delay, but it would simply have to wait.

"We could go back tonight," Alexi said. He had been staring out the window of the cottage—code-named Aspen—as if waiting for a troop of enemies to rush them from the forest.

"We cannot go back tonight," the Russian president corrected him. "We did not come this far to turn and leave before we even ask for help."

"We did not come to serve as targets in a shooting gallery," Alexi groused.

"It's been explained, Alexi."

"Ah. And you believe that story? Men from outer space and World War III?"

"Nobody said we were attacked by men from outer space," the president replied. "I can believe there are fanatics in these days who think the world must end. It's the millennium, Alexi. You should know your history, the kinds of things that happened back in 1899."

Alexi grunted, kept staring out the window. "No one tried to kill me with machine guns back in 1899," he said. "No one used helicopters and cruise missiles to assassinate a president."

"You're right, of course. In Russia, they were throwing homemade bombs to try and kill the czar. An anarchist in the United States used a revolver to assassinate the president. It's all the same."

"It's one thing to avoid a bullet or a homemade bomb," Alexi said. "I don't believe you've been in training to outrun a missile, Mr. President. I know I haven't."

Alexi's fear was palpable, yet it was hard to keep from laughing at the mental image conjured by his words, the two of them sprinting across an open field with a cruise missile panting at their heels. One could die laughing in that strange scenario.

"I'm hungry," the Russian president said.

"It's almost time." As usual, Alexi seemed to know the time of day, within five minutes, without even glancing at his watch.

"I've always wondered how you do that."

"It's a gift," Alexi said. And then: "They're coming."

"With cruise missiles?"

Turning from the window, his adviser and best

friend on earth made a rude gesture, his face deadpan. "The Secret Service," he replied.

"We must not keep them waiting, then." The president picked up his jacket, slipped it on, dispensing with the tie. His host, he knew, would probably turn up for dinner in a polo shirt and sweater. This one—when removed from public view, at least—showed less concern for the trappings of formality than for achieving goals. And what was wrong with that?

The knock came, and Alexi waited for a nod before opening the door. Outside, two Secret Service agents stood facing the Russian guard who would remain on duty at the Aspen cottage through the night. Two more young Russians followed them, completing the escort.

"Ah, gentlemen." The Russian president's expansive smile encompassed all of them. "Shall we be on our way?"

They moved along a gently sloping path, packed earth beneath their feet and trees on either side. Ahead, he saw the clearing that surrounded the primary meeting facilities, including the now-aromatic dining hall and kitchen. They were twenty yards beyond the tree line, halfway to their goal, before his ears picked up the distant whup-whup-whup of helicopter rotors slashing at the air.

THE TIMING WAS a guesstimate, but Icarus was fairly confident in his assumption of the presidential schedule. He had dined at several embassy and White House functions in the past, and service generally began sometime between six and seven o'clock. This day, he guessed it would be running on the early side, with nerves strained by the incident in Washington, his targets looking forward to some badly needed rest before they got down to the crux of their discussion in the morning.

Better luck next time, he thought. Somebody should have told them that tomorrow would never come.

This time, at least, he meant to translate that proverb into a literal expression of the truth.

He had been edgy crossing the Potomac into Maryland, almost expecting to find military aircraft on patrol, seeking the Cobra with a mission of search and destroy. In fact, he realized, the odds were fifty-fifty that the search had moved well outward from the capital and its environs by this time. The brass at Bolling wouldn't rate him as a fool to hang around the area, and their initial grid search would have failed to spot him, either in the air or on the ground. They had to know that if he stayed airborne, his fuel would be exhausted in two hours and thirteen minutes, which would mean he had been forced to land, his tanks bone-dry, more than four hours earlier. At normal cruising speed, he could have reached New Haven, Syracuse, Cleveland, Charleston, Winston-Salem, or some point 150 miles due east of Dover, Delaware, in the Atlantic, if he chose to ditch at sea.

It gave them ample ground to cover, and they had to be concerned—after the scramble for the AGMs— with notions of a pickup team, prepared to haul the Cobra overland, concealed. Where would it turn up next? Unleashing rockets in Chicago or St. Louis?

Strafing shoppers on the streets of Phoenix, San Francisco or Los Angeles?

He wished them happy hunting and he kept his eyes wide open, just in case. One of their chief concerns, he knew, would be Camp David, even as the time dragged on without a glimpse of him so close to home.

Five miles remained, and he could feel excitement mounting, even as he willed himself to stay alert and calm. His hands were rock-steady on the Cobra's controls, eyes constantly sweeping the 180-degree horizon visible from his seat, darting back to the instruments that would warn him of any pursuit from above or behind, including an attempted lock-on by heat-seeking weapons.

It mattered less to Icarus if he was spotted from the ground. One airborne helicopter was much like the next to civilian eyes, and those who could recognize a military chopper wouldn't be surprised, considering the number of bases located in that part of the country. Aside from Bolling and McNair, there was the Marine Corps base at Quantico, the Fort Belvoir military reservation and proving grounds, the Washington Navy yard, Army and Navy medical centers, a huge naval reserve radio station, even the Pentagon itself, all within a thirty-mile radius of the nation's capital.

And, of course, there was Camp David.

"Coming up," Icarus told himself, unconscious of the fact that he had spoken aloud. The fact would not have bothered him, if he had been aware of it. He preferred his own company. After all, who among his various acquaintances was more intelligent, more logical?

Three miles, and he was concentrating on the sky directly to his front now, narrowing his sweep of the horizon to some forty-five degrees. If they had any kind of trap prepared for him, he guessed that it would probably involve deployment of a helicopter force around Camp David, but he saw no sign of any aircraft ahead of him, as yet.

So maybe they were waiting on the ground, prepared to scramble and attack at his approach. Six hours and counting had elapsed since Icarus liberated the Cobra, and no commander in his right mind would keep choppers hovering over a target for that length of time, burning fuel by the truckload, circling endlessly or hovering like giant, prehistoric dragonflies. They would have spotters out, that much was SOP, and they had radar coverage as well, although the Cobra had already beaten that security device by coming in at an altitude below one hundred feet.

If they didn't use helicopters, what was left? The Bolling brass could scramble fighters, armed with everything from 20 mm Gatling guns to "smart" bombs, and while the average jet fighter could double, even triple, the Cobra's air speed, a fighting helicopter wasn't without advantages of its own. For one thing, it could hover in place, a trick beyond the capabilities of any jet fighter plane except the McDonnell Douglas Harrier. Long shots with heat-seeking missiles aside, the jets were sometimes too fast for successful dogfights with slower-moving targets. A chopper, in particular, could bob, duck and weave, rise and fall vertically or spin right around to face backward, while the jets were forced to make sweeping passes, like sharks.

It probably wasn't enough to let him win a dog-fight, most particularly not if there were several jets involved, but at least he would let them all know they had been in a fight.

Below, the countryside was broken up by hills, some dignified as "mountains" by the folk who lived and toiled within their shadows. Much of the forest that once covered that terrain, before the white man came with axes, saws and matches, had long since been razed, the trees converted into lumber or paper, but bits and pieces of it still remained, some carefully watched over now, as if the clumsy stewards feared it would somehow vanish of its own accord.

That miniforest up ahead, he knew had to be Camp David.

He was almost there, excitement mounting as he hurtled toward his target. A rush of adrenaline lifted his spirits and enhanced his perception.

Icarus called up the rough hand-drawn map of his target from a mental archive, examining the layout once again. His best bet, he confirmed, would be a straightforward run at the camp's central facilities, including conference rooms, kitchen and dining hall, Secret Service command post, communications center and a small but excellently stocked infirmary. Dropping a firestorm on the dining hall and conference rooms would be his one true hope of taking out both presidents together. Dodging back and forth to find the several cottages, conversely, would be tantamount to suicide.

So be it, then.

He shaved another thirty feet off his altitude and opened up the Cobra's throttle, racing to the attack.

"ANOTHER BLIP," Grimaldi said. "It's headed in the right direction, though."

The qualifier was required, since they had flown past something like a dozen private planes and helicopters in the short time since their takeoff from McNair.

"Where is it?" Bolan asked, his eyes inadequate for peering miles ahead.

"Approaching two o'clock," Grimaldi said, "off to the south-southwest."

Still nothing when he turned his head to look in that direction, but the Executioner trusted Grimaldi and his instruments. They hadn't let him down before, and if this mission fell apart somehow, he knew the fault wouldn't be Jack's.

"Okay, we got ourselves a chopper!" There was excitement in Grimaldi's voice.

"Let's make sure it's the right one," Bolan said.

While Brognola had telephoned Camp David from his office to alert the President and Secret Service team on-site, he hadn't notified the Pentagon or Bolling Air Force Base as to his plan. He was afraid steps might be taken that would blow the scheme, and so he kept them in the dark. Which meant, in turn, that there was nothing to prevent another military aircraft from pursuing searches in the area, adding confusion to the mix from Bolan's point of view.

"We have a Cobra," Grimaldi proclaimed some thirty seconds later. "Headed west from who knows where."

That still didn't provide the confirmation Bolan needed in his own mind to attack, and there was only one way to be absolutely sure. They needed to make visual contact and try to raise the other pilot on their radio. From his reaction, they would know if he was fair game or a wayward friend.

Grimaldi didn't need instructions as to what should follow next. He had already shifted to an interception course, milking a few more miles per hour from the open throttle as he skimmed across the countryside of rural Maryland. As if by magic below, within a mile or so of Washington, the landscape was transformed from concrete, steel and marble into rolling hills, green grass and trees. It was a different world; but, then again, most any world was radically removed from what went on in Wonderland.

"It's gonna be a squeaker," Grimaldi advised him, sounding tense. "Whoever this guy is, he's almost there."

Bolan didn't reply, since nothing he could say would make the helicopter travel any faster. Jack Grimaldi was the best, and he would give it everything he had.

"There!" The sharp sound of Grimaldi's voice helped focus Bolan's vision on a dark speck ahead of them, flying at treetop height. "The guy doesn't want to draw attention, the way it looks."

And that was passing strange itself. If this had been a normal military flight, excluding any kind of training exercise, the chopper should have been at least three hundred feet above the trees.

"Let's hail him," Bolan said.

Grimaldi tried on several frequencies without result. The Cobra's pilot either had his radio switched off—a major no-no on a stateside military flight—or else he was deliberately ignoring them.

"Yo! There he goes!"

As Grimaldi made the announcement, Bolan saw the Cobra lose another twenty feet of altitude. It seemed to disappear inside a stand of trees, but there was no explosion, no smoke from a crash. They skimmed above some kind of fence, a flash of sunlight, there and gone.

"How long until he's over target?" Bolan asked.

"You kidding me?" Grimaldi's voice came back at him. "He's there right now!"

CHAPTER SIXTEEN

"Cobra, I say again—identify yourself!"

"Fuck you!" Icarus snarled into his microphone, as if it were alive, and took the Cobra down into the trees.

It was a risky move, of course, but no worse than remaining in plain view of the pursuit craft. If he meant to play the game that way, he would have turned to face them in midair. They could have had a little jousting match, with missiles in the place of lances, giving each contestant an extended reach and lethal punch. The end for Icarus, when it arrived, would have been swift and relatively clean.

But that wasn't the game he had signed on to play. The aircraft tracking him was an annoyance and distraction; it was *not* his target. That lay below, somewhere beneath the treetops, as he crossed the boundary line and entered the restricted air space of Camp David.

Any minute now...

He saw a cottage butted against some kind of cliff, another off to his left beyond a grove of evergreens. The sleeping quarters didn't interest him. Now, more than ever, with a hunter on his tail, he needed all his targets in one place.

The trees thinned ahead of him, and he saw tiny figures moving toward a central group of buildings. Even at his present height, he couldn't make out faces and wouldn't have recognized the Russian president on sight, in any case. He had no reason to suspect that these were anything but Secret Service agents on the prowl, perhaps low-level functionaries of the men he sought—but what the hell?

He hit the stragglers with a quick burst from his M-197 Gatling gun and watched the 20 mm rounds rip fist-size divots from the turf. One of the human targets seemed to come apart down there, another sprawling awkwardly, the rest dodging pell-mell for cover that was nowhere to be found.

Icarus left them to it, homing on the structure dead-ahead, which—if his sketchy map was accurate—should be the dining hall. He had no way of knowing whether there was anyone but kitchen staff inside there, yet, but it was plain to Icarus that he would never have a better shot. And if he waited even seconds longer, he might never have a shot at all.

He "painted" the target with his infrared aiming device in the chopper's nose, and instantly unleashed four of the armor-piercing TOW missiles. They were certified tank killers, specially designed to penetrate the stoutest armor worn by any vehicle the Russians or their former client states produced, so wood and plaster offered no protection whatsoever. Hovering, he watched the dining hall as it appeared to swell, like something in a child's cartoon, then blew apart, the wreckage spilling smoke and flames.

"Bon appetit," he said, sneering, and brought the Cobra's nose around to face the conference center. Anyone inside there would have heard the dining hall go up, and would be scrambling for the exits even now. He had no time to calculate the odds against a kill; the hunters would be on him any second now, eliminating any chance at all.

The second target was painted, and he was about to squeeze the trigger for the second quad mount, when his sensors started screaming at him, warning him that he, in turn, was marked for killing fire.

"Goddammit!"

Warning sensors couldn't tell him whether he was being targeted for air-to-air destruction, or by something like a Stinger, operating from the ground. Icarus could have stayed exactly where he was, unloading everything he had into the conference building, while his enemy knocked him out of the sky, but passive suicide still went against the grain. He might not have five minutes left to live, but he would damn well *live* it, take as many of his adversaries with him into final darkness as he could. What did he have to fear from death, when all was said and done?

Icarus held the keys to paradise, and his reward was guaranteed.

THE RUSSIAN PRESIDENT had frozen at the sound of the approaching helicopter. He recalled the recent warning from his host—"Nothing to worry about, I imagine"—and remembered that a stolen military helicopter had been mentioned. Still, that had been hours ago, and even with his meager knowledge of mechanics, he was fairly certain that a helicopter couldn't stay aloft that long without refueling.

This had to be a friendly helicopter, then, one of the flights that doubtless came and went around Camp David at all hours. But if that was true, why were the Secret Service agents drawing weapons from beneath their jackets, making ready to defend themselves?

The helicopter was a hundred yards away from them when its pilot cut loose with what sounded like the world's biggest machine gun. The Russian president saw bullets strike the grass, explosive impacts racing toward him. At the same time, someone grabbed his arm and yanked him back in the direction they had come from, toward the cover of the trees.

His legs responded automatically, but none too swiftly. He was numb with fright and shock, as if this new assault was simply too much for his mind to comprehend and process. He was in America! He was at Camp David! How could lunatics attempt to kill him twice within a single day and come so close?

It struck him that his thoughts, from force of habit, took the form of a survivor's questions; when, in fact, there was no reason to believe he would survive the next few seconds, with the helicopter bearing down upon him, spewing fire and sudden death.

He wondered if the pilot saw his face and recognized him, or if he was simply killing everyone he saw. The Russian president felt slighted, if the latter was the case, and that split-second impulse almost made him laugh out loud, hysterically, at the absurdity of wanting to be recognized by his would-be assassin.

As if it would make a difference somehow when the bullets ripped into his flesh.

He glanced back in time to see the bullets find Alexi. There was panic written on his old friend's face, then nothing, as the heavy slugs tore him apart. One moment, he was running to keep up; the next, a sickly crimson mist enveloped him, his body jerking, as if from the rapid kicks and punches of enraged karate experts. He was spinning, lurching, arms outflung—disintegrating in his tracks before their very eyes.

Behind Alexi, one of the Russian security guards was hit through the legs and went down, screaming as he fell. A Secret Service agent running next to him was struck by what appeared to be a single round in the shoulder, nearly ripping his arm from its socket.

Another heartbeat and the firing ceased, the helicopter sweeping past them, rotors chopping at the air. The Russian president kept running, still uncertain who was leading him, his vision blurred by shock and fear.

They had no sooner reached the tree line than the shock waves of a powerful explosion echoed through the solemn forest of Camp David. "Jesus Christ!" his escort swore, telling the Russian president that he was the surviving Secret Service agent.

Turning back to face the central complex, he was just in time to see the dining hall go up in flames. Amid the rising smoke, he saw dozens of shingles, thrown aloft by the explosion, swirling back to earth, some of them burning, trailing sparks behind them like small comets as they fell.

He longed to ask the Secret Service agent at his side if anyone had been inside the building when it blew, but he was struck dumb by shock. Suppose his host had gone ahead to wait for him. What, then? Was he a witness to another tragedy, the likes of which Americans had almost come to take for granted in their violent daily lives?

The gunship's pilot obviously wasn't satisfied with his accomplishments so far. He held the helicopter where it was, hovering a hundred yards from the funeral pyre of the dining hall, perhaps twice that far from where the Russian president stood watching, one hand braced against a tree to keep his balance. It appeared the pilot had to be angling for another shot, this time at the adjacent conference center, but before he had a chance to open fire, a second helicopter roared past overhead, approaching from the gunship's rear.

"Hey, what the hell...?" The Secret Service agent seemed about to step from cover, maybe try to drop the new arrival with his side arm, but this time the Russian president reached out to drag *him* back.

"Don't be a fool!" he snapped, the younger man regarding him with a mix of anger and surprise.

Across the clearing, just emerging from behind the conference center, half a dozen men in suits—more Secret Service agents—ran into the open. Two of them were armed with automatic rifles, while the rest had long, dark tubes braced on their shoulders, pointed toward the sky.

"Stingers," the agent at his side declared. "We'll show those bastards now."

BOLAN WAS KISSING-CLOSE to target acquisition, ready with a Sidewinder, when Jack Grimaldi blurted, "Shit! Incoming!" and the whole set went to hell.

It had to be ground fire, the Secret Service, Bolan reasoned, since the Cobra hadn't turned to face them yet. He lifted off the trigger, and immediately felt his stomach flip-flop as Grimaldi guided the Apache through a chaotic series of evasive maneuvers, pitching and rolling like some kind of carnival ride.

The gunship had a built-in ALQ-144 infrared jammer, but it was designed for evasion of long-distance shots. Up close and personal, as Bolan knew from grim experience in combat, there was only so much that a jammer could accomplish. Surface-to-air missiles like the Stinger, for example, had an effective range of some 5,500 yards when locked on to a target, but they could easily kill at much closer ranges. From two hundred yards or less, the infrared homing device was almost superfluous, clear targets tracked and nailed by line of sight.

Bolan could do no more than bite his tongue, while Grimaldi worked overtime to save their lives. It galled him, passing on a nearly perfect shot, but he consoled himself with the knowledge that presidential bodyguards below were undoubtedly firing on both helicopters, unable to tell friend from foe, unwilling to take any chances. One of them might get lucky, yet, and knock down the Cobra.

Between the jammer and his own skill as a pilot,

Grimaldi managed to save them from a Stinger aimed in their direction. Bolan caught a flash as it swept past them, looping across the forest to explode somewhere beyond his line of sight. Success was sweet, but any kind of celebration would be premature, he realized. Where there was one Stinger...

Grimaldi nosed the chopper back around, seeking their enemy, and Bolan saw the Cobra pouring cannon fire into a group of Secret Service agents on the ground. Some of the men were down already, others falling as he watched, but the survivors stood fast, fighting back with everything they had. Another missile vaulted skyward, and the Cobra gunship had to disengage, ducking and weaving like a roller coaster riding phantom tracks.

"Get after him!" Bolan snapped.

"I'm already there," Grimaldi said, powering after their intended target, trees and shrubs a green blur below.

"He's running for it," Bolan said.

"It isn't gonna help him," Grimaldi growled. "He can run, but he can't hide."

Bolan was ready with his hands on the controls once more, prepared to unleash fiery death as soon as he had target acquisition. There could be no doubt about the Cobra's pilot after he attacked the presidential compound. At the same time, there could be no thought of taking him alive.

Too bad, Bolan reflected, since the Cobra's pilot might turn out to be their only lead on how and where to find The Two. It was beyond belief that a lieutenant colonel in the Air Force would initiate this kind of action on his own. If there had been a chance to capture him, he might have spilled the names of contacts, something that would have help expose the missing leaders of the cult.

Too late. The only way to stop him was to shoot him down, and Bolan was prepared to do exactly that first chance he got.

The only question, now, was how long that would take, and whether Holt would lead them to a populated area, where he would have an audience. They weren't headed north, toward Washington, and that was a relief. But there were towns aplenty on the rough northwestern course their prey had chosen, any one of them a potential disaster area if one or both choppers went down in their midst.

The Executioner hunched forward in his seat, straining against his safety harness, as if the shift in position would help the Apache exceed its speed limit. The Apache was faster than the Cobra, he knew, by some forty miles per hour, and its range was a hundred miles greater, but Bolan wasn't counting on any kind of lengthy pursuit.

He wanted a kill.

And he wanted it now.

IT WAS A NEAR THING, with the Stingers, but Icarus had pulled his own ass out of the fire at the penultimate moment, a combination of personal skill and the Cobra's infrared jammer defeating his earthbound enemy's best shot. Not only that, but he had given them hell in the bargain, cutting down several of the pathetic guardians with his 20 mm cannon, before a sec-

ond missile forced him to break off, fleeing for his
life.

Now the damned Apache was behind him, closing
fast, and that could only mean one thing.

There was no option but escape, and even that was
looking marginal. It would have been insane to stand
and fight above the presidential compound, dodging
missiles from the ground and from the other helicopter. Even Icarus wasn't that skilled a pilot.

Likewise, there was no question of outrunning the
Apache, leaving his pursuers behind with a sudden
burst of speed. His throttle was wide-open now, and
still the Apache was gaining, its twin engines dou-
bling the Cobra's horsepower, and then some.

The worst part, though, was the Apache's payload.
Icarus assumed that it had been dispatched especially
to destroy him, meaning it would be equipped with
air-to-air missiles, either Stingers or Sidewinders. If
they went with Stingers, the effective killing range
was three miles, give or take; with Sidewinders, they
could nearly quadruple that range.

No Sidewinders, then, he decided, or his charred
remains would already have plummeted to earth, riding the Cobra's twisted wreckage down. As for the
Stingers, they were close enough to try one now, but
any distance shot would give him time and opportunity to dodge, perhaps wasting a rocket that was better
saved for closer range. Icarus took for granted that
the enemy had witnessed his performance with the
Secret Service at Camp David, dodging Stingers
hurled at him from handheld launchers, and his adversaries wouldn't wish to waste munitions on a risky

shot. Better to chase him for a while, draw closer, and improve the odds of a first-shot kill.

His own weapons, by contrast, weren't ideal for dogfighting, but he would make do with what he had. Four TOW missiles remained, with a maximum range of 4,100 yards, and while they were designed for killing tanks on terra firma, they could also blast a chopper from the sky, if he was able to paint the target with his infrared and hold it steady. His 2.75-inch rockets, likewise, were designed primarily for use against vehicles or personnel on the ground, but he could fire all thirty-eight of them at once, if need be, blanketing his airborne target with high-explosive warheads.

But to use any rockets at all, he would have to turn back, face his pursuers, stand and fight. It was an option that he didn't relish at the moment; not until he found the perfect battleground on which to make his stand.

For Icarus, that would ideally mean a populated area where he would be at liberty to do his worst, while his pursuers—theoretically, at least—would feel constrained and, hopefully, distracted by the presence of so-called innocent bystanders. His first impulse was to head back for Washington, fight it out over Pennsylvania Avenue, but practicality had won out in the end, Icarus aware that a northbound course would bring him perilously closer to his enemy, instead of giving him a lead. Likewise, so would a westward run toward Arlington and Alexandria, Virginia.

That left Annapolis, some thirty miles northwest of Camp David, perhaps veering north from there toward

Baltimore, but realistically, Icarus knew he would be fortunate to reach the home of the U.S. Naval Academy before he was overtaken and blown from the sky. In all probability, he would be forced to turn and fight before he got that far, and so he watched the ground below, even as he surveyed his instruments and monitors, watching for any town of substance that could be transformed into a makeshift killing field.

Ahead, perhaps three-quarters of a mile, a sprawl of shops and houses beckoned him. If he recalled his Maryland topography, that should be Forestville, located near the point where Highway 95 met western Pennsylvania Avenue. The population wasn't all that large—around twelve thousand souls, as he recalled—but it would have to do.

The Apache gunship was gaining on him, closing the gap.

Icarus knew that he was running out of time and sky.

"HE'S TURNING," Jack Grimaldi said. "We've got him!"

"Right," Bolan replied. And thought that maybe he had them.

He didn't recognize the town below them, didn't know its name, but he could pick out cars and trucks moving along the roads. Children were playing soccer in a schoolyard, off to Bolan's left. The town's main business district—strip malls and a shopping center reminiscent of a shrunken Pentagon—lay dead-ahead, the Cobra hovering malignantly.

"He's yours," Grimaldi said. "Go for it!"

Bolan held his fire, although he had a lock and could have used his Stingers with a fair degree of confidence. Still, he had seen Holt dodge a missile in the air above Camp David, and he knew that what went up—unless it found its mark—had to ultimately plunge to earth again. Likewise, a kill above the central district of the town below them would insure a rain of fire and mangled steel onto the streets and rooftops.

It had the makings of a no-win situation, but his adversary wouldn't feel obliged to spare the innocent from injury or death. If anything, Holt would be hoping for a body count among the members of his earthbound audience. With that in mind, and calculating ranges on the fly, Bolan determined that he had no choice but to engage the enemy—on his own terms, if possible, but one way or another—to prevent a larger tragedy.

Holt would be firing rockets any second now, but Bolan beat him to it, loosing first one Stinger, then a second, toward the target in his sights. They sped toward impact, rapidly converging on the target he had marked with infrared. The Cobra, meanwhile, was initiating an evasive move, the pilot less inclined toward martyrdom than some fanatics might have been.

And he was swift enough to pull it off, both missiles flashing past him, far enough removed that neither of their automatic proximity fuses detonated the 6.6-pound HE fragmentation warheads they carried. With a three-mile range, Bolan was estimating they should fall to earth somewhere beyond the town in open country, with a minimal risk to civilians.

It was the best that he could do, and it appeared to work, the Cobra veering wide off course and breaking contact, fleeing toward the east. At top speed, the town fell behind them in less than a minute, pedestrians pointing and craning their necks as the gunships flew on, out of sight.

"Get me as close as possible," he told Grimaldi, following the Cobra, tracking as it tried to outmaneuver him. The rogue lieutenant colonel might still be inclined to fight, but he was short of opportunity and combat stretch. If he attempted to reverse directions now, he would present his adversary with a broadside target, virtually guaranteeing a kill.

The only answer seemed to lie in speed, but even there, the Cobra was inferior to the Apache, especially with Grimaldi handling the controls. Another moment, winging over open country, and the Executioner was close enough to try his hand again.

He didn't use the Stingers this time, though. Instead, he emptied one of the rocket pods in a burst of noise and flame, nineteen slender javelins launched toward their target, each bearing a high-explosive warhead. Some of them were bound to miss, he realized, but some wouldn't.

Some didn't, and he watched the Cobra come apart in midair, rocked by a swarm of explosions, each three times the magnitude of a fragmentation grenade. The tail was sheared off, and the motor ripped free of its housing, severed rotors whipping through the air like giant boomerangs. The cockpit nosed over, engulfed in flame, tumbling end over end as it surrendered to the pull of gravity. Fuel tanks exploded when the hulk was still some twenty yards from impact, spraying fiery streamers far and wide across a field of soybeans.

"I'd say that's a kill." Grimaldi sounded satisfied.

"I'd say," the Executioner agreed with him. But he couldn't share the pilot's relief until he found out what the bottom-line damage was back at Camp David.

Even then, he knew, they weren't finished. He had severed one more tentacle, but the malignant octopus was still alive and hiding somewhere, waiting for its wounds to heal. Indeed, another morbid plan to light the doomsday fuse was probably already in the works.

To stop it, to eliminate all future plots and plans, Bolan would have to find The Two and deal with them.

The only problem being that he still had no idea where to look.

CHAPTER SEVENTEEN

Apollo was surprised to find the contact number still in service when he dialed it from a pay phone at a shopping mall in Garden City, Kansas. The voice that answered was asexual, devoid of any accent, possibly the product of an altering device. He didn't know or care.

He gave his star name and informed the operator that he needed to make contact with The Two. He didn't bother telling him-her on the other end that his business was a matter of life and death. The Two would know that if they took his call. If they refused to speak with him, well, then Apollo knew what he had to do.

The operator asked him for his number, and he read it from the telephone, the ageless voice repeating it to double-check. "That's it," he said, confirming that she-he had copied it correctly.

"Can you wait there for a bit?" the operator asked.

"Depends," he said. "How long?"

"Fifteen or twenty minutes ought to do it. Half an hour tops."

"All right." He hung up, felt an urge to wipe the

telephone for fingerprints, then decided he was being foolish. Still, as he retreated several paces from the phone, he checked the face of every passing shopper, young and old, waiting for one to show a spark of recognition at the sight of him. It was his second day on the most-wanted list, and even though he knew the Top Ten fugitives sometimes remained at large for years—or got away entirely—he still felt edgy, as if hostile eyes were tracking every move he made.

Directly opposite the bank of pay phones was a kiosk selling chocolates and coffee. Apollo hoped that he looked casual as he approached the vendor, poured himself a cup of coffee, and rooted through his pocket for change. The youth behind the counter barely glanced at him, his disconnection from the sale encouraging Apollo to believe it just might be all right, regardless.

He had switched cars once again, a short time after murdering the trooper in Kentucky, and had stolen license plates to fit his latest ride in Poplar Bluff, Missouri. He had also found a thrift shop there and purchased clothes that had the lived-in look of someone who was often on the road—not destitute, by any means, but still a far cry from the look of former Special Agent Luther Marx. He hadn't shaved since the abortive strike in Washington, and cheap sunglasses hid his eyes, along with a distinctive little scar that marked the bridge of flesh between them.

Short of putting on a fright wig and a bulbous rubber nose, it was the best that he could do. His story's end wouldn't depend upon his cunning as a master of disguise, in any case.

It would depend upon The Two.

If they rejected him—as they had every right to do, considering his failure at the task assigned him—he would attempt to pacify the Ancients, somehow make his peace, before he used one of the Glaser slugs on himself. It wouldn't be the martyr's death that he had counted on, of course, but neither would he risk a greater insult to The Path by allowing himself to be taken alive. Prison wasn't for him, and while he gladly would have sacrificed himself confronting the authorities, if so instructed by The Two, there seemed to be no point in doing so without instructions.

He had caused sufficient damage as it was, his bumbling at the White House setting back the cause, doing incalculable damage. Why should he believe The Two would even take his call, much less make time to speak with him in person? It was ludicrous. He was a fool for even trying to make contact.

Suddenly disgusted with himself, Apollo dumped his coffee in the nearest trash receptacle and was retreating toward the exit, when the telephone began to ring.

He lifted the receiver.

"Hello?"

"Apollo?" It was no risk giving out his star name, since a stranger wouldn't recognize it, and the first wrong answer on his end would terminate the call immediately.

"Yes," he said, relieved to hear the operator's voice. No matter what came next, The Two had cared enough, at least, to call him back and tell him what to do.

"How's Garden City?"

He hadn't informed the operator where he was, but anyone could presumably work that out, using the area code and prefix of the pay phone's number. He wondered if the operator was trying to impress or intimidate him, showing that The Path could find him anywhere, at any time.

"They've got a shopping mall," he said. "It's all I've seen so far. I don't intend to stick around and take the tour."

"You're right on Highway 60, there, I see," the operator said.

"Uh-huh." So, he-she had a road map. What was next, directions to a charming bed-and-breakfast in the Rockies?

"You could probably be in La Junta, Colorado, in about an hour and a half," the voice suggested.

"What would I do there?" Apollo asked.

"Stop at the Rodeway Inn," the operator said. "Don't register. They have a lounge inside, a combination bar and grill. Sit at the bar and order chili with a beer. The beer should be imported, in a bottle."

"Any special brand?" Apollo asked.

The operator almost laughed at that. Perhaps he-she was smiling. "Doesn't matter," the reply came back. "Someone will meet you at the bar. He's Roy, you're Jim. All right?"

"Got it," Apollo said. There was a sharp click, and the line went dead.

He listened for another moment by force of habit, half expecting to hear the telltale noise of a clumsy wiretapper, but all he got was the dial tone. Paranoia? Perhaps, but he knew how the Bureau and similar agencies worked. Unlike most blissfully ignorant Americans, Apollo knew that at one time, in the Red-hunting 1950s, J. Edgar Hoover's G-men had routinely opened and read every single piece of mail that was posted from Boston to Great Britain. It went on for years, and that was just practice, refining the art. Today, with the technology available, you never really had to tap a line, since there were ways to intercept calls at the trunk—or pluck them out of thin air, legally, if you were stalking someone who was fool enough to use a mobile phone.

There was no reason that the FBI would look for him in Garden City, Kansas, but they might be covering The Path's "secure" contact lines. If so...

Screw it, Apollo thought. He had no options; he would keep the date in Colorado, ordering himself a bowl of chili with a beer. In the bottle. An imported beer, at that.

Why not?

If he was being set up for the kill, at least he could enjoy a fair last meal.

"IT'S HOLT, all right," Brognola said. "At least, we're pretty sure. The ME's waiting on some dental records for the final confirmation, but she might be guessing, even then."

Bolan had no need to inquire about the reason for the medical examiner's conundrum. He had seen the Cobra gunship come apart in midair, shattered by repeated strikes from 2.75-inch rockets, the mangled cockpit plunging to earth from two hundred feet, a seething mass of flame. He was surprised they had a jaw and teeth to work with, even partials, after Nathan Holt had gone to his reward.

"What's the word on Marx?" he asked.

"We're looking at another homicide," Brognola said. "A state trooper in Kentucky stopped a Mitsubishi just across the line from West Virginia, late yesterday afternoon. He radioed the plates in to dispatch before somebody shot him, dumped his body in some trees beside the road and drove his black-and-white in after him. Cops found the Mitsubishi in Missouri, Poplar Bluff, at three o'clock this morning. Plates come back to Horace Crocker, sixty-three, a resident of Arlington. Nobody's seen him since he went to do some shopping yesterday, around the same time as the White House incident."

"Marx took him out and copped the wheels," Bolan said, "then dumped the body somewhere, heading west."

"That's what it looks like," Brognola agreed. "Of course, we're absolutely clueless as to what he's driving now, and where he went from Poplar Bluff."

"Doesn't matter," Bolan said. "He had his shot and blew it in the rose garden. He'll never get a second chance."

"We want him, anyway," Brognola said.

"He's bound to turn up, with his face all over TV and the papers. Right now, I'm more concerned with Locke and Braun."

Brognola's sigh spoke eloquently of a restless night, spent in worry. "Wish there was something I could tell you," he replied. "Those two have gone to ground, but good. I thought we had their hideouts cataloged, but obviously there's at least one that we missed. Hell, they could be halfway around the world by now, for all I know."

"Unlikely," Bolan said. "From everything I've seen, they're true believers, Hal. The last thing either one of them would want is to miss out on the apocalypse."

"I didn't know that was an option," Brognola replied. "We're talking World War III, the way I understand it. That's the mother of all shots heard around the world."

"Agreed. But Locke and Braun won't settle for a passive role. They want a ringside seat. In fact, they want to pull the trigger."

"So," Brognola asked, "where are they, then?"

"We're working on it," Bolan said, thinking about Celeste Bouchet and her computer. It had coughed up leads for Bolan more than once, so far, but now he wondered how far she could push it. If the founders of The Path were really bent on keeping secrets, were they dumb enough to leave a trail of bread crumbs on the Internet?

"Well, anyway," Brognola said, "the presidents are grateful for the save, and that's official from the White House *and* the Kremlin. It was touch and go there for a minute with the visitor, from what I understand, but he's all right. Camp David will be closed a while for renovations, I suspect."

"Your tax dollars at work," Bolan said.

"Strictly on the Q.T., though. Officially, it was an

accident. We've told the press two military helicopters tangled in midair. One went down in the presidential compound, while the other managed to continue for several miles, looking for someplace safe to land, before the pilot lost it.''

"What about civilian witnesses?" Bolan asked.

"That's the slick part," Brognola replied. "It's being called a training exercise that went to hell. Some farmer says he saw two choppers firing rockets at each other, and the Pentagon agrees with him. Of course, they weren't live rockets. Deaths in military training happen all the time.''

"We're covered, then.''

"So far," Brognola said.

Bolan didn't inquire about where the presidents would hold their meeting next, and whether they were amply covered. There was nothing to suggest that members of The Path would mount a fourth attempt, or that they had the wherewithal to pull it off. In any case, he knew without asking that Justice and the Secret Service would be on their toes, brick agents itching for a crack at any members of the cult that had already murdered several of their comrades. And Bolan didn't envy any vocal critics of the President who tried to stage a demonstration anywhere within a hundred miles of Washington, the next few days. He guessed that their reception from the men assigned to guard the chief executive wouldn't be gentle or polite.

His problem, at the moment, was entirely different. If Galen Locke and Helen Braun *had* given up their plan to strike the Armageddon spark by killing off a Russian president in the United States, what would their next attempt entail? Bolan didn't for one brief moment think that they would merely fade away, slip back into the woodwork and give up their plans. Unless...

"I have to check on something," he told the big Fed. "I'll be in touch."

"Okay. Stay frosty, guy."

The Motor Lodge in Annandale, Virginia, had been fresh out of connecting rooms when Bolan checked in with Celeste Bouchet. In fact, they had been unable to get adjoining rooms, and while the balding man behind the registration desk had winked at Bolan, asking if they really wanted two rooms, after all, the Executioner had stared him down and paid for two, rooms 12 and 17 on the ground floor.

He left his room now, walked the few yards to Bouchet's, and gave the coded knock they had agreed on in advance. He had no reason to believe that such precautions would be needed, but it was no great price to pay if it insured the lady's peace of mind.

A shadow moved behind the small lens of the peephole, and he heard the dead bolt disengage a moment later. "Hi!" Bouchet seemed glad to see him, though it had been less than half an hour since they checked in and adjourned to separate rooms.

He saw the laptop on a table near the window, cursor winking on an empty amber screen. "How goes it?"

"Nothing yet," she told him, sounding disappointed. "I was hoping, well, I just keep drawing blanks."

"I'm curious," he said, "about their fallback option."

"I don't follow," she replied.

"Most field commanders count on winning an engagement," he explained, "or else they wouldn't make a move to start with. Even so, if they've got any smarts at all, they plan ahead for all contingencies, including failure. They need someplace to fall back, regroup and try to salvage what they can in case a plan goes sour on them."

"I don't know...wait! You mean the Gathering?" she asked.

"It's Greek to me," Bolan said. "Fill me in."

"Well, it's a Final Days kind of thing," she said. "Before the end, all loyal believers would receive the call, and they would gather at a certain place to wait out the tribulations."

"So where's the place?" Bolan asked.

"No one knows except The Two. Supposedly, directions would be given when they sent the call. I never really took it seriously."

"But suppose they do," he said. "On any scale, they've had a string of major setbacks in the past few days. Could that prompt them to send this summons out?"

"Well, I suppose." She didn't sound convinced.

"And if they did, who would receive it?" Bolan asked.

"In theory," she replied, "all dedicated members of the cult."

"In which case," he went on, "The Two should be on hand to greet them, right?"

"Of course."

"So how do we find out if they've issued this call?"

"Again, in theory, any member of the cult should know. To keep it on the safe side, though, I'd look for someone highly placed, held in esteem."

"And that would be…?"

"Hang on," she said, already moving toward the laptop. "Maybe there's a way I can find out."

APOLLO DIDN'T GET to eat his chili after all. The bowl was barely set before him, piping hot, when he was conscious of a presence at his elbow, and a chunky, thirty-something man sat down beside him.

"Jim!" the stranger greeted him and slapped Apollo on the back, as if the two of them were long-lost friends. "Sorry I'm late, man, but I got hung up in traffic."

"Not a problem, Roy," he told the stranger. "I'm just having lunch."

"No time," the new arrival said. "We gotta roll, you know?"

"Uh-huh." Apollo dropped his spoon into the chili, watched it sink while he was reaching for the frosty bottle of Corona. "You won't mind if I just finish off my beer?"

"Well, uh…"

Apollo didn't wait for a decision, tipping the bottle and taking the beer in long swallows, setting it down empty and rising from his bar stool. "Listen, Roy," he said, "I'm just a little short on cash, if you don't mind…?"

The stranger blinked at him, then mumbled something unintelligible, as he rummaged in his pockets, coming out with several crumpled bills. "How much?" he asked.

"That's fine," Apollo said, relieving him of the cash and fanning the bills on the bar. "Are we going, or what?"

Outside, his contact had a nondescript Toyota waiting in the lot. "Where's your car at?" he asked.

"Back home," Apollo said. "Virginia."

"Oh." Roy seemed to ponder that one for a moment, then gave up and let himself in the driver's side, pressing a button that unlocked the other doors. "We've got about an hour's drive," his escort said. "I'm not supposed to ask you anything about your mission."

"I don't have one," Apollo said.

"Right. I understand."

He didn't think so, the former G-man thought, but he was too damned weary to debate the point. If Roy wasn't supposed to ask him questions, then Apollo could control the conversation—theoretically, at least—by simply keeping his mouth shut. He tried it, and it seemed to work, Roy tiring of the silence after ten or fifteen minutes, switching on the radio to something classical.

Apollo checked the highway signs and landmarks more from force of habit than from any need to know where he was going. He had come to meet The Two, and they were either waiting for him at his destination or they weren't. If they had set him up, so be it. He had been on borrowed time since he had drawn his

Smith & Wesson in the White House rose garden and shot Pete Dickson in the ass.

They followed U.S. Highway 50 northwest until they passed through Rocky Ford. Two miles beyond the town, Roy picked up State Highway 71, due north, and kept on in that direction for the better part of forty minutes, by the dashboard digital. Somewhere in Lincoln County, north of Punkin Center, they turned off the highway to pursue a one-lane access road that led them on a winding course, predominately westward, for another ten minutes. The last leg of their journey was three hundred yards of gravel driveway ending in the front yard of a sandy-colored stucco house.

The place was on the small side, but it had been well maintained, from all appearances. The first thing that Apollo noted was a seeming absence of defenses, though in truth, he couldn't tell how many guns were pointed at him right now, from inside the house. The second thing he saw was that, unless a person dressed in desert camouflage and crawled for miles across the open on his belly, there was no way anyone could sneak up on the house.

Roy broke the silence for the first time since they'd left the Rodeway Inn. ''Let's go.''

Apollo trailed him to the house, letting Roy proceed him through the door—as if it mattered, in the long run. Any kind of ambush that had been arranged for him would be refined enough to keep them from taking out their own pointman. Or maybe not, depending on the skill and smarts of those involved. What difference did it make? If he was marked to die, as punishment for failing in his mission, he wouldn't resist.

Expecting bullets, possibly a strangling wire, Apollo was surprised when Roy conveyed him to the dwelling's smallish living room, where Hermes and Circe stood waiting. The former Fed stepped forward, nearly choking on the lump that had appeared from nowhere in his throat. His legs were trembling, and it seemed entirely natural when he dropped to his knees before The Two, head bowed, tears streaming down his face.

"I failed," he said, as if they didn't know that, and his mind was racing, testing and rejecting sentence fragments at the speed of light. At last, he said, "I'm ready to accept my punishment."

Hermes replied, "How should we punish one who serves us faithfully, but is defeated by imposing odds beyond his personal control?"

Apollo blinked at that, still too terrified to raise his head. What kind of mind games were they playing with him, now?

"You've done your best," Circe said with a voice so soft and sweet that it produced fresh tears. "Arriving here, with every man against you, is no small achievement in itself."

"But I—"

"Enough." Her voice was gentle, but it had the sharp edge of command. Apollo bit his tongue and waited, as she said, "We need your help, Apollo."

"Anything!" he fairly sobbed. "My life for you!"

"Of course."

"Thor's Hammer is without a leader," Hermes said.

"But Cerberus..."

"Is dead. A casualty of war. Are you prepared to take his place?"

Apollo felt the room tilt, was about to pinch himself when it regained a semblance of normality. He didn't trust his ears, and dared not ask Hermes to repeat himself. He had come here expecting death, hoping it would be swift, and now The Two were going to promote him!

"Yes!" he blurted, and raised his eyes for the first time to face The Two directly. "I won't let you down a second time, I swear!"

"We take your oath for granted," Circe told him. "Rise."

Apollo did as he was told, surprised to find his legs a good deal steadier than when he walked into the room. "What would you have me do?" he asked.

"We need your help with many things, right now," Hermes replied.

And Circe stunned him when she said, "We're issuing the call."

THE TRICK, Celeste Bouchet had quickly realized, was finding someone both important to the cult and readily accessible to Michael Blake. If she was right, and Hermes was prepared to sound the call, it would ideally be received and answered instantly by every member of The Path. In practice, though, she realized, the present situation might preclude contact with small fry in the group. Some of them doubtless would have scattered, might be hiding out, and it wasn't as if The Two could commandeer a television satellite to beam their message nationwide. They would be forced to work with what they had, a web of telephones and fax machines that would inevitably leave some gaps, considering the damage suffered by the cult in recent days.

The Two would never lose touch with their A-list, though. Even among the chosen people, Bouchet had discovered, some were more chosen than others. Men and women with fat bank accounts or positions of power and influence were courted with flowery words, glib promises of an oh-so-special place in paradise. A handful bought it, cast their normal flint-eyed skepticism to the wind, and swallowed the whole fairy tale.

As she had, once upon a time.

Whatever else was happening with Galen Locke and Helen Braun, if they were desperate enough to make the call, Bouchet knew they would want as many of their followers as possible around them, and the first ones they would summon were the cult's elite.

She hadn't known their given names while she was still a member of the cult. That information was beyond her "need to know," and her immediate superior had taken pains to safeguard those whose cash and influence allowed The Two to live in style. If it was time to circle the wagons, she knew the inner circle wouldn't be neglected, much less left behind to find themselves another prophet of the Final Days.

Bouchet began with what she knew about the "special'' chosen ones. Their number had included two successful actors—one from television, one from feature films—the vice president of a bank in San Diego, the kooky mayor of a small town in Colorado, the pampered daughter of a Detroit automobile company's CEO, the heir to a national chain of fast-food restaurants, the aging founder of a successful Nevada casino, a San Francisco shock-radio host who immodestly billed himself as ''the next Howard Stern''…and at least one U.S. congressman.

The latter came from California, and while his name wasn't imprinted on her memory, Bouchet knew she would recognize it on sight. Accordingly, she booted up her laptop, logged on to the Internet and made a quick connection with Uncle Sam.

The federal government was nothing if not zealous in maintaining Web sites. Anyone with a connection to the Net could fire off e-mails to the White House— though it might bring Secret Service agents calling, if the message seemed bizarre or threatening—browse through the Library of Congress, check in with the various departments of the presidential cabinet, file tax forms with the IRS, check out the FBI's most wanted fugitives or read a list of congressmen and senators, arranged by state and district, with their voting records on significant issues.

Bouchet had been on-line for thirteen minutes when she found her man. There was no photograph beside his name, but that was easily remedied. She plugged his name into a handy search engine and saw his Web site come up first, among the eighty-seven listings that appeared. Another click, and there he was all smiles and wavy auburn hair.

"Bingo!" she said, and felt Blake moving up beside her.

"Elliot Larson," he read the name aloud. "A congressman? As in the U.S. House of Representatives?"

"His star name's Sirius," Bouchet replied. "I recognize him from a visit he made to the Boulder compound when I lived there."

The web site didn't list a home address in either California or Washington. Bolan spent another moment staring at the monitor, as if to memorize the smiling face, before he said, "I'll need to make a call."

She knew what that meant. He would reach out to the man from Justice once again, Mr. Brognola, and another call or two should nail down the addresses he required. Bouchet could probably have found them, one way or another, prowling on the Internet, but her companion's approach would save them precious time. And what then?

She could answer that one for herself. Once Blake had learned the address, he would pay a call on Congressman Larson. With any luck he would find his quarry in Washington; if not, he would be winging to California, no doubt leaving her behind.

Unless, of course, The Two had already reached out to Sirius and summoned him to join them. In which case, she assumed that Blake would be too late.

There was a chance the congressman might balk at walking out on everything he had without a backward glance, but she remembered him as a devoted zealot, even though he managed to conceal it during party gatherings and speeches for the television cameras. He was a two-faced, lying bastard—which, she realized, was little more than calling him a politician. Still, from what she knew of him, Bouchet believed that he would answer to the call.

The regimen was simple: When the call came, you obeyed. Just that and nothing more. Directions would be given at the time, thus skillfully avoiding any risk that a defector might someday expose the final plan.

That was the hell of it. She still had no idea exactly what the call would mean in terms of concrete action—where those who received it were supposed to go or what they were supposed to do.

But she was going to find out.

CHAPTER EIGHTEEN

The Honorable Elliot Larson (R-Calif.) hadn't been this rushed since his last reelection campaign. Fortunately, since the two-year terms for U.S. representatives meant he was basically campaigning all the time, Larson had never lost the knack of packing in a hurry, canceling appointments with constituents in favor of a meeting with somebody who could lubricate the wheels of his political machine with cash.

This time, however, Congressman Larson almost regarded packing as a waste of time. The call was final; that much had been drummed into his head until he knew the drill by heart. Whatever happened in the next few days, apocalypse or kingdom come, the odds were excellent that he would never see his office or the Georgetown condominium again.

He had no family to think about. His wife of four-teen years had been the victim of a drunken hit-and-run three years ago—and wasn't *that* a surefire grabber for the old sympathy vote. Their union had been childless, and he thanked his lucky stars for that, now that the end was almost here.

His lucky stars.

There was more truth than poetry in that, thought Larson, as he finished piling shirts and slacks and underwear into a Gucci suitcase. He would leave the closetful of business suits behind. Larson wouldn't be needing them where he was going, and neither would anyone else by the time he was missed on the floor of the House.

He thought about the votes that would be coming up within the next few days. There was another raise for Congress, which he had been planning to oppose, secure in the knowledge that his empty protest would be buried in a landslide of approval. Yet another gun-grab measure from the crowd he liked to call the Brady Bunch, after their leader, with another "nay" vote waiting in the wings. A bill designed to curb abuses by the IRS, and he was voting "yea" on that one loud and clear—or would have, rather, if the call hadn't demanded his attention.

But it had, and there was nothing he could do about it. Not since he had learned the truth about the Ancients and sworn allegiance to The Path.

It still amazed him sometimes how the whole change in his life had come about. None of it would have happened in the first place, Larson never would have seen the scout ship, if it hadn't been for Rita, a delightful redhead from West Hollywood who liked his boyish smile. As it turned out, she also liked the rest of him, a circumstance that eased his passage of the big four-o and led to many late-night "caucuses" in out-of-town motels, where Larson's almost-famous face could pass unnoticed by the hoi polloi. They had been driving back from Riverside that night, and he had stopped to take a leak beside the highway when the scout ship zoomed in out of nowhere, hovered long enough to help Larson relieve himself in record time, and then winked out of sight like something from a feverish dream.

Rita had seen it, too, but she didn't appear surprised. In fact, she claimed to see them regularly, and she introduced him to an expert on the subject— someone who, she was convinced, could help him sort it out. The counselor, in turn, had introduced him to The Path. Hermes and Circe welcomed him as if he was the son they never had, advising him to keep his stunning revelation secret for the moment. There would come a time, they promised him, when all would be revealed, and all humankind would know the truth.

Of course, not everyone would handle it as well as Larson had. Some—the majority, in fact—would rage against their destiny, resisting to the bitter end. At that point, he was told, it would be necessary for the true believers to remove themselves, step out from so-called civilized society and let the storm sweep past.

That time was now.

He finished packing, latched the suitcase and slipped on his jacket. After a final look around the condo he would never see again, Larson took his bag, hotfooting it toward the door. He didn't check the peephole prior to reaching for the knob—why should he?—and his swift reflexes barely kept him from colliding with the tall man on his doorstep.

Larson took him in with one quick glance—approximately six feet tall, about two hundred pounds, dark hair, blue eyes, the kind of face that could win arguments without much being said.

"Elliot Larson?"

"Yes, indeed," the congressman replied, "but I'm afraid I don't have time—"

The stranger shoved him backward through the doorway with his left hand, while an ugly pistol showed up in his right, as if by magic.

"Your departure's been postponed," the stranger said.

APOLLO HAD HIS HANDS FULL with the new assignment, but he thrived on rising to a challenge. He always had, from childhood, and the trait didn't desert him now.

His main task, once the call was issued, was to handle preparations at the last retreat. That meant preparing for defensive action in addition to the regular accommodations, grub and medical supplies, truckloads of bottled water, gasoline to run the generators, this and that.

As the commander of Thor's Hammer, he had troops at his command to help with the arrangements, and he delegated some of the assignments. When it came to gearing up for armed defense against their enemies, however, he made time to handle the arrangements on his own.

Ares and Cerberus before him had done much to pave the way, of course; he gave them that, with thanks. It would have been a trial to arm the compound in a hurry, even from black-market sources, and he was relieved to find the armory well stocked.

They had a pair of priceless M-2 HB .50-caliber machine guns—the heavies nicknamed "Ma Deuce," which were equally effective against vehicles and personnel—along with four M-60s chambered for the 7.62 mm NATO round. Individual weapons included thirty-five assault rifles, divided more or less equally between M-16 A-2s and AK-47s; a dozen submachine guns, including Uzis, Ingrams and MP-5s; four Remington 700 bolt-action rifles with ten-power scopes and an effective range of nearly 1,000 yards; a dozen 12-gauge shotguns, mostly Remington 870 pump-action models, and sixty assorted pistols, including 9 mm and .45-caliber autoloaders, with a few .357 Magnum revolvers. In addition to the guns and half a million rounds of ammunition, they had managed to acquire a case of M-26 fragmentation grenades, another case of M-18 Claymore antipersonnel mines and one M-79 grenade launcher, with three dozen 40 mm high-explosive rounds.

It was a formidable stash, backed by gas masks, Army-surplus field glasses and helmets, fire extinguishers, barbed wire and sandbags. The majority of buildings in the compound had been built from cinder blocks and sheet metal, which meant they wouldn't burn. Artillery would knock them down, of course, and air strikes, but the federal government was disinclined to use such tools when it was playing on a home court with a global TV audience.

Waco had taught them that, at least.

Ideally, they would have no use for any of the weapons, but Apollo wasn't one to place his faith in apple-pie ideals. He had seen countless rules ignored and broken by the FBI while he was still an agent in good standing, and it wasn't just the Bureau's game, by any means. Name a police department or a federal agency, and he could rattle off a litany of tales that ranged from laughable to terrifying, with the common thread that each and every one involved departures from procedure that could lead to a suspension or dismissal for the personnel involved—assuming that the brass in charge hadn't demanded some illegal action in the first place.

More important, in Apollo's way of thinking, was the fact that this would be no ordinary showdown, when it came. These were the Final Days; society was on the verge of a convulsion that would write the final page in human history, and that inscription would be etched in blood. Degenerate humanity had come too far along the devolution trail for any but the true elect to welcome home their forefathers and masters from the stars. The popular reaction would be panic and a fierce resistance to inevitable change—resistance which, Apollo had no doubt, would certainly include an effort to annihilate the chosen few who recognized the Ancients as their star-born gods.

A grisly day was coming, and if not for his belief in prophecy, Apollo would have felt like Colonel William Travis, patching up hopeless defenses at the Alamo. This wasn't 1836, however, and the reinforcements he was waiting for wouldn't be held up by the weather, ancient wagons or a spiteful order from the reigning government.

The troops who would relieve Apollo and his brethren of The Path were coming from the stars, and nothing in the man-made arsenal of planet Earth would turn them back.

The Ancients were a race of promise-keepers who would put all others in the shade.

He was prepared to work around the clock, with catnaps when exhaustion wore him down. The job got easier as members of The Path began arriving, singly and in groups, in answer to the call. Each band of new arrivals called upon The Two first thing, paying respect, then stowed their gear and went to work wherever they were needed in the compound—filling sandbags, stringing razor wire on the perimeter, installing mines and range markers to help the gunners do their job when it was time.

Apollo supervised it all and gloried in his role as field commander for these bold defenders of the faith. He didn't know how much time still remained before the last battle was joined, but they would be prepared.

He swore that on his life and was prepared to sign the covenant in blood.

"I DON'T KNOW YOU. What do you want? Is this a robbery?"

The congressman was full of questions, but there was a tremor in his voice, as if he feared someone might have a killing grudge against him. Or, Bolan reflected, maybe it was just the breakdown in his travel plans, together with the gun, that made him seem so agitated.

"Ah," the Executioner replied, "but *I* know *you.*"

"Is that right?" Larson tried to strike a posture of defiance, but was having trouble selling it. "Why don't you tell me what this is about, then? Make it quick, though, if you please. I've got a plane to catch.''

"Smart money says you'll miss it," Bolan told him.

"Listen, you can't walk in here and—"

"When did you receive the call?" he asked, and watched the color drain from Larson's face, as if someone had pulled a plug and let his blood run out.

"What did you say?" The politician's voice had dwindled almost to a whisper.

"That dumb act," Bolan told him, "might get by in Congress. Hey, for all I know, it helps you stay one jump ahead. But I'm not buying it, all right?"

"I don't know wha—"

A short left hook connected with the politician's nose and dropped him in his tracks, blood spurting from his oddly flattened nostrils. Tears of pain and hopeless rage were streaming down his face, mixing with blood that smeared across his lips and chin, as Larson struggled to his knees.

"You broke my nose!" he wailed.

Bolan reached down and grabbed him by his blood-flecked tie, one handed, hoisting him upright. The slip knot on the tie made an effective noose, cutting off the congressman's wind and flow of words at the same time.

"Forget about your nose," the Executioner advised, up close and personal. "Right now, you need to think about your neck. I know about The Path and your involvement. I know all about the Armageddon rap and what's been done so far to make that nightmare come alive. So far, it's been a bust. If we were betting, I'd lay odds The Two are feeling more than slightly paranoid, right now. In fact, my guess would be that they've sent out the call, which would explain your sudden rush to catch a plane at—" Bolan paused to check his watch "—at 10:19 p.m. The only thing I don't know, Mr. Larson, is your destination."

"So?" The politician's voice was strangled, but with eyes wide open, he still retained some of the raw defiance Bolan would expect from any zealot or fanatic.

"So," he said, "I need your help to finish planning my itinerary. Now, I understand your feelings in this matter, and your natural resistance. Which is why I've come prepared to do whatever might be necessary. Understand?"

"Whatever?" There was more fear than defiance showing now, but Larson wasn't broken yet.

"I don't believe in torture as a rule," Bolan said. "It's a messy way to go, for one thing, and the plain truth is, you can't trust what you hear most of the time. Still, there are some occasions when resistance simply must be...overcome. I'm sure you understand."

As Bolan spoke, he carefully relaxed the drag on Larson's tie, allowing him to breathe more freely, but retained his grip, as if the politician were a mongrel on a leash.

"Now we can do this either one of two ways," he went on. "The easy way for both of us would be for you to tell me what was said when you received the call, where you were ordered to report."

"I don't—" the congressman began, but Bolan choked it off and left him gasping.

"If you'd rather go the other route," he said, "we'll do it your way. It takes more time—and frankly, that upsets me—but we'll wind up with the same result. I'll know what you know, only you won't know it anymore."

"I won't?"

"Come on," Bolan said, smiling grimly. "After all that, you don't think I could afford to leave a witness, do you?"

"Witness?"

"Hey, it's nothing personal. Just cleaning house, you understand."

"And if I tell?" the congressman replied, squinting to catch a ray of hope.

Bolan stared back at him. "You talk, you walk."

"This isn't right," Larson complained, tears brimming in his eyes once more.

"It's not exactly kosher when you try to kill six billion strangers, either," Bolan said.

"I won't live anyway," the politician blubbered. "It's the Final Days!"

"At least that's plural," Bolan said. "You stonewall me, *this* is your final day, right here, right now. Look on the bright side, Congressman—The Two may have it wrong."

"DAMMIT!"

Celeste Bouchet was sick and tired of playing with her laptop. At the moment, she could cheerfully have flung it through the nearest window, except for the disappointing fact that she was still on the ground floor of the motel. For maximum effect, she would have liked to drop it from the top of the Washington Monument and watch it explode on impact.

With her luck, she thought, it would drop on a future President of the United States. That image, in turn, set her to wondering if the United States—or planet Earth, for that matter—would even have a future. Most people, she knew, would find the very question foolish and irrelevant. But most people weren't aware of how their daily lives hung by a thread within a wilderness of razor blades.

Until the last few months, even while living with the cult and soaking up their rap about the Final Days, Bouchet herself had been blissfully ignorant to the true state of affairs. She knew that wars were constantly erupting somewhere on the globe, and that the so-called superpowers spent the best part of their time bickering, insulting one another like bullies on a playground, but she never really thought that anything would come of it. She had grown up with televised reports from Vietnam, the Middle East, Grenada, Panama, Belfast, Afghanistan, El Salvador, Sudan, the smoking ruins that had once been Yugoslavia. Indeed, the woman believed she wouldn't recognize the TV news without at least one coup or genocidal massacre to let her know that everything was normal in the world.

She had awakened only lately to the side of life where anything could trigger an ungodly holocaust—

not merely children dead or dying in some Third World country most Americans had never heard of, but a shattered world in flames, surrounded by a cloud of fallout that would drift across the wasted land for years on end. A world devoid of life unless, perhaps, the cockroach finally lived up to its advance publicity and weathered the nuclear storm.

She lived in fear now; not of muggers, carjackers or rapists, but of faceless men and women she would never meet, who spent their every waking hour moment plotting global strategy, one finger on the doomsday button, aching for a chance to let it all hang out.

None of which helped one iota with her original problem, at the moment. Bouchet was looking for another hideaway, some piece of property The Two held, either in their own names or through some paper company formed as a cover.

And she was coming up empty.

There were limits, of course, to the public records available on-line. They seemed infinite, sometimes, but in truth, most local jurisdictions and governments were still tinkering with basic Web sites, assuming they cared enough to bother. Direct access to deeds, plans and similar data was still the rare exception, rather than the rule. Elite hackers and the havoc they caused from time to time, preyed mostly on large corporations and federal agencies for the simple reason that they had no access to the county recorder's office or small-town police department. Even the best computer wizard couldn't work his magic where the Web did not extend.

Bouchet had started with Stargate, gone in through the back door as usual, but she was getting nowhere fast. The fear of being traced had given her a headache, she was on the line so long, and still without result. Each piece of cult-related property she had identified was either a commercial operation or it had been swept by the authorities in the wake of the nerve-gas attack in L.A.

She knew there had to be more—The Two were hiding somewhere, after all—but she was still coming up empty at every turn. The secret kept eluding her, and Bouchet was forced to admit the possibility that she would fail. It all made perfect sense: why should The Two record their deepest, darkest end-of-time secrets on the Web, where any traitor to their sacred cause could come along and read the details for herself?

Reluctantly, she switched off the laptop and slumped back in her chair, rubbing her face with clammy hands. So much for doing her best. When was it ever really good enough?

Whatever hope remained, it all came down to Michael Blake, now, and the congressman. Blake had gone off to "take a meeting," moments after Hal Brognola called back with a Washington address for Elliot Larson, reporting that the congressman—a widower—was thought to be at home, presumably alone.

And if Blake missed him, if their man hadn't received the call or if he simply chose to die instead of spilling what he knew...then what?

Bouchet refused to think about that now. She could

jump off that bridge when she came to it. In the meantime, there was always hope.

Please, God. There had to be.

BOLAN HAD STATED no more than the simple truth when he described his personal disdain for torture to the frightened congressman. There was a universe of difference, though, between disliking a particular technique and swearing off it to the point that he would sacrifice a mission rather than resort to some distasteful means. In point of fact, some of the predators he dealt with on a daily basis could only recognize select stimuli. Some motivations—altruism, generosity, a selfless love—were so bizarre and foreign to their personal experience that they were easily dismissed as scams or fairy tales. The predators had grown up angry, hurting and afraid, so they became adept at recognizing—and at using—anger, pain and fear. They also understood the tidal pull of lust and greed, the weakness, which in their world, supplied the final motive for most actions that weren't impelled by fear or rage.

In dealing with an enemy, Bolan had early learned that he had to speak the adversary's language. That didn't mean that he had to literally speak Vietnamese in Vietnam, Spanish in Bogotá, or Ebonics in South-Central L.A. For he had learned that predators across the board, regardless of their race, religion, politics or sexual proclivities, all understood the language of brute force.

When blood was spilled, they got the message loud and clear.

Of course, the nature of their answers varied widely and wasn't always predictable. Like now.

The congressman had that milquetoast appearance normally associated with the "civilized" virtues of concession and compromise. In the beginning, Bolan thought he would break down with minimal effort, but Larson seemed to draw strength from adversity, finding an odd kind of courage in pain.

Speaking of pain, Bolan had barely scratched the surface in his handling of the congressman. A few slaps, hard enough to keep his hostage focused, but without a serious intent to harm. Twisting his broken nose between two fingers brought a howl from Larson and a stream of fresh blood from his nostrils, but it didn't make him talk.

His stated arguments aside, the main reason why Bolan hated torture was the power trip—one party with the muscle or authority inflicting agony on those without the choice of fight or flight. It was a kind of rape and it disgusted him.

Almost as much as global holocaust, which might yet be prevented with assistance from this man, who still believed that he was absolutely in the right.

"You're pretty tough," he told the congressman at last. "Too tough for me, I guess."

"What do you mean?"

"I mean, it's clear to me that I could kick your ass around this place all night, and you won't spill your guts. I mean, I'm giving up. So, here's what happens next...."

"You're going to shoot me," Larson said.

"Shoot you?" He shook his head. "Why waste a

bullet? The way it works, a deal like this, is that I pass you off to my connection, and they get you all fixed up. This time tomorrow, you should be fit to travel. Then, they cut you loose.''

"You'll follow me."

"Oh, sure." Bolan forced a smile at that. "As if you'd lead us where we want to go. No, Congressman, once you're released, you're on your own."

"Suppose I tell the press?"

"Two problems with that plan," Bolan replied. "The first one is, what would you tell the press? I mean, you don't know me from Adam, and you'll never see my face again this side of Hell. And then, the only way to make your story worth more than fifteen seconds on the tube would be to tell them why you got roughed up. Which is a major no-no, right?"

Larson was glaring at him now, remaining silent as he fumed in rage.

"The good news, though," Bolan continued, "is that you don't have to tell the networks anything. We've got it covered."

"What's that supposed to mean?"

"It means we've got a press announcement already prepared," Bolan replied, "expressing Uncle Sam's appreciation for your help in this emergency."

"What help?" Larson demanded.

"Why, the information you supplied about your fellow cultists after they were dumb enough to try and kill you," Bolan said. "It was a lucky thing for us they only broke your nose and banged you up a little bit. They haven't had much luck that way, the past few days. Seems like whoever's running the show can't find his ass with both hands.''

"I didn't say anything!''

"Hey, I know that, and you know that," Bolan agreed, "but they don't know it. And it gets a little tricky, issuing denials on a deal like this. I mean, if you admit association with the crowd that tried to kill the President, the media will have you for dessert, and no one's going to believe a word you say in self-defense. You could deny it all, of course, but then you're left explaining what went down, and where the story came from in the first place. Either way, one look at you on television, and The Two will change your name from Sirius to Judas in the time it takes to reach for the remote control.''

Larson was silent for a moment, weighing options. Then he said, "All right, you prick. What do I have to do?''

CHAPTER NINETEEN

It was tough going, for a while, to keep Hal Brognola from sending in the cavalry. His first impulse, quite naturally, once they found the cult's retreat, was to surround the place with men and guns, have ambulances and emergency rescue teams on standby, ready for anything. It was Bolan's persuasiveness—combined with memories of Ruby Ridge and Waco—that finally convinced him to chill out.

Brognola couldn't simply sit on the report, of course. If it had blown up in his face, and word leaked out somehow that he had known about the gathering before it hit the fan, he would have been crucified by the press and in Congress. His career would be history for starters, and any remnants of a pension that he managed to retain would be devoured by lawsuits from the relatives of cultists in the compound. Even flying in the face of logic, it wouldn't take much, in today's atmosphere, to convince a middle-class jury that Brognola—and by extension Washington—should have "done something," whatever that was, to avert yet another replay of Masada.

So, the FBI and ATF had special teams on standby,

hanging back a mile or two from the compound itself, while Jack Grimaldi ferried in Bolan to do his thing. Now, all the Executioner would have to do is figure out what that "thing" was, and how to pull it off.

Unfortunately, at the moment, he didn't possess a clue.

But at least he knew where he was going.

It was Colorado, Yuma County, twenty miles east of the border with Kansas. In essence, the county was twelve hundred square miles of nothing, quartered by interstate highways that sliced across the flat land like old keloid scars. Bolan had checked a road atlas before they left Washington and found that only nine towns in the county rated any kind of recognition; half of those were concentrated in the southern quarter near the county line, and his target was miles away from anything that might be called a human settlement.

Which, he supposed, was the original idea.

The congressman had told him everything, then wept as he was led away by federal agents to a safehouse, where he would remain until the smoke cleared. Bolan could have iced him, but there seemed to be no point. Whichever way it went in Colorado, Elliot Larson was terminally compromised. He had betrayed his country and his oath of office, on the one hand; and he had directed Bolan to his fellow cultists. He was anything but innocent, no matter what went down, and if it turned into a bloodbath, the spin doctors at Justice would paint him bright crimson, along with the rest of the team.

"Seems to me like your ass is hanging out a mile," Grimaldi said.

They were using the Apache once more, with Bolan in the gunner's seat, but this was simply transportation, not a strafing run. He smiled at his friend's expression of concern and answered through his microphone.

"It's been out in the breeze before," he said.

"This is a different kind of breeze," Grimaldi reminded him. "If Larson was telling it straight, you'll be looking at more than just soldiers."

And that was the problem, Bolan recognized. According to the congressman, there were whole families inside the compound, waiting for a sign from heaven or the second coming of the Ancients, something that would mean a fresh start for the planet and their own ascension to the role of chosen people in a brand-new world. Thor's Hammer would provide the first line of security, the soldiers, but each member of the cult had been indoctrinated—brainwashed, if you like—to expect a government assault. The sect had stockpiled weapons; Larson wasn't sure how many or what kind, but he admitted to illegal sources in the U.S. military. When push came to shove, most of the men would fight, perhaps some of the women, too.

And their children would be caught in the cross fire.

That was enough for Bolan to oppose a Waco-style assault, and Brognola had finally relented, unwilling to spill the blood of youngsters. At the same time, though, he knew that Justice couldn't simply watch and wait if leaders of The Path turned suicidal, taking their disciples the way of Jonestown, Heaven's Gate and the Order of the Solar Temple.

If it came down to a slaughter from within, someone would have to move. Bolan, for his part, hoped that he could stop the action short of self-immolation, but for that, he had to get inside.

"Five miles," Grimaldi said. "I still think we should—"

"Never mind," said Bolan, interrupting him. "It's down to me."

And he would have to live with it, no matter how the hand played out.

APOLLO WAS SURPRISED, to say the least, when he discovered the stockpile of cyanide, while taking final inventory of the arms and ammunition in the compound. He had tried to visualize the poison's use as an offensive or defensive weapon, but had come up empty. Even if they were besieged inside the camp— especially if they were cut off from the outside world, in fact—the only means of using cyanide against their enemies would be to dip their bullets in the poison, and the very notion seemed so odd that he dismissed it as preposterous.

Apollo had consulted Hermes in an effort to resolve the mystery, and while his questions had been answered, he had come away from their discussion filled with new doubts, puzzling over the grim turn his assignment had taken.

The twenty-five gallons of cyanide, he was told, had been purchased for use in the last extremity, if there was no more hope of defending the retreat against their enemies outside. In that case, rather than submit to torture, rape and degradation, it had been decided by The Two that all loyal members of the sect would end their earthly lives and wait in peace for that day when the Ancients summoned them from dreamless sleep to rule a world reborn.

Apollo hadn't argued, but he wondered whether he could carry out that order, if and when it was delivered to him. It was one thing, after all, for an adult to make the choice of sacrifice—as he himself had done in Washington—and pay the final price that was required for some grand gesture on the sect's behalf. It troubled him to think of wiping out the children, though, and he was forced to wonder if the choice was really theirs, or if they would feel trapped, like minks penned for slaughter, when the cyanide was passed around.

It hadn't fazed him, previously, to imagine those incinerated by a global holocaust, because he knew they would be unbelievers, lost in any case for their rejection of the Ancients. This was different, though: a conscious plan to liquidate the offspring of The Path. And somehow, even with his firm belief in paradise to come, the notion left him feeling vaguely ill.

Which didn't mean Apollo would refuse to carry out the order. He wouldn't enjoy it, but a soldier did as he was told by his superiors. The same way he had done while he was drawing paychecks from the FBI.

He watched two members of his team prepare the last of the M-2 HB .50-caliber machine guns, securing its heavy tripod behind a rampart of sandbags, the long barrel with its ventilated cowling pointed northward, past the chain-link fence and coils of razor wire that marked the camp's perimeter. From where he stood, Apollo couldn't see the Claymore mines out there, but he knew where they were, prepared to detonate by radio-remote control. Each had been mounted with the FRONT TOWARD ENEMY, as indicated on the outer casing, so the load of steel ball bearings would erupt like hellish shotgun blasts toward the advancing troops, the mines concealed from view by scattered shrubs and tumbleweeds.

And now, Apollo asked himself, where *was* the enemy?

Granted, he knew the call hadn't been broadcast publicly, but even with his own great faith, it still defied all logic that the gathering could have been carried off without a leak at any point across the nation. Someone surely had to have heard something by now, especially considering the heat that had come down since the theft of Air Force missiles and his own abortive action at the White House.

So, where were they?

He had been expecting SWAT teams, Hostage Rescue from the FBI, blacksuited ATF commandos, maybe even Delta Force. It would have been a showdown to remember, putting Waco and Montana's so-called 'freemen' in the shade. Apollo had been looking forward to it, even in the expectation that his side wouldn't prevail. Faith told him that his enemies would be the real losers, whatever happened here. The Ancients would return, and those who had revered them from the start would be exalted over all the doubters of the world.

Amen.

And still, he had to wonder where their adversaries were. How could the Feds, with all their bugs and wiretaps, their informers and computers, fail to know that remnants of The Path were gathering to make their final stand against the lame-duck masters of old Earth?

Forget about it.

It wasn't Apollo's job, after all, to direct their enemies and get them to the starting gate on time. If they were clumsy, inefficient, he would gladly take advantage of their negligence. It simply meant that when they did arrive at last, his own troops would be that much more prepared, and they could serve up bloody hell on earth to those who would destroy them.

Even if it didn't save them in the end.

Even if they were forced to feed their wives and children cyanide.

Apollo's first and foremost job was to prepare the camp for battle—and to make that battle costly for their enemies, once it began. Prolong the action if he could, until the arid plains around the makeshift fortress drank their fill of blood.

He left his soldiers to complete their preparations in the gun pit, moving toward the next emplacement, and the next. Despite their tardiness, the enemy might still arrive at any moment, and Apollo wouldn't have it said that he had wasted precious time.

He had a job to do.

The children, he decided, weren't his problem.

They would have to take care of themselves.

BOLAN HAD PHOTOS of the compound, from an SR-71 Blackbird overflight, the high-resolution black and whites revealing an anthill of activity as photographed from six miles up. The place was fenced—chain-link and razor wire, from what Bolan could see, perhaps electrified—and there were gun emplacements going in. The big guns looked like .50-calibers, and that spelled bloody havoc for advancing troops if they were forced to storm the wire. No body armor known to man would stop a .50-caliber full-metal-jacket round, with an effective killing range of 2,000 meters, and some high-tech projectiles for the fifty were specifically designed for killing armored vehicles.

Smaller machine guns were spread out along the camp perimeter, some posted on the roofs of certain buildings in the compound. They were probably M-60s, but might also prove to be HK-21s, British L-7 A-2s, or even—an admitted long shot—the Belgian Minimi squad support weapons. Whatever they were, they were manned and they had the compound amply covered with interlocking fields of fire.

So far, so bad.

He didn't know what else the cultists had in there—no doubt a small arms smorgasbord—but it made no real difference, in terms of Bolan's task. Whatever they were packing, he still had to find a way inside and see what he could do to take down the shooters without touching off a general bloodbath.

Good luck.

His first step would be waiting for the wee small hours of the morning, when the most determined sentry felt his concentration start to wander, wishing he was tucked in a nice, warm bed, instead of walking post alone and waiting for the shadows to divulge a lurking enemy. An airborne drop was out, which meant Bolan would have to crawl for something like a mile across the open plain avoiding spotters, snakes and any traps his quarry might have laid out to receive an uninvited visitor. They kept the compound dark at night, and that was something in his favor, though he still had no idea about alarms or sensors, and the photos showed him floodlights ready to blaze bright in the event of an emergency at night.

The fence was something else, and he would have to take his chances. Bolan took a pair of insulated cutters with him, just in case the chain-link was electrified, and while the rubber handles on his wire cutters would save him from electrocution, they wouldn't prevent alarms from going off, if any were wired to the fence. They wouldn't shield him from explosive charges if he cut a trip wire by mistake, nor would they save him from machine-gun bullets if the lookouts were roused.

Each field of battle had its bonuses and drawbacks. One bonus for the Executioner this night was that a crawl across the open desert didn't lead through swamps of reeking undergrowth, where cobras lay in wait to strike at him from hiding, and the drip of rainwater felt like Chinese water torture, endlessly striking his head. The bad part, ironically, was a flip side of the same coin: he had no cover to speak of on his long crawl toward the compound, nothing but the night to shelter him while he worked his knees and elbows raw, humping over dry, rocky ground.

There was no moon, and that was good. Bolan hadn't been able to discover if the military stash collected by his adversaries included night-vision goggles for the sentries—and if they did, that, potentially, was very bad. One of the gunners could be watching him right now, an insect scuttling over a benighted moonscape, all tinged green by the goggles. The shooter could have warned his superiors, sounded the alarm; he could be lining up a shot or whispering coordinates to the nearest gun emplacement, waiting for one of the fifties to hose Bolan down.

But none of that happened, and he reached the wire intact, aside from minor nicks and bruises he had picked up on his crawl across the desert floor. No one had seen him yet, as far as he could tell, nor were there any sentries he could see on roving foot patrol along the fence. Plainly, the cultists thought their enemies would show up by the carload, flashing lights and wailing sirens, maybe even tanks and helicopters. They hadn't prepared themselves to face a single man.

They hadn't counted on the Executioner, and that was a mistake.

He used his insulated cutters, half expecting some alarm as he snipped through the chain-link fence, but nothing happened. Moments later, taking care to make no noise, he slipped into the compound, wriggling on his belly like a snake.

HERMES WAS RESTLESS, pacing in the quarters that were visibly less plush than he had grown accustomed to the past ten years. It wasn't comfort that prevented him from sleeping, though. In fact, he was afraid to sleep. Afraid that he would dream.

And more particularly, it was one recurring dream that kept him pacing now, his features carved into a scowl, hands clenched behind his back. One dream, which Hermes now regarded as a prophecy, and thus more terrible.

It was a dream of failure and defeat, humiliation and the loss of hope. Each time, he woke up just before the grim, inevitable climax, drenched in clammy sweat, his muscles twitching as if he was lying on a live electric wire.

The dream could trick him, starting out in different ways, with different scenes, but each beginning led him to the same result. At some point in the early stages of the dream, his plans began to fail, fair-weather disciples abandoning him, while the faithful were driven before their enemies into the final refuge. They surrounded Hermes, weeping and pleading, still expecting him to save them, somehow. They were trapped, cut off. Their enemies attacked relentlessly— sometimes with swords and maces, other times with modern weapons; the result always carnage. Hermes felt himself boxed in, with no escape. He was afraid that he would die, and even more afraid of what would happen if his enemies took him alive.

The mother ship came, then, and this part of his dream was always identical, with no variation at all. The first time, Hermes had experienced a sense of sweet relief, but now the massive ship's appearance filled him with an aching, nameless dread.

The craft was vast, perhaps three football fields across, its length from stem to stern incalculable from his line of sight. Its mere arrival filled his enemies with awe and put their troops to flight, scrambling to get away before the Ancients fell upon them with an all-consuming wrath. The first time he had seen the mother ship, Hermes felt vindicated, rescued from an evil fate. He cheered and beckoned, calling out his praise to anyone or anything inside.

More recently, forewarned by grim experience, he merely stood and watched the mother ship loom over him, its shadow blotting out the moon and stars. He knew what to expect, now, when the forward hatch slid open, and a beam of brilliant light lanced toward the earth.

It was some kind of transport beam, he realized, too late. The dreaded Man in Black was coming, not like any of the characters from urban legends who were sent by some anonymous government agency to intimidate and silence UFO witnesses, but someone—some*thing*—infinitely worse. This Man in Black was tall and muscular, his features vague to the point of near invisibility, but there could be no doubt about his mission.

He was sent to punish Hermes.

And the hell of it was, Hermes still had no idea what he had done to deserve punishment.

The deadly Man in Black was nothing if not efficient. From the moment he touched feet on solid ground, he went about his killing business with a vengeance, slaughtering whoever crossed his path. Sometimes he used an ax and sword, sometimes a laser weapon from the future yet unimagined, but it was all the same. He left a trail of blood and broken bodies, mowing down enemies and the faithful alike, implacable in his search for Hermes. It mattered not at all how Hermes prayed for help or understanding. He was helpless in the face of this new enemy.

Inevitably, he was cornered—sometimes in the smoking ruins of a building, other times in what appeared to be a wooded glade, with cliffs behind him. Once as he recalled, the dream had found him running for his life across a barren desert, stumbling at the final moment into a deep gully from which he couldn't escape.

Again, the details hardly mattered. The thrust of the dream was destruction, coming for him as the Man in Black, and that grim hunter always found him in the end, no matter how his subconscious mind altered the playing field. His final moments in the dream world were always the same, sprawled on his back with the shadow figure looming over him, the hunter's eyes burning into his, into his soul, like white-hot ingots lifted from a blast furnace. With sword or laser ray, the Man in Black always prepared to finish off his prey…

At which point Hermes woke up, sometimes screaming in the darkness of his bedroom, sometimes biting off the panicked cry before it could escape.

Their was an old wives' tale, recalled from childhood that said that any man who actually saw himself die in a dream would die in fact, and never wake. As far as Hermes knew, there was no scientific evidence supporting that belief, but then again, how could there be? If it was any more than idle superstition, the unlucky dreamers would be dead, and no one but psychic mediums could know what they were dreaming when they died.

Sometimes he went for months on end without the dream—almost a year one time, in the late eighties— but it dogged him almost every night, these days, and had for several weeks. The grim, relentless Man in Black was haunting him. Now, here he was, preparing for what might turn out to be his final stand against the unbelievers, and a dream had very nearly robbed him of the confidence to lead.

He almost wished the Man in Black would come and show himself, appear before him in the flesh, and get the blasted waiting over with.

"Can't sleep?"

The sound of Circe's voice surprised him, almost made him jump, but he was smiling when he turned to face her. "Too much on my mind," Hermes replied.

"The dream again," she said, not asking him.

Hermes said nothing, simply turned back toward the window. He could feel her close beside him, seconds later, as she took his hand in both of hers.

"He's not out there, you know," she said.

A frown etched furrows in his face. He said, "I wish I had your confidence, my love. If only—"

The explosion jolted him, more shock than shock wave, since the blast had echoed from the far side of

the property. A moment later, scattered bursts of gunfire could be heard from all around the compound.

Hermes turned to Circe with a smile that trembled
on the razor's edge between hysteria and sweet relief.
"What were you saying, dear?"

APOLLO WAS RELAXING in his quarters for the first
time since he woke at half-past five that morning
when the blast went off. He hadn't gone to sleep yet,
so he knew that it wasn't a dream. Already on his
feet before he started thinking of the possibilities, he
struggled into clothes that needed laundering, tugged
on his boots without lacing them and grabbed an
M-16 on his way out the door.

Beyond his line of sight, from the southwest corner
of the compound, gunfire stuttered fitfully, light
weapons at first, the big fifty joining in seconds later.
The .50-caliber aside, Apollo couldn't tell if the gunfire was friendly or hostile, assuming the worst as he
sprinted toward the sounds of combat, prepared to
find enemies storming the wire and invading the
camp.

Had the explosion been a Claymore mine? Perhaps
a hand grenade? Apollo didn't know and couldn't say,
his racing mind a jumble of prospects and possibilities.

At the moment, none of them looked good.

He came around a corner, skidding to a halt. In
front of him, the gunners on the perimeter were unloading with everything they had, firing into the darkness beyond the wire, tracer rounds drawing brilliant
trails in the night. Incredibly, he saw no evidence of

an attack in progress, nothing in the way of muzzle flashes, lights or vehicles, no troops advancing toward the fence.

What were they shooting at?

Apollo held his automatic rifle at the ready, sprinting toward the gun pit where the .50-caliber was roaring, spewing death into the desert night. He dropped into the pit and saw the backup gunner swing around to face him, wide-eyed, with an Uzi in his hands.

Apollo froze, waiting for recognition in the soldier's eyes, before he leaned close and shouted to be heard above the racket of machine-gun fire. "What are you shooting at?"

"Out there!" the backup gunner told him, pointing vaguely to the desert beyond the wire. "One of the mines went off, I think."

"You think?" Apollo grabbed the shooter roughly, jerked him backward and away from his weapon, almost spilling him into the dirt. "Hold your fire without targets!" he bellowed, lunging out of the pit and repeating the order as he moved along the line. "Hold your fire without targets, goddammit!"

It took him several moments, but the firing stopped at last, leaving an eerie silence in its place, together with a stench of cordite that was nearly overpowering.

"All right, now! Where did the explosion come from? Did anyone here see anything?"

Before Apollo got an answer to that question, yet another blast echoed across the desert, this one from the northeast corner of the property. At once, the sentries stationed there unleashed a hail of automatic fire into the night, Apollo cursing as he tried to figure out exactly what was happening.

"Listen to me!" he told the troopers within earshot. "No one fires without a solid target! Do you understand me? No one fires without a target!"

And whether they understood it or not, the men were on their own, Apollo sprinting across the compound toward the latest source of gunfire.

It had to be the enemy, in some guise, but where was he? How had he become invisible? What if—?

Apollo managed to derail the train of thought before it carried him away to Panic Land. He had enough to think about right now without indulging any fantasies. He had to stop the firing somehow, or at least direct it toward a target.

And one other thing, of course.

He had to find out if The Two had started doling out the cyanide.

CHAPTER TWENTY

The trick was relatively simple: just lob a frag grenade over the fence and wait for it to blow, letting a pack of nervous sentries do the rest. They didn't need a target in the state of paranoia they had managed to achieve. The flash and noise were all it took to set them off and concentrate their full attention on the midnight world beyond the wire.

He had already taken out two gunners in the camp, but silently, using his fighting knife, dragging them into the shadows for concealment. He was trying to avoid a general confrontation with the enemy until he knew where the "civilians" were, specifically the children of the sect, in an attempt to spare them from the line of fire. It might not be within his power to save them, Bolan realized, but he was bound to try.

He was returning from the northeast corner of the compound, leaving chaos in his wake, when Bolan saw a group of children moving in the open, following a man armed with a rifle, while two others lagged behind them, bringing up the rear. He watched them from the darkness, while the gunfire sputtered on behind him, would-be soldiers wasting ammunition on thin air. Someone had managed to restrain the first group, but he didn't care. There was enough confusion at the moment to permit him to follow the group of children to their destination, herded as they were like sheep.

Bolan was watching as the pointman brought them to a prefab shed no more than eight feet square. The gunner ducked inside, came out a moment later and began to wave in the children. They hurried to obey him, several of them glancing fearfully around the camp and cringing at the sounds of gunfire. Bolan counted heads and made it seventeen, all told. There was no way for them to fit inside the shed, which told him it had to be a cover for the entrance to some kind of structure set below ground, out of sight and relatively insulated from attack.

It could have been an effort to protect the children, but somehow he didn't think so. There had been too many other cases in the recent past of cults that chose to sacrifice their young in the bizarre conviction that their life on Earth was somehow not worth living. It was one thing, Bolan thought, for an adult to make that choice—even a group, deluded as they might be from commitment to some half-baked holy man—but when those same fanatics dealt the death card out to children "for their own good," Bolan was prepared to intervene with force, whenever possible.

Beginning now.

A woman suddenly appeared out of the darkness, moving in from Bolan's left, when all but half a dozen of the children had been ushered through the open door and down below. She called out to the men

and spoke a name—Eddie, Freddie; he wasn't sure—
racing to join them as another child was shoved inside
the shed. One of the gunmen moved to intercept her,
tried to catch her with an outstretched arm, and failing
that, lashed out to club her with his rifle butt.

The woman staggered, but she kept her balance,
shrieking out the name again, no more intelligible this
time, as her mouth filled with blood. Her armed as-
sailant saw the last two children disappear inside the
shed and turned to strike at her again, his rifle gripped
in both hands, raised above his head.

He made a perfect target standing there, and Bolan
didn't hesitate. A 3-round burst ripped through the
gunner's chest and took him down, stone-dead before
he hit the ground. His two companions swung to face
the sound of gunfire, but they weren't fast enough to
save themselves. Bolan was close enough by then that
he could drop them both with short bursts from the
hip, not bothering to aim.

The woman gaped at him, still groggy from the
clubbing she had taken, looking wobbly on her feet.
She didn't seem to know if she should thank him, call
for help or maybe light into this stranger on her own
with tooth and nail against his M-16. At last, she settled for a tearful plea.

"Don't hurt my boy."

"I won't," he promised her. "I want to get the
children out of here while there's still time. I need
your help."

It was a gamble, but he didn't care for the immediate alternative, which would require that she be si-
lenced where she stood. The woman blinked at him

for precious seconds, used a hand to wipe the fresh blood from her lips and said, "Just tell me what to do."

"Are there more children in the camp?" he asked.

The woman shook her head emphatically. "Just these," she said.

"We need to get them out of there," he told her, nodding toward the shed and bunker below, "and find a way out of the camp."

"The trucks?" she asked him, brightening, as if with hope.

"Sounds like a plan," the Executioner replied. A long stride brought him to the shed, and he threw back the door. Inside, another door resembling the hatch to an old-fashioned storm cellar stood open on a rectangle of artificial light.

"I'll cover you," he said, deciding that the last thing any of the children needed was a black-clad stranger shouting orders at them. "Go ahead and get your boy."

"I CAN'T BELIEVE it's come to this." There was an unaccustomed quality to Circe's voice, as if she had been stripped of hope for the first time since they had met.

"We always knew it might," Hermes reminded her.

"It's one thing knowing," she replied. "It's another thing believing."

Hermes tried to put his arms around her, but she pulled away from him and moved to stand before the window, listening to sounds of battle from outside.

He almost called her back, afraid she might be hurt or killed, then realized it didn't matter.

"Were we wrong?" she asked him. "All this time?"

"Not wrong," he said, refusing to accept that notion, even now. "I might have made a small miscalculation as to when the mother ship will come."

"You still believe, then."

It wasn't a question, but he felt compelled to answer her regardless. "Certainly I still believe! The prophecies are crystal-clear, the evidence irrefutable. If an error has been made, it's mine and mine alone. The Ancients will return! We will see them in paradise!"

"I hoped to meet them in the flesh," Circe replied, an aching sadness in her voice.

"You will," he said. "New flesh. We'll be reborn."

At last she turned to face him, smiling. "You sound like a Christian, Galen. Honestly."

It was the first time she had used his given name in...what? Six years? Seven? "Helen—" he said, and then stopped short. He couldn't think of anything to say.

"They must be near," she said, and nodded toward the window where the sounds of battle had grown louder by the moment.

"Yes," he agreed. There seemed no point in lying now.

"I won't be taken to their prison," Circe told him. It was nothing that he hadn't heard before, but she was letting Hermes know her nerve was still intact, that she hadn't forsaken their agreement.

"No," he said. "They'd only try to break us and humiliate us there."

Better to die, they had decided long ago, than to surrender and submit themselves to judgment by the unbelievers. Hermes, for his part, had sampled life inside an "institution," and wouldn't have wished it upon his worst enemy. It made no difference, to his mind, whether they were convicted on criminal charges and sentenced to prison—perhaps to death— or whether they squeaked by acquittal on an insanity plea and were consigned to some warehouse for the criminally deranged. In either case, it meant confinement, separation, a protracted living death.

Why suffer that when they could rob their adversaries of the satisfaction and be done with it?

"It's sad about the children, though," she said.

"Would you prefer them to be taken from their families and taught to worship fairy tales? Have them forsake the Ancients, even when we know the Final Days are close at hand? What would become of them, their souls?"

"I know," she said. "You're right, of course. Still, they're so young...."

"They have eternity in front of them," Hermes replied. "Tonight is nothing but a minor interruption. A detour along the road to paradise."

"I wish we had a child," she said, and he could see bright tears brimming in Circe's eyes.

"They're all our children, dear one," he replied. "You know that. They know it."

Startled by the sound of yet another loud explosion, Circe moved to stand beside him, color draining from her face. "It must be time," she said.

"I think so. Yes."

He led her to the counter of the breakfast nook—their quarters were the only dwelling in the camp to boast a private kitchen—where two bottles and two glasses stood together. One bottle was a soft drink, the stout two-liter size. Beside it, smaller and unlabeled, with a metal screw-on cap, the second bottle had been filled with cyanide.

"Is it supposed to hurt?" she asked.

"I don't think so." The answer was a reflex. Hermes didn't have a clue concerning death by cyanide. He only knew it worked, and relatively quickly. Short of bullets in the brain, it was the best that he could do.

He poured them each a glass of cola, three-quarters full, then put the cap back on and opened the second bottle. Instantly, he caught a scent of bitter almonds in the air. His hand was trembling slightly as he topped up the glasses, pouring approximately half the poison into each.

"My dear?"

He took one glass and handed it to Circe, took the other for himself, and they retreated toward the nearby sofa, holding hands as they sat.

"To paradise," he said, and raised his glass, waiting for Circe to clink hers against it in a toast.

"To us," she said, eyes shining as she raised the glass and drained it.

Hermes held her afterward, and felt his own nerve

faltering. Her death hadn't been easy, as he would have wished, and now he was afraid to follow in her footsteps, terrified of suffering, more so of being found in that condition by a group of strangers who would mock his corpse, defile his memory.

But then what difference would it make when he was dead? The Ancients would be coming soon, and they would settle all accounts, insuring that his enemies were made to pay their debts, with interest.

It was embarrassment, as much as anything, that made him follow through at last. How could he shirk his duty now, when Circe had possessed such courage?

"Here's to life," he said.

And drank the poison cocktail.

IT WAS A GAMBLE, bringing the children out in the open, but Bolan reckoned there were greater risks in leaving them below ground in the bunker. There was no time for him to inspect the place, find out if it was wired with explosives, maybe rigged for gas to be piped in, and he wasn't inclined to take the chance. Even without such preparations, leaving them penned inside the bunker was a hazard. It would take only one soldier with a frag grenade or automatic weapon to transform the bunker from a hideout into a slaughter pen.

Protecting them in place would mean that Bolan had to stay and guard the shed, while the camp went to hell all around him, and his adversaries either pinned him down with sniper fire or seized the opportunity to slip away. In either case, the risk was unacceptable.

The trucks.

He had a clear fix on the compound's motor pool, from studying the aerial surveillance photos. It was on the west side of the camp, which meant that he would have to convoy eighteen terrified civilians—all but one of them children—directly through the middle of the camp to reach their wheels.

Okay.

The children started coming out, the first ones stopping short at sight of Bolan, edging back in fear, until the woman joined them, whispering to them that everything would be all right. The tall man was a friend, she told them. They should follow him and do as they were told.

When she appeared to have them more or less calmed, he drew her to one side and asked, "Do you know how to use a gun?"

She nodded. "Yes. We've all been trained."

"You'd better pick one out, then," Bolan told her, glancing toward the dead men on the ground. "We might have opposition coming up."

The woman didn't hesitate, but rather chose the AK-47 carried by the gunman who had struck her with it moments earlier. She wore a smile of something very much like satisfaction as she faced him once again, and said, "All set."

"Okay," he said.

She briefed the children quickly, telling them, "We're going to the trucks. You must be very brave and very quiet now. Whatever happens, I'll protect you. So will Mr...?''

"Blake," he said.

"I'm Stella."

"Pleased to meet you, Stella. Let's get out of here."

He had hoped to settle with the cult's surviving men-at-arms before he left the camp, but now he saw that it wouldn't be possible. The children were his first priority, Brognola's troops could seal off the compound and deal with any mopping up once he had cleared out the children.

A sudden thought arrested him, when they had covered less than forty yards. He beckoned Stella over, leaning close to her and whispering, so that the children wouldn't hear.

"The other women—" he began, before she cut him off.

"Forget about them," Stella said, a tone of bitter resignation in her voice. "They've made their choice. They sent their kids to die."

There was no civilized response to that, and Bolan offered none. Instead, he concentrated on the trek that lay before them and the dangers they were likely to encounter on the way.

Their path lay through the middle of the compound, winding in and out past buildings that had been constructed out of cinder blocks, with corrugated metal roofing. Floodlights were mounted at strategic points around the camp, but no one had seen fit to turn them on, as yet, and Bolan hoped the oversight wouldn't be soon corrected. Darkness helped to shield his little troupe from prying eyes, as he and Stella led the children toward the motor pool.

The distance, overall, was something like three hundred yards. Alone and unopposed, he could have run that far in about thirty seconds. He wasn't alone, however, and they could expect fierce opposition from anyone they encountered along the way.

He guessed that most or all of the adults inside the compound knew the children were supposed to die in the event of an attack, but he was betting that the rank and file hadn't been briefed on the specific plans. Cult leaders thrived on mystery, particularly when the details of a plan might tend to make their sheepish minions hesitate, perhaps start thinking for themselves again. He guessed that Galen Locke and Helen Braun had probably avoided any grim specifics of the "sacrifice," leaving the details to their personal gestapo. And if that was true, then who, besides the triggermen he had already taken down, would be inclined to question "orders" for removal of the children to the motor pool?

Once they were out of there, he could relay a message through Grimaldi, bring the cavalry to ring the camp with guns and armored vehicles, and let it go from there. If those remaining in the compound chose to shoot it out or kill themselves, it meant a headline for the next day's papers, but the memory would fade in time.

As for the children, even with the burden they would carry from this place, at least they had a chance to sample life and see what it was all about, without a madman preaching poison to them every day.

They reached the halfway point before a member of the home team intercepted them and called a halt to the parade. He was a young man, nervous-looking in the circumstances, brandishing an M-16.

"What's going on?" he asked them, voice cracking with the strain.

"We have the children," Bolan said, as if that answered everything.

"I see that. What I mean—"

"We have to take them through," Stella said, interrupting him. "It's time."

"Oh. Right." His manner changed, as he lowered his weapon. "You'd better go on, then. There isn't much time."

Grim-faced, the young man turned away and let them pass.

APOLLO HAD COMPLETED one full circuit of the camp's perimeter, and he had still seen no one even vaguely resembling an enemy. The sentries were excited, some of them nearly hysterical, but none of them could tell him who or what they had been shooting at. As for the source of the explosions that had gone off in the desert waste beyond the fence, no ready explanation came to mind.

Two things were crystal-clear now in Apollo's mind. He recognized that they weren't under attack, at least by any kind of enemy in force, and he was equally convinced that it was now too late to save the camp. He knew the kind of stress The Two were under, and he realized they would have issued final orders from the moment they heard gunfire out on the perimeter. Apollo didn't have authority to overrule those orders, although he could still present his findings to The Two if it wasn't too late.

If they had started dishing out the cyanide, however, he would have a choice to make: whether to join the others in oblivion or save himself again, ignore his standing orders for the second time and try to get away.

But get away to what?

Before he had a chance to think the question through, Apollo was distracted by someone calling his name. He turned in the direction of the sound and saw two soldiers running toward him, the expressions on their faces close to panic.

Now what?

Instead of snapping at them, though, he used restraint and simply asked, "What's wrong?"

"We've lost three men!" one of them blurted.

"Lost?" The word seemed alien, incomprehensible. "What do you mean?"

"They're dead!" the other told him, gasping as he spoke. "Back there!"

Apollo stared in the direction his informant pointed, hesitating but a heartbeat. "Show me," he commanded.

There were three of them and they were dead, all right. From what he saw, it looked as if all three were shot at relatively close range, with some kind of automatic weapon. Nor, he instantly determined, could their deaths be written off as any kind of accident related to wild firing on the camp's perimeter. This was precision work by someone who had killed before and knew the ropes.

But who? And why?

Another moment passed before Apollo saw the answer right in front of him. The narrow doorway of the prefab shed was standing open, pale light spilling from inside. He ducked his head to clear the doorjamb, leading with his rifle, though he had no doubt of what would be revealed. There was no ambush waiting for him, no sign of a living soul, in fact.

Where had the children gone?

Apollo knew about the plan, conceived, Hermes assured him, via inspiration from the Ancients. They would bring the children all together if the compound was attacked, and soft drinks spiked with cyanide would be passed out to them before the doors were closed and locked. If anything went wrong, a hand grenade or two would do the job as well, if less tidily.

Retreating from the shed, he looked around the bodies scattered on the ground and saw no evidence that they had carried any beverages. More to the point, he saw that only two of the corpses were armed, though all three wore cartridge belts and bandoleers.

Where had the missing rifle gone?

Apollo didn't know who was responsible, but logic told him that the interloper's first impulse would be to get the children out of camp, as quickly and as far away as possible. Since no vehicles had approached the camp, as far as any of his sentries could determine, that meant anyone who planned to drive away—and who would choose to walk with better than a dozen children, under fire?—had to find his means of transportation somewhere in the camp itself.

The motor pool.

"Come with me!" he told the others, sprinting through darkness toward the far side of the camp.

It didn't strike Apollo as ironic that he was about to "save" the children from escaping death. His own doubts seemed to vanish as he found new purpose in the chase. His old faith in the Ancients and The Two hadn't deserted him, he found. It simply took a crisis for him to perform at optimum efficiency. Once he was stripped of time to think and brood, once instinct took over, Apollo knew he had made the right choice.

He would do his duty and retrieve the children from their enemies, or he would die in the attempt.

THEY WERE WITHIN a dozen paces of the motor pool when someone started shooting at them from the rear. Bolan fell back to cover the advance and called to Stella, "Take whatever suits you if it's got a key in the ignition and enough room in the back. Head for the gate and keep on going. You'll find people waiting for you."

"What about you?" she asked, hesitating.

"I'll catch the next one," Bolan said. "Now *go!*"

She did as she was told, with bullets whipping after her, some of the children squealing as they ran for cover in between the half-ton trucks. Bolan returned fire with his M-16, spotting the muzzle-flashes, counting three opponents. If the three had spotted him and knew what he was doing, though, the numbers would be growing momentarily. He had to buy time for the children, but the best thing he could do—

A bullet snapped past Bolan's face, perhaps an inch off target to the left. He sent a burst right back, then dodged toward the nearest structure, hoping the shooters would stick with him and let the children go.

It took about ten seconds to discover that his plan hadn't worked. One of the shooters sprayed his hiding place with bullets, while the other two broke off and headed for the motor pool, intent on closing the escape route. Bolan chased them with a short burst from his M-16, but they were dodging, weaving, and the sniper left behind to cover him cut loose as soon as Bolan showed himself, driving him back to ground.

Cursing, he ripped the compact walkie-talkie from his belt and keyed the button that connected him to Jack Grimaldi. "Wings!" he said.

"Right here," Grimaldi answered.

"Lock and load, my man. You should have friendlies headed your way in a half-ton any minute now. Whatever's left is yours."

"You mean—"

"Repeat! Whatever's left is yours!"

He severed the connection, picturing the Apache gunship as it lifted off, and knew that nothing the pilot could do would help the kids and Stella in the next few minutes.

They were on their own—with just a little booster from the Executioner.

He palmed a frag grenade and yanked the pin, gripping the high-explosive egg in his right hand as he broke from cover, the M-16's pistol grip clutched in his left, with the stock clamped tight against his ribs. He triggered off a short burst, hoping it would draw the sniper's fire, and lobbed his grenade toward the bright muzzle-flash that came back in reply. He was flat on the deck when it blew, barely registered a stranger's dying scream as he vaulted to his feet and went after the others.

Downrange, a pair of headlights blazed to life beneath the corrugated metal canopy of the truck barn. Bolan saw his targets in silhouette, but the truck was directly in line with them now, as they moved in to block it. Bolan couldn't fire at them, for fear of missing them—or shooting through them—and endangering the children in the vehicle.

He started running all-out, bent on sweeping them aside by hand, if necessary, but a determined Stella beat him to it. Shifting the half-ton into first, she plowed forward, ignoring the loud bursts of fire from two automatic weapons, bearing down on her assailants like a savage juggernaut.

One of the shooters dodged aside to save himself, and that was all the opening that Bolan needed, firing on the run, watching his target dance a little death jig, with the 5.56 mm tumblers tearing into him. The other guy stood fast, still firing from the hip, and that turned out to be the worst idea he'd had all day. The half-ton flattened him without a hitch and kept on rolling, swerving toward the gate.

The cult had sentries at the gate, but they were so confused by this time that they didn't know exactly what was going on. One waved an arm, as if to flag down the half-ton's driver, then both men stood aside and watched the truck blow through that flimsy barrier as if it had been made of paper, trailing chainlink fencing for a hundred yards behind it.

Bolan ignored the latest corpses, as he ran toward the motor pool in search of anything that he could use to put that place behind him. He got lucky with a Jeep, found keys in the ignition switch and got it rolling in a flash.

The Executioner was halfway to the shattered gate and reaching for his M-16 again when he heard Jack Grimaldi passing overhead. The two guards on the gate were staring up at the Apache, barely conscious of the Jeep approaching them until he switched the headlights onto high beams, blinding them. The truck before him had already taught them how to handle such emergencies, and Bolan saw them scramble clear, one leaping off to either side as he sped through the gate and out across the flats.

Behind him, fragmented and shrunken in the Jeep's three jiggling mirrors, he could see the doomsday compound catching hell. He could have called off Grimaldi at that point, left it to Brognola's SWAT team, but why bother?

The pilot would cover his retreat, but he wasn't a savage. Brognola would probably turn up survivors in the wreckage, if the cultists didn't take their own lives first. At least, whatever happened, they weren't about to take the children with them.

They had done enough in that regard already, twisting young, impressionable minds with sci-fi gibberish presented as the sacred word of ancient gods from outer space. Bolan could only guess what kind of therapy would be involved in sorting out that mess, together with the fact that every one of the survivors would grow up without birth parents, knowing Mom and Dad preferred to die—and would have killed their children, given half a chance—instead of working with the lives they had.

Some future, Bolan thought. Some paradise.

And yet, at least the children *had* a future now. There would be pain and tears, but that was part of living. Those who never felt or wept were either dead, or they were monsters on a fast track to oblivion.

Bolan had helped a few of them get there this night, and Grimaldi would hold the door for others, giving them a little nudge along the way. It was a grim night's work, but necessary.

And the next day, Bolan thought, could damn well take care of itself.

EPILOGUE

"Nineteen adult survivors," Hal Brognola said. "Some made a conscious choice to skip the cyanide and some of them were shaken up so badly by the air strike that they couldn't get their act together for the final scene."

"They won't give up," Bouchet reminded him.

"I'd guess you're right," he said, relaxing in the air-conditioned motel room outside of Burlington. "They're all on suicide watch until further notice, with arraignments coming up. I don't know if the counts we've got in mind will stick or not, but either way, we've got a strong case for involuntary commitment on the obvious suicide risks."

"Good luck teaching them the error of their ways." Bouchet seemed downcast, even though the mission was completed now, the threat removed.

"We've got a couple of deprogrammers on tap," Brognola said. "Beyond that...well, we can't watch everybody all the time."

It hadn't been the clean sweep Bolan would have liked, but then again, The Path hadn't been a traditional enemy. Most of its members were deluded, bar-

ring a few in the upper ranks who might have lusted
for power over others, but not all of them were violent, self-destructive. Stella had proved that, at the
end, and she was still cooperating with authorities,
helping them unravel the secrets of the cult's final
days.

So far, they knew that Galen Locke and Helen
Braun were dead, both suicides, while former G-man
Luther Marx had done his last turn in the form of
roadkill, after Stella ran him down. The cult's computer brain, one Ingrid Walsh, was also found among
the forty-three who chose to kill themselves with cyanide inside the camp. Tax men and other Feds were
busily dissecting Stargate Enterprises, following the
many paper trails, and more indictments were expected down the line, of businessmen who had found
ways to profit from the cult illegally.

"We're done, then," Bolan said.

Brognola thought about it for a moment, frowning
to himself, then nodded. "Yeah, I'd say."

Bouchet was silent, trying not to stare at him. He
had a fair idea of what was going on inside her
mind—some of it, anyway—but he wasn't about to
tackle it in front of Brognola.

As if in answer to his thoughts, Brognola said,
"Well, hell, I've still got umpteen meetings lined up
for the next two days. Everybody from the Russian
embassy to Colorado State Police is after me. Looks
like I'm back in style."

He rose to leave, and Bolan walked him to the
door. Before he left, the big Fed dropped his voice a
notch and said, "The Oval Office sends a special

thank-you, and I'm told we also have a brand-new friend in Moscow.''

"Hey," Bolan replied, "it couldn't hurt."

Brognola nodded toward Bouchet. "You think she'll be all right?"

The soldier considered it a moment, nodding as he said, "I wouldn't be surprised."

"Too bad about Morrell."

"Too bad," Bolan agreed.

"Well, hey. I'm out of here." And so he was.

"What now?" Bouchet asked Bolan, as he closed the door and moved back toward the sofa where she sat.

"Now, everyone relaxes and goes back to normal life," he said.

"Not everyone."

She had him there, but Bolan didn't dwell on it. Life was a game of chance, not always fair, and there were losers every time you rolled the dice. Most of the players who survived a roll broke even, while a few came out ahead. The catch, however, was that no one was allowed to leave the game alive.

"It's time to look ahead," he told her. "Put the old business behind you."

"I've already tried looking ahead," she said. "It's hard to see, though. I can't tell if I'm alone, or what."

"Some things you have to answer for yourself," the Executioner replied.

"A unilateral decision, that would be?"

"If it's the only kind available," he said.

"That's tough. Suppose I choose togetherness,''

she asked him, "and the other party has different ideas?"

"Maybe you compromise."

"I don't know if that's possible," she stated.

"The only way to learn things—"

"Is to ask," she interrupted him. "I know."

"Well, there you go."

"I guess you have someplace you need to be," she said.

"Not right away."

"It's been awhile since I had a vacation," she remarked.

"Vacations can be nice," he said, and smiled. "As long as they go one day at a time."

James Axler

OUTLANDERS™

OUTER DARKNESS

Kane and his companions are transported to an alternate
reality where the global conflagration didn't happen—and
humanity had expelled the Archons from the planet. Things
are not as rosy as they may seem, as the Archons return for a
final confrontation....

Book #3 in the new Lost Earth Saga, a trilogy that chronicles
our heroes' paths through three very different alternative
realities...where the struggle against the evil Archons
goes on....

Shadow THE EXECUTIONER®
as he battles evil for 352 pages of heart-stopping action!

SuperBolan®

#61452	DAY OF THE VULTURE	$5.50 U.S.	☐
		$6.50 CAN.	☐
#61453	FLAMES OF WRATH	$5.50 U.S.	☐
		$6.50 CAN.	☐
#61454	HIGH AGGRESSION	$5.50 U.S.	☐
		$6.50 CAN.	☐
#61455	CODE OF BUSHIDO	$5.50 U.S.	☐
		$6.50 CAN.	☐
#61456	TERROR SPIN	$5.50 U.S.	☐
		$6.50 CAN.	☐

(limited quantities available on certain titles)

TOTAL AMOUNT	$
POSTAGE & HANDLING	$
($1.00 for one book, 50¢ for each additional)	
APPLICABLE TAXES*	$ _____
TOTAL PAYABLE	$ _____
(check or money order—please do not send cash)	

To order, complete this form and send it, along with a check or money order for the total above, payable to Gold Eagle Books, to: **In the U.S.:** 3010 Walden Avenue, P.O. Box 9077, Buffalo, NY 14269-9077; **In Canada:** P.O. Box 636, Fort Erie, Ontario, L2A 5X3.

Name: _____

Address: _____ City: _____

State/Prov.: _____ Zip/Postal Code: _____

*New York residents remit applicable sales taxes.
 Canadian residents remit applicable GST and provincial taxes.

GSBBACK1